T0194142

A NOVEL by

Sergei Miro

Order this book online at www.trafford.com
or email orders@trafford.com

Most Trafford titles are also available at major online book retailers.

Edited by Courtney Luk
Book Cover by Sergei Miro
Type Setting & Book Design by Courtney Luk

Print information available on the last page.

ISBN: 978-1-4907-5543-4 (sc)
ISBN: 978-1-4907-5542-7 (e)

Library of Congress Control Number: 2015902380

Trafford rev. 05/05/2015

www.trafford.com

North America & international
toll-free: 1 888 232 4444 (USA & Canada)
fax: 812 355 4082

Contents

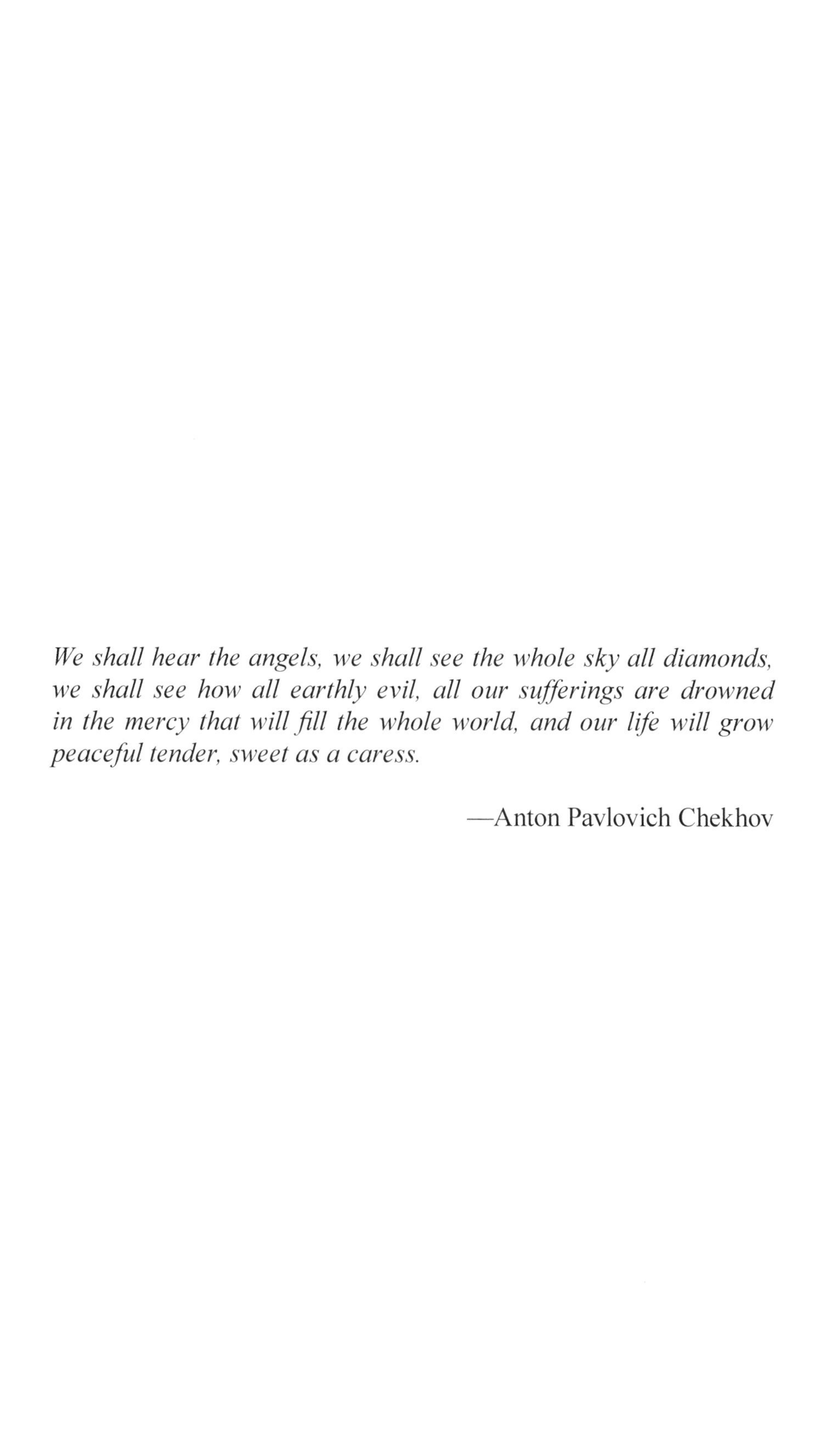

We shall hear the angels, we shall see the whole sky all diamonds, we shall see how all earthly evil, all our sufferings are drowned in the mercy that will fill the whole world, and our life will grow peaceful tender, sweet as a caress.

—Anton Pavlovich Chekhov

Prologue

Y*our father was arrested by the Gestapo today.* The words kept echoing in Kare's mind, and there was nothing he could do to stop them.

Kare Hoffmann had been in class when the school secretary had come to tell him that he was wanted on the phone. When Kare picked up the line, he learned that the caller was his father's colleague at Humboldt University in Berlin. The conversation was short and brief. Kare was shaken and in disbelief of what he had just heard. When the secretary saw the look on Kare's face, she asked, "Is everything okay?"

Kare thought back to the countless conversations that he and his mother had had about this topic. "If your father is ever arrested by the Gestapo," she had directed him, "you mustn't tell anyone at all. You must tell them something different to protect our family. Go to our friend, Max, at the gourmet shop and wait for further instructions."

He quietly and quickly composed himself and replied to the secretary, "No. My uncle in Holland is very sick, and I must travel to see him." Kare sighed heavily, turned on his heel, and walked out the door to the fate that was awaiting his family.

Kare

It was early in the morning when his father woke him up for school. "Kare, it's seven o'clock. Wake up or you will be late for the gymnasia." Kare leapt out of bed. He had a busy schedule today at his high school. He grabbed his breakfast while glancing at the open newspaper on the dining room table. The headlines in 1937 sang praise and congratulations for Hermann Goring, the German minister of economy and the director responsible for "The Nazis Economic Miracle."

Goring's prescription for Germany's economic miracle was a policy of "guns and butter" for self-sufficiency. He shifted state resources to the rearmament industry, kept wages stable, crushed trade unions, and kept unemployment and inflation low. It lifted the standard of living and enriched the Germans.

Kare picked up his school bag and ran out the door. It was a typical, sunny spring day in Berlin, and he walked briskly to the nearby U-Bahn station. Kare lived in Dahlem, a tranquil suburb of Berlin. It was a cultural and affluent neighborhood with large estates and residential buildings, yet it still retained its twelfth-century gothic charm. Kare was a third-year student at the Kino and Cinematography Academy. He was studying to become a director of photography.

Previously, in Nazi Germany, Kare had been required to join Hitler's Youth Organization; however, at the age of thirteen, Kare had not understood the Nazi racist ideology against gypsies, homosexuals, liberals, artists, and Jews. It was through this youth movement that he learned about Nazism. He was politically programmed to obey orders, cultivate "virtue," and stand at attention and say, "Yes, sir!" The elders of the group had prepared him for his future role as soldier for the "Fatherland." Lila and Eric, his parents, explained that, while they disagreed with the Nazi ideology, he had no choice but to participate.

As a young man, Kare was the splitting image of his mother—tall and broad shouldered with brown eyes and light brown hair streaked with blonde. He was a handsome young lad.

On Kare's thirteenth birthday, Eric surprised him with an expensive gift, an 8-millimeter Agfa Movex camera. Kare loved movies and had wanted to become a cameraman ever since he had seen a documentary called *Day of Freedom*, the German Armed Forces propaganda movie that he'd watched at Hitler's youth group meeting. He had written down the name of the director of photography, Leni Riefenstahl. From that moment on, he wanted to see more of her films. He found her approach to filming new and imaginative, a modern way to shoot a movie.

In 1936, Leni Riefenstahl had filmed a documentary of the Berlin Olympics, *The Triumph of the Will.* Kare rushed to the movie theater to see it. He was glued to his seat watching Leni's masterful sport photography, especially the shots of the torch procession relay. She became his artistic inspiration in cinematography.

Eric had also taken Kare on a tour of the grounds of the United Film AG movie studio in Babelsberg. Kare had seen the movie, *The Blue Angel*, with Marlene Dietrich and Josef von Sternberg, which had been produced in Babelsberg. As he walked through the studio, Kare said to himself, *One day I will be working here*.

Kare and his camera were inseparable. At one of the Hitler Youth rallies, he asked his group leader for permission to film the rally on his Movex. He filmed his group marching and saluting the German Nazi flag. The Girls' League was nearby, marching and saluting, "Heil Hitler!" He noticed an ideal Aryan maiden in a black Nazi uniform and zoomed his camera in on her. She was a beautiful, blonde-haired, blue-eyed young woman with pigtails and the face of an angel. Her image filled up Kare's viewfinder; his camera was like Cupid, the son of Venus, the cherubic winged boy shooting arrows of love and desire from his bow at this Aryan maiden. She must have noticed him because she blushed, smiled, and looked away. Kare felt his heart bulge. It was *le coup de foudre,* and he knew that he needed this angelic face in his life. Kare approached her and asked for her name. "Monika," she said just as he was waved away by a large woman, whom he found out later was the group leader. The Hitler Youth Movement was obsessive about gender separation. Boys did not speak to girls and vice versa. The opposite sex was considered taboo. From that moment forward, Kare worshipped Monika's image on film, but she hardly noticed him.

During Kare's first year at Kino Academy, Hitler's Youth Movement took control of his life. Kare rebelled and quit. He was fed up with his drill instructors. Kare joined the *Swing-Jugend* (Swing Youth). They offered independence and a modern lifestyle. The fact that girls were involved attracted him. He shed his black pants and brown shirt and replaced them with a checkered shirt, dark trousers, and white socks. He grew to love jazz, American and British music, and he learned to dance to "enemies' tunes." He rejected the German *volks* music and dancing that were favored and promoted by Hitler's Youth Movement.

The police and the Gestapo harassed the groups, branding them as wild. There were several other rebellious groups with names like The Roving Dudes, Kittelbach Pirates, and The Navajos. They were similar to neighborhood gangs. These groups took trips to the countryside and confronted Hitler's Youth patrols. Being a part of this scene was dangerous for a young man living under the Nazi regime.

Eric allowed Kare to rebel as long he did not participate in physical confrontations with other groups.

When Kare was fifteen, his father sat him down for a discussion about Adam and Eve. He said, "Humans are profound sexual beings. They have natural sexual urges. It is what drives us in the world. We all have innate energy and desires for physical pleasure." He lectured Kare about teen sex, promiscuity, and abstinence and asked him to delay his first time.

In the Swing Dance Hall, Kare notice a beautiful girl dancing. Her performance on the dance floor caught his eyes. Kare took his Movex camera and zoomed the lens on her. Through the viewfinder, he filmed her provocative gyrations and sensual dance movements. She acknowledged him with an endearing grin as she moved in front of his camera, twisting to the sounds of jazz. When the music stopped playing, she approached him. "Why were you filming me?" she asked in a serious voice.

"I am a student at Kino Academy, and I have an assignment to film dancers and musicians for homework. I hope you don't mind."

"Not at all, but on one condition. You have to show me what you filmed."

"It's a deal," Kare replied, shaking her hand. "What is your name?"

"Daniela. Do you dance?"

"Yes." Kare swung the camera onto his shoulder and held her hand. He glided across the floor with her. "Where did you learn to dance like this?"

"I am a student at the Contemporary Dance Studio. Did you see the American dancer, Josephine Baker, the 'Black Pearl,' in *Zouzo*? I want to be like her, a 'Creole Goddess.'"

"I am impressed," Kare said, twisting his body to the sound of the saxophone blaring from the stage. After that night together, they started dating. In one of their rendezvous in the park, Daniela taught Kare all about carnal desires. He gave his virginity to Daniela on a park bench. However, Daniela was a free spirit and hated to be attached to one person. Like a butterfly, she flew from one flower to the next, collecting sweet nectar. The couple became like planets orbiting one another but never colliding. They drifted apart and stopped seeing each other. Only her dance routine recorded on the black-and-white film stayed in Kare's memory; her face faded away.

As the Nazi regime harnessed more power, the conversation in the Hoffmann home turned toward leaving Germany. Their liberal political views conflicted with the views of Nazi Germany. Eric's brother, Peter, who was the head of the Hoffmann family's textile business in Leipzig, joined the German Labor Front, and in the same year, joined the Nazi Party. Eric rejected Peter's Nazi views and refused to join the family business. Eric loved teaching, and his professorship at Humboldt University in Berlin was his life. He was an eternal optimist and was hoping for better days to come; though, when the university fired all of the Jewish professors, Eric was so upset that he almost quit himself. One of his colleagues stopped him from making this foolish decision by telling him that being sent to the labor camps would be a waste of his talent.

Most ordinary German citizens loved the Nazi government. It had restored prosperity by investing heavily in public works and the military. Hitler had hypnotized his audience with his oratory abilities, thus controlling public opinions. Lila saw doom and gloom for Germany's future and viewed Hitler as the Devil.

Mom and Dad

Lila Esther Schonkoff was born in 1901 in the small town of Apeldoorn. It was located in the province of Gelderland, Netherlands, sixty miles east of Amsterdam. Lila's ancestors, who were German Jews, had arrived at Apeldoorn in small groups in 1770. She was the daughter of Miriam and Solomon Schonkoff. Her father had two older brothers, Jakob and Avraham. Jakob resided in Amsterdam with his wife, Rivka, and their three daughters. He was a well-to-do man, a progressive Jew, and oversaw successful import/export businesses in Holland, Canada, and Argentina. Avraham, a successful diamond dealer, was married to Rivka's cousin, Nehama. They had two daughters and lived in Antwerp. The brothers did not have any male heirs, but Lila had two older brothers, Adam and David. Adam had moved away to London while David stayed in Apeldoorn to work with their father, who had a shop that sold fur coats in a town where there were about 1,500 Jews.

As a child, Adam had been a gifted student. In order to further his education, he had moved from Apeldoorn to Amsterdam to live with his Uncle Jakob's family. A decision was made to groom Adam in business and law and to give him the best education that was available at the time. They sent him to study law and business at St. Gallen University in Switzerland. Adam became an erudite lawyer, one of the best in his class. Upon graduation, Adam returned to Amsterdam and joined his uncle's businesses. It was the end of World War I. Jakob and Avraham sent him to London, the financial and banking center of Europe, to secure the finances for the expansion of their businesses.

In London, Adam met Sally at a Jewish function. She was the daughter of a wealthy banker and financier. They fell in love and got married, and he changed his name to Andrew, a Christian-sounding name, so he could blend in with genteel members of London's banking world.

Lila's father was a pious man; he had a zeal for the study of Talmud and the Torah, the law of God. His outlook on life was reflective of the Orthodox Jewish faith. He believed that women were to be in charge of the home's integrity from the inside while men were to provide means for that home from the outside; therefore, he hardly participated in household chores.

Lila became motherless at the age of ten. After the passing of her mother, Solomon hired elderly women to shop and cook their daily meals. For cleaning and washing, he hired a local Dutch maiden by the name of Yara. She and Lila found common interests and became close friends. Solomon noticed this relationship and become concerned. He forbade Lila from spending leisure time with Yara. As an orthodox man, he believed in a clear division between "others" and the Jewish world, but Lila continued the friendship behind his back anyway.

Her father encouraged her to go to the house of prayer morning and evening. He insisted that she scrupulously obey the roles applied to religious Jewish women: modesty, sanctity, and reverence. He forbade her from wearing modern fashions. As an adolescent girl, Lila rejected her father's Orthodox outlook on life. She rebelled. He did not know how to respond and interpreted her behavior as being a "difficult child." He decided she needed a motherly figure in her life, so he sent her to live in Amsterdam with Jakob and Rifka, who were educated and progressive Jews.

Apeldoorn was a small, backwater provincial town in comparison to Amsterdam. By the 1900s, Amsterdam had seen growth in liberal and social traditions, but the norm in an Orthodox Jewish family at the time was for women to complete primary school and not enroll in higher education. That was reserved for males only, like Lila's brothers. She excelled in her studies, and Adam took charge of her education in earnest. He enrolled her in a progressive public school, where she was able to complete her secondary education.

Adam developed a love for art and introduced Lila to the Amsterdam museums. They spent many hours in the Rijksmuseum viewing paintings and attending lectures on the Dutch masters, such as Rembrandt, Vermeer, Van Dyck, and Jan Steen. During this time, Lila discovered her love of art and knew that she was destined to become an artist. Adam recognized his sister's talent; he encouraged and financed private art lessons. The two developed a tight bond. She reminded him of their beloved mother in looks and temperament.

To further her knowledge, she started spending time at the library, reading literature, newspapers, and magazines. She also listened to jazz music. In the Keizersgracht district of Amsterdam, at the library, Lila discovered the writings of the Dutch pacifist feminist, Aletta Jacobs, and was drawn to the cause of the women's suffrage movement in Holland.

She kept these activities secret, hidden from her father. At home in Apeldoorn, Lila often had long, passionate arguments with Solomon about Jewish traditions, especially women's place in a changing world and the rabbi's control in society. She often asked, "Why can't a woman be a rabbi? Why must the rabbi in the community be consulted about everything?" In their community, the rabbi was to be consulted on many things, including who people should marry, what clothes they were allowed to wear, which doctor they could visit, and what food-related utensils they should use. Lila argued that, even without violating the Jewish laws and traditions, she could answer all of these issues and questions. She also rejected many of the Jewish practices and beliefs that dictated that a woman should only be a homemaker and a man should be the breadwinner. She told him that in Persia, Esther had saved the Jewish people from annihilation as is written in the Megillah—the Scroll of Esther. Vashti and Esther exemplified the roles of women in Judaism and embodied feminist consciousness. Lila proceeded to tell her father that the biblical Esther was her role model.

As an Orthodox Jew, Solomon was always horrified listening to her feminist arguments and her desire to become a professional artist. That was not what he had in mind for his daughter, but she was determined to be different. He expected her to obey him, follow the traditions, marry a Jewish boy, and raise a family. She told her father that marriage was of no interest to her. She did not want to be dominated by a man, emotionally or physically. She said, "The real commitment of a union is to have equal respect for one another."

When Lila was eighteen, she asked her father to let her study fine arts in Weimar, Germany at a newly founded art school called Bauhaus. He vehemently denied her request and told her to get those foolish thoughts out of her mind. Lila was determined to change the course of her life and devised a plan for herself. She contacted Adam in London who had become a successful and wealthy businessman. Lila's plan was to have Adam support her financially and pay for her tuition, which would allow her to pursue her dream. Adam agreed, and they vowed to keep their plan a secret from the rest of the family.

In May 1919, at the end of World War I, Lila packed all of her belongings and left a note on her bedroom mirror. It read:

Dear Father,

Forgive me. I am leaving for Germany. I don't know if I will be back. Marriage is of no interest to me.

Art is my calling, and I am determined to follow my destiny. I hope that someday you will understand me.

Goodbye.

Love,
Lila

Once she arrived in Berlin, she dropped her middle name, Esther, which in Hebrew means "hidden," and hid her Jewish identity. Lila also needed to assemble her art portfolio for school. Berlin had the finest art museums in Europe. She rented a simple flat in Prenzlauer Berg, an impoverished and densely populated working-class district. The rent was cheap and suited her budget. The '20s were roaring around her. Lila enjoyed the café scene, where she often met other artists, writers, and poets. She did not bob her hair, do her nails, or learn swing, but she did start smoking. She quickly became bohemian.

***

Eric Hoffmann was born in Leipzig, Germany in 1896. He was a Roman Catholic from a well-to-do family. They traded in the cotton industry. The family cotton business dated back to the time of German industrialization in the 1800s when Saxony's wood industry made its home in Leipzig.

The Hoffmanns traded in Silesian cotton, which at the time, was Germany's most important export. They also traded with Polish Jews, importing furs from Poland. At that point, a business dispute developed between the Hoffmanns and their Jewish partners that left bad blood that lingered until the early 1900s when the Hoffmanns built a large weaving and cotton mill based on the model of the English textile technology and continued to modernize their manufacturing techniques. After World War I, they were the major supplier of cotton products in Saxony, Germany.

Eric had no interest in becoming part of the family business enterprises. Instead, he decided to study law at Leipzig University and become an atheist—religion was an anathema to him. Then he began studying for an advanced degree in law at Humboldt University, Berlin.

On a sunny day in June of 1919, Eric decided to take a break from his studies and take a stroll along Unter den Linden. The streets were crowded with Sunday strollers. Eric walked down the Palace Bridge that connected Lustgarten and the museum island. He stopped to look at the massive neo baroque Berliner Dom Cathedral. He marveled at the reflection of the cathedral and the beautiful ripples forming on the Spree River. Eric continued to walk along the riverbank and then turned onto Bodeststrasse and stopped in front of the Altes Museum's monumental colonnade. He considered the building to be one of the most beautiful neoclassical structures in Germany.

Eric was an art lover who admired Greek and Roman classical antiquities. On this particular day, acting on impulse, he decided to amble through the museum galleries. Sunday was the museum's busiest day, and the halls were bustling with visitors. Eric walked into the center of the building, a two-story, sky-lit rotunda. The domed coffered ceiling was surrounded by Corinthian columns. Between the columns stood the museum's collection of Roman and Greek statues. It resembled the design of the ancient Pantheon in Rome. He proceeded to walk toward the Roman and Etruscan exhibits, viewing clay and bronze figures, when he noticed a young female artist sketching in her notebook. He decided to take a sneak peek at her artwork.

Eric stopped behind the artist's back and stood quietly, admiring her work. She was drawing a Greek warrior's head with charcoal. Her back was bent, and her long white scarf flowed down her round shoulders and over her long, dark blue dress. The artist must have felt his gaze from behind her because she turned around. When their eyes met, Eric was taken by the artist's exotic beauty. Her image seemed somewhat familiar, although he could not quite place it at first. Then it hit him. She reminded him of Diana, the Roman Goddess of hunting and the open sky. Her face was fair, adorned with large brown eyes, slim red lips, and a high forehead. The white scarf looked like a moon crown over her dark-brown hair.

Eric stood paralyzed, looking at her like a child watching an exotic animal at the zoo for the very first time. "Sorry to disturb you, *fräulein*," Eric said meekly. "I was admiring your artwork."

The artist smiled. "Do you like classical antiquity?" she asked.

"Yes," he replied. He extended his hand and introduced himself. "I am Eric Hoffmann."

"Lila Schonkoff. It's nice to meet you."

"What a beautiful and unusual name you have."

"It's Dutch. It means 'night.'"

Her name matches her mysterious beauty, Eric thought to himself. With a nervous gesture, he asked, "Would you join me for a cup of coffee at the museum café?" He was afraid of her rejection but took a leap of faith anyway.

Lila hesitated at his request for a long moment. She displayed the demeanor of one not accustomed to having conversations with strangers. "Yes. I would love to have coffee," she replied. Eric was pleasantly surprised. He felt that there was something special about this connection.

Eric courted Lila for several months. Throughout their courtship, Lila and Eric built a sweet and loving relationship. They became inseparable, spending days taking romantic strolls in the park, visiting art museums, and having passionate conversations about their hopes, dreams, and deepest desires. They seemed to be a perfect match for each other, each one the missing piece to the other's heart, and they knew that they wanted to spend the rest of their lives together. Although Eric was five years older than Lila, they had fallen in love, and she decided to move in with him.

***

Lila was naïve about sex, since her life in Apeldoorn had not prepared her to live in the real world. She had always been told that girls must remain virgins until they were married. For a Jewish woman coming from an Orthodox family, breaking this rule was the ultimate sin. If her community found out she'd had premarital sex, all doors would be slammed in her face.

Lila did not believe in these rules and wanted to be liberated. She felt no guilt for her pleasurable desires and gave herself to Eric, who proposed marriage to her for fear that he might lose her to another man. Lila felt both resistance and temptation from the marriage proposal. She hesitated, not because of a lack of love for him, but because of the fear of word getting out that she had married out of her faith. If this were ever to be found out, she would be ostracized from her family in Apeldoorn.

She told Eric, "We are already equal partners. We love each other. I gave myself to you without any reservations. We are already one, and we do not need a marriage certificate to prove it." Lila wanted to finish her studies in Bauhaus and did not feel that she could stay and deal with Eric's marriage proposal. The following day, she left Berlin for Weimar.

During the school year, Lila found herself pregnant with Eric's child. She had strong beliefs about women and pregnancy and wanted to keep the child. Although her roommate encouraged her to abort the pregnancy and finish her studies, she refused.

Lila wrote to her brother in London about her situation and asked for his advice. He told her that, under no circumstances should she abort this pregnancy. He believed that life was sacred, and he was also concerned about the health risk she would be taking. As for his feelings regarding her promiscuity, he was very disappointed in her behavior. He also felt that, since Eric was the father, he must be told about the pregnancy.

When Lila told Eric, he was elated. He encouraged her to finish her art studies in Berlin. He repeated his proposal of marriage, and she told him that they would get married eventually, just not at the present time. She moved back to Eric's apartment in Berlin.

In 1920, Lila gave birth to a healthy baby boy. She named him Kare, which means "strong" in Dutch.

Escape

In the spring of 1937, the dreadful day arrived when Kare needed to remember the instructions given to him such a long time ago. The words that his mother had told him echoed in his mind: "In case anything ever happens to your father or to me, you mustn't come home." After receiving the phone call, Kare left school in a hurry. Lila's instructions proved that she had had a premonition for things to come, and she had confided her thoughts to her friend, Max.

Max Van Devel was of Dutch origin and a personal friend of the family. He resented the Nazi regime but kept his views to himself. Kare had worked part time in his gourmet shop during his Keno Academy school years, and the family knew that he was a trustworthy man.

Kare's mind filled with many thoughts. *Why did they arrest Dad? Was Mom arrested too? What will happen to me?*

Kare took the U-Bahn metro to Max's gourmet shop, which was only a few train stops away from his home. As he walked from the station, his curiosity got the best of him, and he decided to walk past his house. He strayed toward the opposite side of the street and noticed two black cars parked next to his driveway. In one of them sat a sinister looking man with greasy black hair and a perfectly groomed, equally greasy, moustache and beard. Kare recognized the infamous Nazi insignia sewn onto the right sleeve of his shirt. He lowered his head and walked past his house quickly, not daring to look back.

When Kare arrived at Max's gourmet shop, he told Max what had happened. Max was surprised to hear the terrible news but remained calm and reassured Kare that everything would be all right. Max was a short, plump, grey-haired man in his sixties. He sported a moustache and had pleasant, friendly green eyes. "Just listen to me and follow my instructions," Max said as he walked Kare to the basement of the shop. In the basement was Max's office with a filing cabinet, a desk, and a small sofa. He instructed Kare to stay there for the night. After closing the store, Max brought down some food and a blanket. He lived in an apartment above the gourmet shop with his wife and did not want her to know that Kare was staying there.

As Kare lay on the sofa, the room was quiet, except for the sound of the clock on the wall. *Tick tock, tick tock.* His eyes were wide open, as he thought about his mother. He realized that she had been right. They should have left Germany when they'd had the chance. When Uncle Andrew was in Berlin last year, Kare had overheard a conversation between his father and Uncle Andrew. Andrew had told Eric to move to London. He had been able to line up a job for him and was convinced that things would not get any better in Germany. Kare had dismissed this conversation at the time, but it now weighed heavily on his mind. He now knew that they should have left Germany long ago. If father had only listened, he would not be in this predicament now. Eric was stubborn, loved his teaching job, and didn't care for money. He spoke his mind, which is what had gotten him arrested. Kare could not believe that his father was sitting in jail at that very moment. He wished that it was all a bad dream, but the sound of the clock snapped him out of thought. *Tick tock, tick tock.* As a single tear trickled down his cheek, Kare's eyelids slowly closed, and he fell asleep.

Kare woke up early and heard Max coming downstairs. The man entered the room holding a towel and soap and said, "*Guten Morgen* (Good morning). How did you sleep?"

Kare nodded his head. "I slept well, thank you."

Max instructed him to wash himself and then come upstairs to help in the store. When Kare arrived in the shop, he was told to work in the back room chopping and preparing salads. The employees knew him and thought nothing of having him there. The day passed uneventfully, and when night fell, Kare retreated back to the basement.

The next day, at noon, Max asked Kare to come help in the shop again. This time, he would be helping the customers. As Kare looked at the line of people waiting to pay, he noticed his mother in the back of the shop. Max whispered to Kare that he could not show any sign that he knew her or show any favoritism toward her. He thought the Gestapo might be watching her since Eric had been arrested. When Lila got to the front of the line, she ordered half a kilogram of veal sausage. When Kare handed her the meat, she handed him twenty reichsmarks and slightly squeezed his fingers. "Keep the change," she said in a hushed voice. Kare had a strong feeling that his mother was saying goodbye to him for the last time. He held her hand just a little bit longer without saying a word, and then let go as tears filled his eyes. As he put the money into the cash register, he noticed a folded paper tucked between bills. Kare took it to the storage room and unfolded it slowly.

Dearest Kare,

Leave as soon as possible for Apeldoorn, Holland. Go to your Uncle David Schonkoff's home. You will find him in Solomon's Fur and Coat Shop near Orange Park in the center of town. Once you have contacted David, contact your Uncle Andrew in London. He will instruct you on what to do.

Your father was arrested at the university. He gave a lecture to the students and criticized the Gestapo's use of the Schutzhaft. Ask Max for the envelope.

Your Loving Mother

Kare folded the note back up and put it in his pocket. He knew about the law of protective custody. He went to the front of the store and asked Max for the envelope. In it, he found their passport and a photo of the two of them together. The envelope also contained 1,000 reichsmarks. Max told Kare that his mother had had a premonition that this would happen, and he was glad she had been wise enough to prepare for this day. Max gave Kare a small suitcase and urged him to empty his school bag into it. He bade Kare farewell and advised him to leave immediately.

Kare left the shop and blended in with the pedestrians on the street. He took the U-Bahn to the Berlin central station, Anhalter

Bahnhof, near Potsdamer Platz. Kare stopped at one of the shops near the train station and bought himself a pair of black slacks and a grey jacket. Then he quietly waited for his train to arrive.

The connection from Berlin to Amsterdam was an easy one. Trains left every two hours. It was an eight-hour ride. Kare settled into one of the cabins, which was already occupied by two other passengers. He introduced himself and took a seat next to the window. He had hardly slept the previous night; thus, exhausted, he fell asleep. The conductor and a Gestapo officer, who was dressed in civilian clothes, awakened Kare. For a moment, he had fear in his eyes. Then he heard, "Documents!" The Gestapo officer demanded identification and tickets. Kare was relived. Then, just as quickly as they had come in, they were gone, and Kare fell back asleep.

The train suddenly jolted to a stop. This time, it pulled up at Duisburg Hauptbahnhof. Here, Kare had to transfer to a train to Amsterdam. It was nighttime, and the large station was almost deserted. As he ambled through the station, Kare was stopped by a Gestapo officer in civilian clothes, who began to question him. "What is in your suitcase?" he demanded.

Kare tried not to let the officer hear his voice shake as he answered. "It is just my personal belongings."

"Open it up."

Kare placed the suitcase on the platform floor and opened it. He held his breath while the officer surveyed the contents of the suitcase.

"What is this?" the officer asked, pointing his fingers at the Movex.

"This is my camera and film. I am a student at the Kino Academy."

"Your documents, please" he said. Kare handed him his German identification. There was no *J* stamped on his passport. "Why are you traveling to Nederland?" he asked.

Kare swallowed the huge lump in his throat. "To see my sick uncle in Apeldoorn. I have a letter from my school for a month-long leave of absence."

Kare handed the letter to the Gestapo officer. He glanced at it quickly and gave it and the identification back to Kare, then he reached into Kare's suitcase and picked up one of the movie cassettes. He opened it up, unrolled the 8-millimeter film, and held it up to the light. Kare's heart started pounding. One of the films was a movie he had taken of his father at home. Kare pondered what the chances were that this officer would recognize his father from the film. The officer stopped looking at the unrolled film and said, "You were at the Hitler Youth Movement?"

"Yes, I filmed one of the rallies a few years ago."

The Gestapo officer threw the cassette back into the suitcase, said, "Heil Hitler," and walked away. Kare replied with the Nazi salute and boarded his train to Amsterdam, his heart still pounding.

At the border, the Dutch customs officer checked him again. Kare showed him his Dutch passport and was cleared to continue his journey. The next day, he arrived at Amsterdam's Central Station. It was a large and busy terminal located on a manmade island in front of the open harbor. Kare proceeded to buy tickets to Apeldoorn on the Dieren Line. The ride to Apeldoorn was about an hour and a half long.

Kare arrived at the Apeldoorn central station in the afternoon, and soon after, boarded a local bus for the last part of his journey. When he stepped onto the bus, he asked the driver if they would stop at Orange Park. "You can walk from here. It is only a few blocks away," said the driver dismissingly.

"*Bedank* (Thank you)," Kare said as he got off the bus. At the bus station, Kare asked a passerby for directions to Orange Park. He followed the directions and arrived at the park. Looking across the street, he saw a sign: Solomon Furs & Coats. It was a typical eighteenth-century Dutch building—a three-story brick façade with large windows and an apex ball gable rooftop adorned with stonework and cornucopia decorations.

As Kare entered the store, a bell rang, announcing his entry. The first floor was long and narrow with wooden plank floors and a high ceiling. The smell of fur and glue was in the air. The narrow shop served as both store and workshop. Fur coats were hanging on both sides of the counters. A man behind the counter looked at Kare and said, "Can I help you?" He was wearing grey overalls and glasses and sported a long beard.

"I am looking for Mr. Schonkoff," Kare said.

"And whom, may I ask, is looking for him?" the man snarled.

Kare took a deep breath. "I am Kare Hoffmann. I have come from Berlin."

The man's expression changed. He was silent for a moment and then broke out with a smile. "Is your mother's name Lila?"

Kare's face lit up as he nodded. The bearded man came out from behind the counter and greeted Kare with open arms. "What a surprise. Welcome, Kare. I am your Uncle David, your mother's brother. I must call Sarah to tell her this good news. When did you arrive?"

"Just half an hour ago from Amsterdam."

"How are your parents?"

Kare told him of his father's arrest and his own quick escape from Germany.

"Terrible, terrible news. How long are you planning to stay with us?"

"I need to contact my Uncle Andrew. In the meantime, my mother wants me to stay with your family."

"You are welcome in our home. Stay as long as you like." David closed the shop, and they headed to his house. Kare remembered that he had to send a telegram home to tell his mother of his safe arrival in Holland. He decided that he would do it the following day.

Apeldoorn, 1937

It was a tranquil, late afternoon. Uncle David's house was a thirty-minute walk from the shop. They turned toward Burgemeester Tutein and strolled halfway down the block to his front porch. Kare was exhausted from his long trip from Berlin. The day's tension had given him a pounding headache. Sarah, David's wife, had been told of Kare's arrival, and she greeted them at the door. "Welcome to our home," she said as she invited him inside.

Kare had never met Sarah. She was older than his mom and did not dress as his mom had. She wore a long dress with long sleeves, and wore a neat, colorful scarf on her head. She had a pleasant face and did not wear makeup except for a hint of red lipstick. She was an Orthodox woman; modesty was her norm.

The tantalizing, warm, and savory aroma of simmering chicken soup filled the room and aroused Kare's appetite. For the past few days, he had eaten only cold sandwiches. Home cooking would be a welcome change. Kare was seated at the table. Being polite, he waited for his uncle to start the meal. David proceeded to change his hat to a small black *yarmulke* (skullcap). Then he gave one to Kare, who hesitated, pausing for a moment, not knowing what to do. David motioned with his hand to place it on his head. Putting it on, Kare thought to himself, *Only Jewish people wear yarmulkes. I am not a Jew.*

Sarah went back and forth from the kitchen to the dining room table, fetching food. "How are your parents?" she asked.

"They are fine," Kare replied. He was unsure if he should tell Sarah of his father's arrest. Then his uncle answered for him.

"His father was arrested by the Gestapo."

Something fell and crashed onto the kitchen floor. Sarah popped out from the kitchen. She held her two hands on her cheeks, reminiscent of Edvard Munch's *The Scream.* Distressed, she asked, "When did this happen? Your father is not Jewish. Why?"

"A few days ago," Kare replied.

"Sarah, darling," his uncle interjected, "let him eat now. He is tired and hungry. We will continue this conversation tomorrow when Kare has rested and unwound." Then his uncle picked up a loaf of bread, held it in his hands, and started praying. He slightly raised the bread from the table and uttered words that did not sound familiar to Kare's ears. It was not in German; it was not Dutch. *What language is that?* he wondered.

Sarah asked Kare, "How long do you plan to stay in Apeldoorn?" Kare shrugged his shoulders. "I don't know," he replied. "I need to hear from Uncle Andrew."

His eyes were focused on the chicken soup in the bowl. He lifted his spoon and slurped his soup. After he'd swallowed a few spoonfuls, Sarah proceeded to serve meat and potatoes. He wolfed them down as well, chewing and gnawing at his food in a hurry. It was delicious and comforting. His uncle and aunt looked at him in bewilderment. He lifted his eyes from the plate and felt ashamed for pouncing on the food. He slowed his chomps. Sarah said, "God bless you! You have a healthy appetite. Eat more!" She proceeded to stuff his plate with more food.

When tea was served, Uncle David said, "I haven't seen Lila for more than twenty years. The last image I remember is when she was your age and left for Berlin. A beautiful young woman. She was unbound, free-spirited, noncompliant, and a real rebel. She was always arguing with our father. I miss her. Did you know that your mother was your grandfather's favorite?"

"No, she did not tell me that," Kare replied. "She has not spoken much about her family in Apeldoorn. I asked her once why she never visited her family in Holland; she told me that she would tell me why someday. She never did."

Sarah placed her hand on Kare's shoulders and said, "It is okay. Now that you are here, you are part of our family. I remember your mother as a young woman many years ago."

"I met Uncle Andrew in London three years ago when I visited him with my mother. I liked him."

"My brother hasn't visited Apeldoorn for years. I met him several times in Amsterdam when he was there for business. Did you know that you have two uncles besides me?" asked David.

"No," Kare said, his eyes widening in surprise.

"Your Uncle Jakob and Rivka live in Amsterdam. Uncle Avraham and Nehama live in Antwerp."

"I didn't know that. I should visit them someday," Kare said.

"You must be tired. Come upstairs, and I will show you to your bedroom," Sarah said. The bedroom was sparsely furnished with a bed, a desk near the window, and a dresser, but Kare did not pay any attention to the room décor. The only thing that he wanted now was to stretch out on the bed. His eyes were heavy, and he yawned when he heard Sarah say, "This was your mother's room when she lived here. Your grandfather, Solomon, bless his soul, died last year. He had kept this room just as it was when Lila left us long ago. You know, sometimes he would come here, lock the door, and sit quietly for a long time. His heart was broken by grief when your mother married your father. She was dead to him."

Sarah's words astonished him. He had been unaware of the close, deep relation between his mother and his grandfather. He asked, "Why? She's not dead."

"You know, Kare, for us Jews, marriage outside of our faith is forbidden. It hurt your grandfather."

"What happened to Grandmother Miriam?"

"She passed away. God bless her memory. She died when your mother was ten. It was terrible. Your grandfather was left to take care of your mother. Did you know that your mom's Hebrew name was Esther?"

"No."

Sarah continued talking while placing clean linen sheets on the bed. "Your grandfather gave your mom the Hebrew name of Esther because it was his mother's name. Your mother loved the name. During Purim, she loved reading the Megillah aloud, pointing out her heroine, Queen Esther, as her role model for women. Have you read the Megillah?"

"No."

"You should. It was your mother's favorite book," Sarah replied quietly. "Go to sleep now. We will have plenty of time tomorrow to talk. You must have a good rest, *Goedenacht* (goodnight)," and she left the room silently.

Sunlight was playing on Kare's face when he woke. For a moment, he needed to find his bearings. *Where am I?* His eyes landed on the low ceiling, then panned and focused on the peeling yellow paisley wall covering. Tree branches cast shadows on the wall. They swayed back and forth, back and forth. Kare's mind drifted, recalling last night's conversation with Sarah. "This is your mother's room," he remembered her saying. He had a pleasant feeling. He was home in his mother's bed and wrapped the blanket around his body. Holding it tight and closing his eyes, he felt like a child in his mother's arms, safe and secure. The feeling lasted for just a moment, and then reality sank in. Kare jumped off the bed. He had things to do today. Washed and dressed, Kare walked into the kitchen. Sarah was baking. The smell of fresh pastries permeated the house. "*Goed morgen* (good morning)," she said.

"Good morning," Kare replied.

"How was your sleep?"

"I slept like a log."

"Sit down. What would you like for breakfast? I just baked a *kridkoek* (spice cake). Would you like a piece?"

"Yes I would," he said.

"How about two fried eggs and a piece of cold meat?"

"That would be fine," he replied.

Sarah placed a hefty piece of *kridkoek* on Kare's plate.

"*Bedank.*"

While frying the eggs, Sarah pointed to the tea that was on the stove.

"Can I have a glass of milk?" Kare asked.

Sarah stopped frying. She turned around, holding a spatula in her hand. "We do not eat meat and milk products together. We observe a kosher tradition in our house."

Kare had heard the word *kosher* before but was unaware of what this Jewish law was about.

"Did your mother observe a kosher house?"

"No," Kare answered. "She never told me that she was Jewish. At home, we did not practice any religion."

"We do not eat pork or shellfish and do not mix meat and milk."

"Mother hated pork and would not eat it, but she served it to my father and me."

In the morning, Kare headed to the Post, Telegraph and Telegram office. He sent a telegram to his mother with these words:

TELEGRAM DEUTHE REIHSPOST BERLIN
The uncle feels better stop hoping to see you soon
KH

Then he sent a second telegram to Uncle Andrew:

TELEGRAM WUTRAVBURO LONDON
Arrived at Apeldoorn yesterday stop G-men arrested Father 4 days ago stop Mother instructed me to travel to London to see you KH "XU" [I await your reply.]

Kare window shopped in the vicinity of the post office. He needed undergarments and stopped at a haberdashery to pick up a few items. He then remembered Sarah's words. "Today is Friday. Your uncle will be home at noon. Tomorrow is the Sabbath, and the store will be closed. Come home before five in the afternoon."

In the evening, Uncle David rushed to go to the local synagogue. It was the only place for Jewish worship in town. David asked Kare to join him for the service to which Kare agreed. He remembered the pleasant experience he'd had with Uncle Andrew in a house of prayer in London. There had been a choir and music, and he'd enjoyed the scene.

This synagogue was a small, brick-faced building with large, rectangular windows. There was a simple Dutch-style door. The chapel was full of worshipers dressed in their best, each wearing a white *tallit* (shawl) and praying loudly. They faced a simple cabinet with open doors, in which the Torah scrolls were stored. In front of the cabinet was a *Bemah* (elevated platform), where a Torah scroll was unwound. A bearded rabbi stood at the Bemah and prayed in unison with the congregation. Kare noted that there was neither music nor a choir. This was so different from the worship service he had attended in London. This was an Orthodox synagogue. This was only the second time he had observed Jewish services. There were no more synagogues in Berlin, and his Jewish classmates had emigrated from Germany several years before. Kare remembered the anti-Semitic posters on shop windows and around the city. Here in Holland, the Jewish life and traditions continued uninterrupted and without fear. *How strange*, he thought. *Just a few hours by train and you are in another world.* He felt like an outsider observing the services. He did not consider himself as one of them, as a Jew. There wasn't a *J* stamped on his German ID papers. *It's strange that mother never told me of her past and her family in Holland.*

After services, Uncle David introduced Kare to the rabbi, Bernard Rosenthal. He was a short, bearded man in his sixties and spoke perfect German. "Please come tomorrow evening to my home. I would like to hear the latest news from Berlin."

Kare nodded his head and replied, "I will."

Back home, at the dinner table, Sarah lit two candles. As she spread her arms in the warm candlelight, she said a prayer in silence with her eyes closed. "Amen." She finished praying and then rubbed her warm hands on Kare's shoulders. Kare sat and observed the ritual with open eyes and keen interest. It reminded him of when his mother lit two candles in silence at the kitchen table on Friday nights. He had never asked her why. Now, it all began to make sense to him. Uncle David prayed over a glass of wine and a loaf of bread. It was *Shabbat* eve. Kare asked about the meaning of the Shabbat (Sabbath). Uncle replied, "Shabbat is a period of timelessness set off from the rest of the week when our daily hectic activities come to a slow halt, and a sense of unutterable peace, calm, and tranquility takes its place. We refrain from our daily activities and *melakhah* (work)."

On Saturday, Uncle David invited Kare for a walk. He wanted to know more about Lila and Eric's life together. He also told Kare that news from Germany was disturbing. "There are rumors of possible war in Europe. The Germans have always considered the Dutch people a German tribe. The anti-Semitism rattled the Jewish community in Holland, and the outlook of them is not good. There are rumors that they will need to register with new ID cards. I am thinking of selling my business and emigrating to America, where my two daughters reside now." David then asked Kare what his plans were for the future.

Kare responded, "I hope my father's arrest is a temporary setback. He is not a criminal, not a communist, and not a Jew. When this is clarified, they will release him. As for me, I would like to finish my studies in cinematography. That is my life's goal."

"You cannot go back to Germany."

"Not now, I know. Maybe soon. The situation is only temporary."

"No, Kare," David said. "I read the *Nieuw Israelietisch Weekblad*—the *New Israelite Weekly*. Things in Germany will not get better for the Jews."

"But I am not Jewish."

His uncle fell silent for a while. Then he said, "Kare, you are considered Jewish to the German authority. You are a Jew. If they find out, they will deport you or arrest you and send you to a labor camp."

Kare stopped walking. "What do you mean? I am a Jew?"

"Kare, I will let Rabbi Bernard explain that to you." They continued walking in silence.

Kare wrestled with the question, *Why is Uncle saying that I am a Jew? I don't practice the faith.* He was eager to meet with the rabbi and ask him the question himself.

It was late afternoon when they reached the rabbi's home. He invited them into his study. His wife offered tea and cake. The rabbi sat at his desk, which was laden with books and newspapers. It was a dark room lined with bookcases. Rabbi Bernard asked Kare and his uncle to sit in the chairs next to his desk. A single light bulb illuminated the table. *He looks like Saint Nicholas,* Kare thought.

The rabbi said, "Your uncle told me all about your mother, and I understand she was a talented artist. Is she still painting?"

"Yes," Kare said. "She used to teach art in the Berlin Campus of the Bauhaus before it was closed by the Nazis."

"And your father," continued the rabbi, "what does he do?"

"He is a professor of law at Humboldt University."

"Yes, Moses was our law giver, a noble profession for a man to pursue. Why was your father arrested?"

"He gave a lecture at the university to the students and criticized the Gestapo's use of the so-called *Schutzhaft*—the law of protective custody."

The rabbi nodded his head and said, "It is a dangerous time in Germany, especially for Jews."

Kare replied bitterly, "My father is not Jewish."

"I know," the rabbi said, "but your mother is Jewish."

"She does not practice Judaism, and she never told me she was Jewish." He then asked the burning question that had been bothering him all afternoon. "Rabbi, my father was born as a Roman Catholic. My parents were atheist and did not practice any religion. What am I? Am I a Jew?"

The rabbi answered, "It is an old question that has puzzled our sages for centuries. Who is a Jew is interpreted in our Jewish laws and customs. The *Halakha* ruling—interpretation of the laws of Scriptures—says that if the mother is Jewish, even though there is no certainty that the father is a Jew, the child is a Jew. You are one of us. Your mother married a non-Jew. Such is life. Were it not for the prohibition of interfaith marriage, were it not for the *Halakha*, who could have withstood the disappearance and the problem of the Jewish existence in the Diaspora? What would happen if there was no assimilation? Within a few generations, our people would have been doomed. They would have disappeared. The *Halakha* ruling forbade us from intermarriage unless a conversion was performed in front of qualified *battei din*—a panel of judges—and accompanied by circumcision, immersion in *mikveh*, as well as acceptance of the Torah commandment. That decision was your father's to make."

Kare said, "I am not circumcised."

David, who, until now, had been sitting quietly listening to the conversation, interjected, "Let me tell you a joke. Why are Jewish men circumcised? Because no Jewish woman will touch anything that isn't at least twenty percent off."

They all laughed, and Kare began to admire his uncle's wit.

"Now, young man, you need to answer this question: 'Am I a Jew?' Now that I have explained this to you and have laid out the law, you decide. You should be aware of the German Nuremburg Law, which passed in Germany in 1935 and forbade contact between an Aryan German and a Jew, especially a marriage. It strips Jews of

German citizenship. This Nazi law is to protect German blood and rescue German honor, so they say. It also applies to the children of such marriages; they are deprived of the rights of citizenship. Now, young man, my advice to you is not to go back to Germany."

Kare recognized how naïve he had been. He now understood the facts that the rabbi had laid out in front of him, painting a bleak picture. He knew he could not go back to Germany. He would not finish his courses in the Academy of Film. He would not see his friends again or walk the streets of Berlin. He would never have the opportunity to date girls like Monika. He realized it would be impossible to go back to the times before his father's arrest. He felt anger. His hope of seeing his father began to fray. The sordid truth hit him like a bombshell. *Why wasn't father careful in choosing his words at his university lectures?*

Kare stood up ready to leave. Then he asked the rabbi if he had a German translation of the Book of Esther.

Rabbi Bernard answered, "Yes. I have the *Ketuvim.* It is the Old Testament that contains the Book of Esther. It tells the story of a Jewish girl named Esther. You can borrow it." The rabbi retrieved the book from the shelf.

Kare promised to return it once he had finished reading. He said goodnight to the rabbi. Uncle David and Kare walked in silence back home. By the time he reached the house, Kare's mind was cleared of angry thoughts. Reason prevailed. After all, his mother wanted him to be in a safe place. Kare felt safe and "at home."

London

Kare received a night letter from London. It was from his Uncle Andrew:

Dear Kare

In two weeks you will receive your travel documents stop we are waiting for you

Love Andrew & Sally

Kare sent a reply back:

TELEGRAM WUTRAVBURO LONDON

Dear A & S

I received your instructions stop any news from Berlin stop regards to all

Love KH

Kare settled into a routine at Uncle David's home. He spent his free time exploring Apeldoorn. It was a small, provincial town in Holland. There were no shops where he could buy 8-millimeter film for his movie camera, so he ordered it from Amsterdam.

Kare loved nature and took advantage of the nearby forest known as the De Veluwe. He hiked through heavy woodlands on narrow paths that threaded their way among tall trees of pine, birch, and oak. Occasionally, an uprooted root on the trail blocked his course. Kare scrambled over fallen trees. Then he stopped to sit on a fallen trunk for a long time, observing striking strips of light streaming through tree branches. He panned his movie camera to capture those natural moments on film.

Kare also visited the Dutch royal family palace known as the Paleis Het Loo. There, he practiced filming "Dutch angle shots." This technique originated in Germany and was widely used. The tilting of the camera created distortion and a movie montage that gave viewers an overall impression of the passage of time. When he ran out of film, Kare spent his time with Uncle David in the fur shop. Kare watched him work and helped him with chores at the store, packing customers' orders and cleaning. Kare also practiced Dutch by conversing with customers. Strangers gravitated toward him, as he was charming and friendly.

In May 1937, two weeks after his arrival from Berlin, Kare received a "night letter" from London:

In a week's time, come to Amsterdam to pick up your travel documents from my business associates at the law firm of Single and de Klerk. You will meet with your Uncle Jakob Schonkoff to assist you with your travel arrangements. They are located at Nieuw Zijde on Kalverstraat. I will meet you on May 28th at Liverpool Line Railway station in London.

Greetings to Sarah and David. Good luck!

Love,
Andrew and Sally

P.S. No news from Berlin.

Kare left for Amsterdam to meet his Uncle Jakob at the law offices for the first time. Jakob was a tall, grey-haired, clean-shaven, well-dressed gentleman. He was excited to meet his nephew and received him warmly. "Welcome to our family, Kare. You are so grown up. We haven't seen your mother for a long time; you are a splitting image of Lila."

"Thanks. I am pleased to meet you, Uncle. I heard so many good things about your family from David."

"David is a good man. I had a long conversation with Andrew and heard the bad news. God willing, they will free your father soon."

"I hope so."

"You know, Kare, your mother lived with us. We consider her our daughter." Uncle Jakob turned to the attorney, Mr. Single, and said, "Let's help this young man with the travel paperwork."

Mr. Single made Kare sign legal travel applications and advised him that the passport and visa would be ready in approximately a week's time. While waiting for his documents, he stayed with his uncle and aunt in Amsterdam.

Kare was astonished to hear about his mother's past from Rifka; it was all a discovery for him. She told him she had treated Lila as her daughter, and Rifka questioned Kare about his mother's life in Berlin. She wanted to fill in all of the blanks in Lila's life. Rikfa showed him a folder of Lila's watercolor paintings, which she had kept for the past twenty years. She offered it to Kare and said, "It belongs to you."

Uncle Jakob told Kare that the Nazi persecution of the Jews in Germany eventually would spill into Holland. Although Jews had lived with the Dutch in harmony for centuries, Holland was a small country and had a weak military. Jakob was planning to relocate his businesses in Canada, where his daughter and son-in-law had a satellite export/import office.

Kare spent a week with his uncle's family, cementing his relationship with them. He wondered why his mother had hidden all of this from him. He noted that he must ask her once they were reunited as promised.

A week later, Kare received all of his travel documents. He thanked his uncle's family, who had treated him as one of their own. He called Uncle David in the store and thanked him for his hospitality. Kare said, "Please send my warmest regards to Sarah. I will call you from London."

Jakob stuffed one hundred pounds into Kare's jacket pocket, saying, "This is your spending money." As he hugged Kare, he said, "Give our warmest regards to Andrew and Sally."

That morning, Kare took a train to Rotterdam and boarded a ferry from the Hook of Holland to Harwich, England. He arrived at Harwich Port and took a train to London. His uncle had instructed him to wear a red scarf so he could recognize him and to meet him at Liverpool Landing Train Station under the World War I monument.

The train pulled into the Liverpool station on time. It was crowded with passengers. As he was approaching the monument, he recognized Sally and Andrew. They waved to him.

Kare kissed Aunt Sally on her cheeks. She smelled of a flowery, sweet scent. It reminded him of his mother's perfume. *It must be Guerlain, the French perfume,* he thought. Her lips were colored bright red with a blue undertone. Her crystal-clear eyes sparkled on her welcoming face. Sally hugged Kare tight. "You are so grown up. I almost did not recognize you," she said, smiling. Sally wore a beautiful printed, full skirt reaching just below her knees—a shirtwaist with big sleeves tucked neatly into her bodice. Her hands were covered with short ivory gloves, and an ivory summer hat rested neatly on her blonde hair. She looked like a typical aristocratic British woman.

Andrew extended his hand and greeted Kare. "Welcome to England, my boy. How was your crossing?"

Kare replied, "Fine. Everything was on time."

His uncle was dressed in a blue striped suit and a white shirt. He looked he had stepped out of a magazine page—an English gentleman. He pointed his furled umbrella toward the exit and said, "Let's go."

Sally grabbed Kare's hand, and they headed toward the street. Andrew waved for a taxicab. He said to the driver, "Eaton Square, please." Kare's uncle was a wealthy man. Eaton Square was an upper-class address, not as grand as Mayfair or Belgravia, but still, Eaton Square ranked high as a fashionable neighborhood. The square predominantly consisted of three bay-wide classical buildings joined together and was almost wholly residential. The black taxicab stopped in front of a white stucco neo-Greek classical, four-story townhouse dating back to the 1800s.

Under an Ionic colonnaded portico entry, Thomas, the butler and valet, greeted them. Dressed in a black frock coat with a white bowtie, he was an elderly gentleman with graying hair. He took Kare's suitcase and invited him into the house. At the door, Kare's cousin, Laura, was waiting for him, grinning. Laura looked so mature, dressed in a schoolgirl uniform. It had been four years since Kare had last seen her. Now she was glamorous with blonde hair and blue eyes. Like her mother, Laura had an Andalusian guitar figure, a Belle Tourneur, hoity-toity. Laura greeted him with a kiss on the cheek, grabbed his hand, and invited him into the salon.

The townhouse was luxurious and large. In the salon, Andrew offered him a glass of port. Kare's eyes wandered over the salon's walls and décor. Andrew was an art lover and a collector of fine paintings and art objects, including furniture, from the Art Nouveau and Art Deco periods. The blue-hued walls were adorned with the artwork of Aubrey Beaudsley, Alphonse Mucha, Georges Braug, and two twentieth-century avant-garde painters, Pablo Picasso and Marc Chagall. In the adjacent dining room, a large oval table with chairs designed by the Dutch artist, Henry van de Velde, sat in the center. A large Tiffany chandelier hung over the table. There were also Tiffany and Daum vases displayed throughout the ground floor.

Sally and Andrew had good taste. They collected visual art for pleasure; they were not building a collection of art as a shrine to these artists. They were not "high-brow snobs." They were verbally and socially sophisticated. In England, at the time, the cultural differences between the elite and the rest of the middle class were not so great. Shakespeare, museums, and operas enjoyed mass appeal.

Kare carried a glass of port as Laura gave him a tour of the stately ground floor rooms. The library was full of books, plump leather sofas, and a beautiful, unusual piano. Laura told him that it was a replica of a Bechstein Art Nouveau grand piano and a favorite of her sister's, Gabriella. She was not present to greet him today, as she was attending the all-girl Headington Preparatory School in Oxford and only came home on holidays. The smoking room was her father's inner sanctum. He spent his private time there at his desk.

The rest of the house tour was given by Thomas. On the second floor, there were three bedrooms. The first one was for his uncle and auntie. In the rear was the girl's boudoir. Adjacent to it was the ladies' sitting room. The guest rooms were on the third level. Thomas showed Kare his room and private bathroom. *What luxurious accommodations*, thought Kare. The fourth level was Thomas' domain; his quarters were adjacent to the maid's room.

Two staircases connected the ground floor to the upper levels. There was a grand staircase at the front of the house and a service staircase at the back. In the basement, there were storage rooms and a set of stairs to the sidewalk.

The next morning, Kare woke up early. He dressed and walked down the stairs to the dining room. Uncle Andrew was already at the table reading the *Daily Express*. Putting his paper down, Andrew spoke in German, "*Guten Morgen Wie hast du geschlafen mein junge* (How did you sleep, my lad)?"

"*Dunnke, ich habe gut geschlafen* (I slept well, thanks)."

Thomas, standing by, invited Kare to sit down. "What would you like for breakfast?" he asked.

"Just coffee and toast with marmalade, please."

Kare sat at the table, and Uncle Andrew began to speak. "Kare, I decided to hire an English language tutor so that you can improve your English. As of next week, you will meet with your teacher twice a week in the library."

"I am much obliged," Kare said. "Uncle Andrew, is there any news from my mother?"

"Not yet, but no news is good news. I made some inquiries through my business associates in Berlin. I should hear from them soon."

"Thanks."

Andrew stood up ready to leave. Politely, Kare stood, putting his cup of coffee on the table. His uncle said, "I am going to my office. I will be home early today for Friday dinner. Sally wants to take you shopping at Harrods Department Store today. She said you need new clothes. My chauffeur will take you there. Have a good day, my lad."

Kare sat back down at the table to finish his breakfast, wondering why he needed a new wardrobe.

In the afternoon, the chauffeur drove Kare and Aunt Sally to Harrods. Kare had not experienced that kind of luxurious shopping before. Sally was like a child in a candy store. She wanted Kare to have everything. She had a good eye and impeccable taste for couture clothing. Jackets, pants, shirts, and shoes all flew from the shelves. She insisted that Kare be dressed as a proper English gentleman. Boxes and boxes of new clothes were delivered to the house that afternoon. Kare found out later that Sally had always wanted a son in her life.

Dressed in his formal evening clothes, Kare sat down for dinner with the family. Sally lit two candles, said a prayer, and welcomed the Shabbat. His uncle and auntie were liberal, progressive Zionist Jews, unlike David in Apeldoorn. They belonged to a reformed synagogue near the Marble Arch in London. They attended services for the Jewish High Holy Days but did not keep a kosher home. They did, however, refrained from eating pork. They believed in Jewish tradition integrated with non-Jewish insights. They drove on the Sabbath. Kare felt at ease with this kind of reformed Judaic practice.

At the dinner table, all conversations turned to discussing the day's news. Former King Edward VII, now the Duke of Windsor, had married Mrs. Simpson.

After dinner, Uncle Andrew invited Kare to his study/smoking room. They sat in the leather chairs. Andrew lit a cigar. He looked at Kare as he puffed the smoke. "My lad, what are your plans for the future?"

Kare replied, "I would like to finish my internship in cinematography and find work in the movie industry."

Andrew smiled, puffing the cigar and exhaling smoke. "What a coincidence. I know some of the movie studio owners. They are clients of our bank, and I invested in Alfred Hitchcock's thriller, *Young and Innocent.* In fact, I have tickets for tomorrow's show. Would you like to see the movie?"

Kare's eyes lit up. "Of course! I love Hitchcock's movies."

"You can take Laura with you," Andrew said.

"How long can I stay in the UK on a tourist visa?"

"As long as you want. I have a connection in the Home Office. If you want to stay permanently, I can arrange that too. You are not going back to Germany, my boy."

Kare lowered his head and said, "I know." Then he thanked his uncle for the day's shopping.

"You are welcome, my boy."

The next day, Kare took a walk in the neighborhood to familiarize himself with his new surroundings. He walked toward Buckingham Palace, only eight minutes from the townhouse. Then he passed by the Wellington Arch, admiring its imposing structure. From there, he passed the Victoria underground tube station and ended his walk at the east end of the Eaton Square to admire St. Peter's Church.

London is so different from Berlin, he thought. London had interconnecting squares and many curved streets with classical, delicate buildings. Berlin was less crowded, a smaller city, and had straight, wide boulevards bordered by large, imposing buildings.

On Saturday evening, Laura and Kare hopped into a taxicab and made their way to a music hall to see Hitchcock's 1937 masterpiece, *Young and Innocent.* The movie was based on Josephine Tey's novel, *A Shilling for Candles.* The movie was a major film starring Nova Pilbeam and Derrick De Marney. It was a hit in London. Kare loved the cinematography by the talented Bernard Knowles. In a cameo appearance, Alfred Hitchcock appeared in the movie, outside the courthouse, holding a camera, sixteen minutes into the film.

At the theater, Laura was dressed in the latest Christian Dior black A-line, layered, strapless dress. She looked like an actress from Hollywood and caused a major stir of attraction. Her appearance to men was like honey to bears. During intermission, in the lounge, Kare watched in amazement as she flirted with men.

Over the next few days, at the townhouse, Kare fell into a routine. He took his English language lessons seriously and spent hours polishing his English and practicing conversation with Laura. When he was not studying, he found German books about Jewish history in the library. He read them all. The subject fascinated him, and he wanted to know all about these "chosen people." Kare learned in the simplest terms that the relationship between God and the Jewish people is a covenant, a kind of legal binding contract. God's reign is like a constitutional government. The citizens pay taxes, and the government provides services. Parents give rewards for students who achieve good grades, a mutually obligatory contract. God promised a fulfilling life, and in return, the Jewish people must keep their vows. On the other hand, when the "chosen people" disobey God, He punishes them.

In the library, there were many books on diverse subjects, from economics, law, and philosophy to the classic works of Plato, Aristotle, Gottfried Leibniz, John Locke, and Baruch Spinoza. One day, Kare found Adolf Hitler's *Mein Kampf* tucked away on a bookshelf. He asked his uncle why he had such work on his library shelves.

Andrew said, "I needed to understand my enemy and to know what makes him tick. This book is a shallow combination of documentary and fiction. It is an ideology of venom and anti-Semitism. It is a ticking bomb. I can't understand how it can appeal to the rational German mind. This book is a racial, biological science of toxins."

Kare's uncle also owned a country estate in Borehamwood Town in southern Hertfordshire. It was situated seventeen miles north of London. The town was home to the film studio known as Elstree Film Studios. The Schonkoffs spent their summer months at the estate. It was a modest, two-story Victorian building situated on twenty acres of land. In the summer season, they mingled with their business associates and neighbors. They hunted, played tennis, rode horses, and visited each other's gardens. They had receptions and private concert balls, dinners, and parties.

It was the end of school for Laura and Gabby. Gabriella was a fifteen-year-old, blue-eyed, blonde-haired angel. She was reminiscent of a Venus de Milo figure, beaming with beauty. Gabby had a friendly personality and a sharp wit like her father. She was an excellent student, and her father was grooming her to take over his businesses.

Laura was meant to be a society girl, a modern-day Gibson Girl—beautiful, kind, spoiled, and manipulative. Laura knew how to get her way with Uncle Andrew. He played her game and was planning to marry her off to one of his business associate's sons. Laura had a character and temperament like *fraises des bois* (fragile woodland strawberries).

Kare loved his cousins, and they loved him in return. Laura taught him how to play tennis while Gabby taught him all about horses, introduced him to literature, and instilled in him a love for poetry. She was fond of female writers and made sure he read *Wuthering Heights* by Emily Brontë and the work of Jane Austen, *Sense and Sensibility*. Now, she had a new literary hero, Hermann Hesse; she gave Kare the book *Siddhartha*, in which the author explores the struggle of the human soul. From the start, Gabby and

Kare gravitated toward each other. He was her best friend, one to whom she could confide her thoughts, and he was a good listener.

On July 7, 1937, the British Peel Commission made propositions for changes to the British Mandate for Palestine. Andrew introduced Kare to one of his Jewish causes, supporting the Zionist Congress. Kare was introduced to many important people. One of them was Dr. Chaim Azriel Weizmann. Andrew was a big supporter of Dr. Weizmann, who would become the first president of the state of Israel.

In August, the family was in the Borehamwood Estate, enjoying a summer evening. Andrew had come up from London to spend the weekend with the family. He was preoccupied with deep thoughts. At the dinner table, Kare felt that something bothered his uncle, who seemed to be putting on a brave face in front of the ladies.

After dinner, Uncle asked Kare to join him in the study. He locked the door. Kare made himself comfortable in a leather armchair, opposite his uncle's. Uncle Andrew lit a cigar and puffed in silence. Kare was familiar with this type of behavior from him; he knew his uncle was trying to choose the right words to say about what was on his mind. He took a chair and faced Kare. Looking straight into his eyes, Andrew said, "Bloody awful news I have to say to you. Sons of bitches, they arrested your mother."

Kare's heart stopped beating. Blood drained from his face. His torso sank deep into the armchair. "Why?" he asked in a whisper.

Andrew swallowed hard, took a long puff of the cigar and said, "Bloody hell! Your Uncle Peter, your father's brother from Leipzig, betrayed your mother to the Gestapo devils." Kare could not believe what he had heard. Andrew continued, "He traded your mother for your father's freedom. Like a sacred goat, he sent her into the wilderness—the concentration camp."

"Impossible," Kare said. "My father loved my mother. He had principles. He would rather die than let this happen. It is not true!" He stood up from his chair, angry.

"Sit down. It is bloody true! I received a detailed letter from my investigators. It cost me a bloody lot to find out this devastating news! As you know, your Uncle Peter is well connected with the Nazis. His factory in Leipzig is cranking out fabric for the Boss Company. They, in return, make all of the SS and army uniforms for the Germans. He convinced the Gestapo devils that your mother was the one responsible for your father ranting against the Gestapo laws at the university. He convinced them that she was a subversive liberal, a secret communist sympathizer and, worst of all, a Jew in hiding."

"Impossible!" Kare said. "Father would not agree to this."

"Bloody Peter! He has a Machiavellian mind. He made sure to expunge the rest of your father's documents and substitute them with new documents, attesting that your father was arrested for a nervous breakdown. Bloody Peter! I wonder how much this cost him. Son of a bitch!" Andrew threw his cigar into the ashtray and continued ranting in an exacerbated tone. "Then he took responsibility for your father's well-being. He moved him to Leipzig and made an accommodation with the Gestapo. Your father is now staying in Peter's custody under house arrest for bad behavior. Then he convinced your father that you and your mother had left Germany and abandoned him in the prison."

Kare couldn't believe Peter's lamentable behavior. He snapped. As he quickly stood up, he knocked against a small table, sending a drinking glass tumbling onto the floor. Kare leaned his head against the wood-paneled wall and then banged his fists in anger. The pounding reverberated on the wall; it reminded Kare of how fragile life was.

"Why? Why is this happening to me?" he cried. "Peter, why did you betray my mom and dad and hurt me? I loved you, and you, in return, didn't love me. I hate you!"

Andrew paced around the room like a lion in a cage. "Bloody Peter! If I get a hold of him, I will ring his neck!" Pointing a finger, Andrew continued, "You know, he never liked our family. He always thought that your mother trapped your father into marriage with her pregnancy. He got back at her this way and got rid of her by sending her to a labor camp. I always knew that he hated Jews."

Kare was distraught. He was completely adrift. With tears in his eyes, he said, "Why are the Jews so hated? I do not want be considered a Jew!"

Andrew placed his hand on Kare's shoulders. "Sit down, my boy." Andrew pointed a finger in Kare's face. "Remember what Churchill said: 'If you are going through hell, keep going.' You need to be strong now. Let me tell you something. Jews have lived through a long history. They have been on the receiving end of what some call the longest hatred of the Jews. It is not that Jews want to suffer; rather, Jews have constantly been made to suffer. In Yiddish, we say, '*Shver tzu sein a yid'*—it's hard to be a Jew. Why is your mother punished for being a Jew? Some say that God occasionally hides His face from His people. I say no! There is no divine judgment. My boy, that is why I work so hard for the cause of Zionism, so our people will have a safe home of their own. Bloody Nazis! Even here in Britain, they aren't happy to receive the Jewish refugees fleeing Germany. Last year, we had our own Battle of Cable Street riots with the Blackshirts. The Nazis are among us. Bloody hooligans! The scum of the earth! Now, listen to me, Kare. I've always wanted a son of my own. Sally cannot have more children. She almost died giving birth to Gabby. Consider yourself my son. I love you as I love your mother." Andrew lit another cigar as Kare composed himself. The sordid news had hit him like lightning, and he had lost his inner balance. He turned to the door, indicating that he wanted to be alone.

"Before you go," Andrew, said, "not a word of what I said in this room to the ladies. It will upset them and make their days sour. We men need not distress our women."

Kare nodded his head and left the room in a hurry.

Denham Studios

Through his business connections, Uncle Andrew arranged an apprenticeship for Kare in Denham Studios located on a 165-acre site near the village of Denham, Buckinghamshire. The studio had been founded by Alexander Korda. Construction of the site had just been completed, and it was the most up-to-date and largest facility of its kind in the UK.

Kare was assigned to be an apprentice for the film, *The Citadel.* The screenplay was adapted from a novel of the same name written by A. J. Cronin. Kare was part of the cinematography crew, and Harry Stradling was in charge of the filming. This would be Kare's first hands-on experience. It was an opportunity that he had always dreamed of, and he took the apprenticeship seriously. He wanted to learn everything about filming. His basic knowledge of cameras, lenses, filters, and lighting helped him to adapt to the needs of the film crew. Andrew rented a flat for Kare in the village of Denham, next to the studios, since Kare would be working without pay for the next six months. Uncle Andrew also financed his studies, for which Kare was grateful. During the week, Kare spent long hours on the studio grounds learning the trade.

It was a real challenge for Vidor and Donat during filming. Donat had come from the theater, and acting for movies was not his forte. He argued with the director on set daily. Other stage actors criticized him for improvising the script. Some were afraid of the technology and anything mechanical. They dubbed it as a crude, modern necessity, not the product of intense thought capable of transmitting superlative acting to the screen. Kare watched all of this unfold and took it as a lesson for the future.

Kare learned how to arrange a single glance shot in the camera to form a character, other various camera angle shots, and the relation of the camera to the actor's performance. He learned that the actor must gauge his movement as a close-up, not looking into the camera itself, but at a spot close by. His head must be still, and his eyes would tell the story. Kare learned that, on stage, actors could communicate with the audience via stage presence and eye contact; in movies, actors used a more consciously coded performance.

Kare spent hours watching the camera crew and the director in action on the set. There was so much to take in. He stayed late into the night and arrived early in the morning to observe and make mental notes. He spent numerous hours learning all about various movie cameras and observing camera repairs in the studio equipment shop.

Kare was taught the most important yet basic concept—the five Cs of cinematography: camera angles, continuity, cutting, close-ups, and composition. He had good eyesight and an excellent ability to judge distances. He collaborated well with the production team and cast members. The cameramen liked Kare and took him under their wings. After a few months, he was allowed to glance through the camera viewfinder on set.

Laura would come to visit him at the studio. He gave her a tour of the sets and introduced the actors to her; she loved to schmooze with the stagehands. With her femininity and sense of chic, she always found admirers.

These were happy times for Kare; he tried to suppress the pain of missing his parents. He let his mind go blank when he heard bad news from Germany on BBC. Soon enough, Kare stopped listening to the radio. His heart and mind were in the movie studio.

In September, Kare was back in London for the Jewish High Holy Days. He went to the synagogue with his family for Yom Kippur, the holiest holiday on the Jewish calendar. He asked Uncle Andrew to explain the meaning of the holiday, to which Uncle Andrew told him a simple story: "On the day of Yom Kippur, a simple tailor sought forgiveness from God. The rabbi asked him what he had said to God. The tailor said that he had told God that he wished to repent for his sins and that he had committed only minor offenses. He had kept leftover cloth, and he may have eaten in a non-Jewish home without washing his hands. He had told God that He himself had committed grievous sins, such as taking away babies from their mothers and mothers from their babies. 'You forgive me, and, God, I will forgive you.' On this day, we repent for all of our sins."

Kare replied, "Why did the tailor let God off so easily?"

"It is a tradition with God. The Jewish people, through centuries, invite and encourage us in rational discourse."

Uncle Andrew informed the family that his brother, David, had sold his business in Apeldoorn and was planning to stop in London on his way to America to be reunited with his daughters in Brooklyn, New York.

The families celebrated the New Year in 1938 in London. The movie production of *The Citadel* was suspended over the holidays. Kare was enjoying his break from work and was happy to announce to his uncle that the studio had given him a position as an apprentice to the camera crew with modest pay, but he still needed his uncle's financial support. There was no news of his mother's whereabouts, but Uncle Andrew was trying to find out. It had gotten harder and harder to communicate with family in Berlin.

Laura was in her last year of high school and was looking forward to her graduation in June. Kare saw Gabby only on school holidays. She was now sixteen. When she was home, Kare enjoyed her company, listening to her piano playing in the music room or sharing a poem. They spent hours discussing the latest literature, which she encouraged him to read. Most of the time, he listened to her. Laura was into jazz, swing music, parties, boys, and dinners.

The talk of possible war changed the mood in London. In March, German troops marched into Vienna. The Anschluss happened; Germany annexed Austria. Uncle Andrew said, "During World War I, Austria's and Hungary's army of eight million had among them twenty-five thousand Jewish officers. Thirty years later, the surviving officers were rounded up and banished into concentration camps." In the same month, the prime minister, Neville Chamberlain, announced that Britain would fight for France and Belgium if they declared war on Germany. Uncle Andrew worried about the looming war. He decided to move some of his sensitive business documents to the country estate and installed extra telephone lines as well.

In April, the filming of *The Citadel* was complete. It was a successful production and ready to be shown in November of 1938. Kare was assigned to another movie, *Goodbye, Mr. Chips.*

Uncle David and Sarah arrived in London. They stayed for a month before leaving for America. Kare was happy to see them again. Sally made changes in the house to accommodate her brother-in-law. She changed her dishes to new ones, and the food preparation in the kitchen was strictly kosher. She hired an observant Polish woman to help Ethel, the cook, with the preparation of kosher meals.

One day, Uncle David and Uncle Andrew asked Kare to come to the study with them. Uncle David said, "Kare, you know I sold the business and our home in Apeldoorn. The money from the sale is to be divided three ways. As of today, we still don't have any news from your mother. We know she is in a concentration camp, and there's nothing we can do about it. Her portion of the proceeds will be given to you. Andrew decided to forgo his portion of the proceeds and is giving it to you as well."

Kare was surprised. "I would like you to keep this money for my mother," he replied.

Uncle Andrew interrupted Kare. "I don't need the money. Her inheritance is yours. Let's be realistic. It is bloody terrible that your mother is in the camp. A few months ago, I found out that she is in Bergen-Belsen Camp. There are as many as sixty thousand inmates. The conditions are bloody atrocious."

Kare's face turned white, and he ground his teeth. He sank into the armchair. "Bloody Nazis!" He banged his fist on the armchair and cried, "Why is my mother being punished? She doesn't deserve this! It makes me angry! I feel empty inside."

Andrew lit his cigar, puffing thick clouds of white smoke into the room. He paced back and forth. He said, "I did not want to upset you. I kept this news a bloody secret. Please forgive me. Listen to me, my boy. Take this money and use it. These few thousand pounds will help you with your needs."

Uncle David prayed in a hushed tone, eyes closed rocking his body slowly: "*Shema Ysrael!* Hear, O Israel! The Lord is our God is one …" It was the opening words of *Shema*, the prayer at the heart of Jewish daily worship.

Kare composed himself and wiped his tears. "Please forgive me for my outburst. Can I have a glass of port?"

"Of course, my lad."

Uncle David stopped praying and said, "I will have a schnapps, please."

They raised their glasses, and David said, "Let us say grace. Amen. *L'chaim,* for life!" They emptied their glasses.

Kare broke the brief silence. "Uncle Andrew, you are very generous to me. I would like to repay the expenses that you have provided for me."

Uncle Andrew raised his hand. "Don't be silly, my boy. What I will do for you is what I would do for Laura or Gabby. Your mother's inheritance is yours to keep."

With the money, Kare bought a 1928 Morris Minor M.G., a small two-seater sports car, which gave him some independence and made it easy for him to travel from the studio to the country estate. He loved the car and zipping along country roads. Sometimes, he took Gabby for rides through the country. They both sang the latest hit songs at the top of their lungs and stopped for fish and chips in small towns. He drove Laura to tennis matches with her male admirers at the neighboring estates. Kare invested the rest of the money with Uncle Andrew at his bank.

Back in Denham Studios, Kare started working on the set of *Goodbye, Mr. Chips*. It was a British film directed by Sam Wood and based on the novel by James Hilton. The plot takes place in 1933. Mr. Chips, age eighty-three, has flashbacks. When he was twenty-two-years-old, as a teacher not liked by his students, his friend and German teacher, Max, take him on a holiday in Austria. There, Chips meets Kathy while climbing a mountain. They meet again in Vienna, fall in love, and get married. Back in England, she takes up residence where Chips teaches, conquering everyone with her warm personality. Abruptly ending the short marriage, she dies; however, she has shown Mr. Chips how to be a better teacher. Mr. Chips becomes much loved in school. In 1913, he retires at age sixty-five but returns to serve as headmaster due to the shortage of teachers during World War I. England is attacked by German

Zeppelins, and Mr. Chips reads the school's honor roll of those former students who died in battle.

The film was released on May 15, 1939, and was nominated for seven Academy Awards. Kare and Laura attended the premier in London.

Uncle Andrew foresaw and predicted "an incipient World War II." He traveled to Switzerland and moved some of his assets to the vaults of Basel. Uncle Andrew remembered Winston Churchill's speech in the House of Commons. He had warned, "We must expect that, under the pressure of continuous attack on London, at least three or four million people will be driven to the open country around the metropolis."

In June 1939, Andrew removed all of the precious possessions from the townhouse in London and stored them at the Borehamwood Estate. Kare attended Laura's graduation from City of London School for Girls. The family celebrated the event with afternoon tea at The Savoy Hotel.

Kare was assigned to a new movie production, *The Thief of Baghdad.* This was a British Technicolor fantasy film produced by Alexander Korda. The film was based on flashbacks, mimicking the style of *Arabian Nights.* Kare was given a job as a second camera trainee to the first assistant camera known as the focus puller. He was responsible for focusing the camera lens as actors moved within the frame of each shot. The studio built a large set of the city of Baghdad and started to shoot scenes of Ahmad, the naïve King of Baghdad.

On September 3, 1939, an announcement was made in the studio: "BBC announced Germany has invaded Poland. Britain has declared war on Germany." The producers of the movie decided to move the production to California, in America.

Kare was given the choice to go to Hollywood, but he decided to stay in the UK and enlist in the British Army. The government looked at the film industry as a war effort and a public morale booster and encouraged all employees in the movie industry to stay on the job. Kare moved to Borehamwood Estate and got a freelance job as a film editor at Elstree Film Studios, which was just a few miles from his uncle's estate.

In August, Uncle Andrew's entire family moved to the countryside. London was a target for the Luftwaffe. Despite the Polish bravery, the German army had overrun Poland. The Poles surrendered to Germany on October 4, 1939. Next was Norway on April 9, 1940. France followed shortly afterward on June 22, 1940. The Nazis were looking forward to a parade on Bond Street in London. The war was going badly for the British army.

From July to September 1940, the Luftwaffe tried to gain air superiority over the Royal Air Force in the Battle of Britain. The RAF managed to gain the upper hand in the air. The British outperformed and out produced their enemy counterparts by replacing aircrafts as they were lost. The German invasion of Britain stalled.

Beginning in September, the Luftwaffe continuously bombed the city of London for fifty-seven consecutive nights. This happened to many other towns across the country as well. One million homes were destroyed or damaged, and 40,000 civilians were killed, almost half of them in London. The financial center of London was heavily bombed, and Uncle Andrew's office was severely damaged in the blitz. Uncle Andrew's family had escaped the horrors of London's destruction. Although their Eaton Square townhouse escaped damage, except for broken windows, it was now vacant and boarded up. Andrew had evacuated his entire household and moved them to the Borehamwood estate.

The year 1941 was a sober affair. The family spent their time in the country estate. Gabby now volunteered for the Women's Home Guard, and Laura, to the surprise of all, joined the Red Cross and enrolled in a nursing program. Kare said that she would be a perfect nurse; she just needed to hold the sick or wounded soldier's hand, look into his eyes, and he would be cured. Sally, in her way, was the model 'chin up, eyes ahead' British woman. She collected clothing and sold war bonds to the rich. Kare worked for the BBC, editing and sorting documentaries in the BBC library. Occasionally, he would shoot army recruiting and training films.

In the spring of 1941, while working at the BBC studio, Kare was summoned to his superior's office. To his surprise, he was introduced to a British officer from the Special Operations

Executive (SOE)—Her Majesty's Major Stanley. "I would like to ask you a few questions," he said to Kare.

Kare sat down, and his superior left the room. The major locked the door. The major introduced himself and said that he was from the Special Intelligence Office, a British World War II organization that specialized in recruiting agents to work behind enemy lines. They trained these agents in guerilla warfare, economic sabotage, propaganda, acquiring intelligence behind enemy lines, and weapon research. Kare was not surprised because he had met many officers of this type at the BBC studio. He had worked with them; they had vetted him.

Major Stanley asked, "May I speak in German?"

"Yes," Kare replied.

The major interrogated Kare on his background in cinematography, including his experience and schooling. Then he asked about his parents' background and his childhood in Berlin. He asked about Kare's father's arrest. Kare wondered where all of this questioning was leading, since the major already knew all of his answers. Then the major switched to English, put his pen down on the pad, looked at Kare and said, "You have been selected for a special mission to get information from Germany."

"Hold on, what mission?"

"Of course, if you accept it."

"Sir, accept what mission?" asked Kare again.

The major removed his hat and placed it on the table. He had bushy black hair, deep-set eyes, and a black moustache. His image was typical of a British officer that one might see on the silver screen. He pulled a document from his briefcase, placed it on the table, and said, "You must sign this document. You are required to keep this conversation and information a secret. Breaking this secrecy will place you behind bars."

Kare was not surprised. At the BBC, he had signed several "for your eyes only" documents. Kare signed it, and the officer placed it in his briefcase. "May I smoke?" the officer asked.

"Go ahead," Kare replied.

Major Stanley pulled out a pipe, packed some tobacco into it, lit the pipe, and began puffing. A sweet and smoky aroma filled the room. "If you accept it, I will divulge the mission in full. Our counter-propaganda office needs advanced knowledge about what is being planned in Babelsberg Studios. As you know, the studio is part of the Ministry of Propaganda, and Joseph Goebbels is in charge of it. Their work is swaying the world's opinion, especially in America. The studio has cranked out hundreds of films, mostly propaganda films. We, in Britain, need to have advanced knowledge about what is in the works and what the plots of the movies are. This way, we can prepare counter-propaganda. The Germans want, at all costs, America to stay out of this war."

Kare asked, "And how am I coming into the picture?"

"You are to get a job in UFA film studios—Universum Film AG—in Babelsberg, Germany, and report to us."

Kare smiled and countered, "And why should they hire me?"

"It is up to me to make an interesting offer that they cannot refuse."

"What offer?" Kare asked.

"I will divulge that to you if you accept the mission."

Kare was silent for a long time and then said, "I am sorry. I am not interested in this mission."

"Why, may I ask?"

"It is too dangerous. The Gestapo has already arrested my father. My mother is in a concentration camp. They have my name, my background, the school I attended, and I would be arrested as a spy and then shot."

Major Stanley considered this for a moment and then said, "We don't think so. We believe that your success in the mission is guaranteed."

"Yes? How?"

"You need to accept this mission, and then we will give you all of the details. You will also need to have special training in our secret facilities."

"Why should I do this?" Kare replied.

"We need to win this war for your parents, for your Jewish people, for the Free World. This mission is one small screw in a big machine that will defeat Hitler."

"I am not a Jew."

"I know all about your background." He pulled a folder from the briefcase and pointed to the pages. "We know what you drink, with whom you slept last, the color of your underwear. Our job is to know everything."

"It' not fair," Kare said.

"I'm sorry, my lad. This is war. Winner takes all. And we intend to win. I will leave you to think about this for two weeks. Then I will see you again." He closed the briefcase. "Not a word of this conversation to anyone. Not to your uncle's family. No one. Understand?"

"Yes."

"Good luck, my chap." With that, Major Stanley left the room.

Adieu

One week after meeting with Major Stanley, in the evening, Uncle Andrew invited Kare for a glass of port in his study. After sitting and listening to the latest BBC news, Uncle Andrew stood up and shut off the radio. He pulled his chair closer to Kare and said, "Major Stanley visited me last week." Kare was surprised to hear this revelation but said nothing. "He told me that he had asked you to volunteer for a special mission in Germany but did not divulge any specific details to me. He asked me to probe you and help you decide to accept the mission. It's an honor for the SOE to select you."

Kare listened to his uncle in silence. The glass of port rested in his hand still half full. Uncle Andrew asked, "Can I refill your glass?"

"No, I'm okay," Kare replied and shifted himself in his chair.

Andrew continued talking, "As you know, Kare, the news from Germany is sickening. Now that the Germans have occupied Poland and part of Russia, the SS *Einsatzgruppen* executioners attached to the regular army battalions began systematically liquidating Jews by the thousands. The rest of them, like your mother, have been sent to concentration camps as slave laborers or for later disposal. Who knows? Bloody Nazis. We need to defeat this monstrous regime as quickly as possible. Do you know what will happen to all of us if Hitler succeeds in invading Britain? You, Laura, Gabby—all of us—will be executed or put in concentration camps. Britain will be finished. Our way of life and democracy will be extinct. Bloody awful!" He lit a cigar, his face twitching, showing nervousness. Looking into Kare's eyes, he continued, "I speak to you as a father to his son. I hate for you to go away to war and the unknown. I want you safe, but sometimes we all need to make sacrifices for the good of others. Kare, you need to accept this mission for our 'chosen people.' Do it for your mother's sake, for England, a country that gave you her safe haven so you could be free. Do it for Laura and Gabby, so you all can fulfill your life's dreams and aspirations." He paused and then said, "The decision is yours. I will not pressure you. I will support you in your final decision. After all, it is your life." Andrew said goodnight and left the room.

Kare sat in the study for a long time, his mind wandering back to what his uncle had said. Then his eyes focused on the Marc Chagall painting on the wall. He looked at the headless figures hovering upside down in space, fire with red and grey smoke blowing in the background accentuated by vivid white and yellow colors. *What was the artist trying to convey to the viewer?* he thought. *Is it disorder? Suffering? Is it the end of the world?* He felt a sudden urge to rearrange the composition of the headless Adam and Eve. He wanted to give them back their souls and their heads, pull them down from the air to the ground, make them human again. He thought, *Was Chagall foretelling the present or the future? Was he warning us of what would become of this raging war in the world?*

Kare had read all about the artist's background. He knew that Chagall had witnessed anti-Semitism, discrimination, and pogroms in his native country, Russia. All of it had left deep scars the artist would never forget. The horrors of war and the tragic fate of the Jewish people depicted vivid impressions on canvas. Kare stopped looking. He asked himself why humans make war and destroy life. Although the Bible teaches the precept, "Thou shall not kill," war is ever present. Kare noted that the German Army "Wehrmacht," means "Defense Force," and on the soldiers' buckle is written "Got mit uns," "God with us" or "God on our side." *Is God on the agressor's side?* His mind gave him no answer. His eyes felt heavy. He was tired. He thought about whether or not to accept the mission and decided to make the decision the next day, when his mind would be clearer.

In the morning, Kare made a phone call to Major Stanley. "Sir, after long deliberation, I have decided to accept the mission."

"I commend you for accepting the mission. Prepare to say farewell to your family."

Later that week, Kare met with Major Stanley. The major warned him that the moment Kare stepped into the training facility, there would be no more communication with the outside. In a week, he would need to report for training in a secure facility of the SOE. The place was called The Thatched Barn. It was not too far from his uncle's estate. He would be given twenty-four-hours advance notice before a car would be dispatched to pick him up for training. Kare asked the major, "When do you think I will be back from the mission in Germany?"

"I don't know," the major answered. "It could be a long time. You will know more when we call you back. I say, plan for a year or more. It all depends on the progress of the war."

It was a glorious Sunday in June. This would possibly be Kare's last weekend with his uncle's family. He woke up early and finished packing his belongings. The rest would need to be stored. He packed some personal items into his small suitcase. It was the same one he had carried with him from Holland two and a half years earlier. Laura called him from outside. He looked down at her from his window. She stood on the porch wearing a short-sleeve shirt and white skirt, holding a tennis racquet on her arm. "Hurry up with the packing and join me outside," she said with a grin. "This will be your last chance to beat me."

They walked to the tennis court. "I will try my best," he said. For the past two years, he had never managed to win a game. Laura was the queen of the court. A taxi pulled into the driveway. It was Gabby in her Civil Home Guard uniform; she volunteered for Civil Defense as an assistant in the hospital, public kitchens, and food drives. She waved to them. This was her day off.

After lunch, Gabby asked Kare to take a horseback ride. They had done it many times before. She mounted her stallion and immediately took off in a fury toward the hills. Kare rushed to catch up to her. It took him several minutes to reach her. When he did, he held her horse's reins to slow her down. "What's the rush?" he said. Their horses stopped. Kare gazed at Gabby. She appeared upset and somewhat jittery. "Let's talk," he said.

They walked their horses toward the trees near the brook. Sitting on the grass, leaning against a tree trunk, Kare asked, "Is everything all right? What is bothering you? You look irritated."

"I am so sad that you are going away," she replied.

"You know, it is wartime and it is my duty to go."

"I know. I just have a bad premonition about your going."

"I understand your feeling. I can't divulge where I will be and what I will be doing, but I can assure you that I do not expect to be in combat. I am not going to war to fight on the front lines."

"When will you be back?"

"I don't know. I have a feeling I will be gone for a long time. I wish I had a crystal ball to see the future, but I believe that it is a mistake to look so far ahead. I will try to unchain one link of my destiny at a time."

In her sweet voice, she said, "I am sorry to sour your day. Can I read you a poem?"

"Please do."

She opened her poetry book to a marked page and read W. S. Merwin's *When You Go Away*:

I remember that I am falling
That I am the reason
And that my words are the garment of what I shall
never be
Like the tucked sleeve of a one-armed boy.

"That was beautiful, Gabby. Did you write that?" Kare asked.

Gabby smiled and said, "No, that poem is by W. S. Merwin. He wrote it in 1927. It reminds me of you."

Kare smiled. "I will remember you."

They rode home side by side in silence. Before reaching the house, Kare said, "Gabby, I want you to have my M.G. It will be of no use to me anymore."

"I will keep it for you."

"No," Kare said, "It is for you to keep. I am giving it to you. We had many good moments in the car. It belongs to you."

"Thank you."

Dinner was served. Sally had worked hard with Ethel to cook a farewell dinner. Sally had dismissed the help for this night. She and Laura served the food. For starters, she served lettuce and greens from their victory garden followed by watercress soup. For the main course, she served locally caught trout with boiled potatoes in butter sauce. For dessert, Laura had made a chocolate cake. Uncle Andrew opened a bottle of his best claret and toasted Kare's safe return. Uncle Andrew held the glass and said, "Remember what Churchill said, 'If you are going through Hell, keep going,' my boy. God bless the king, and God bless Britannia. Victory is ours."

After dinner, they all assembled around the piano in the salon. Uncle Andrew asked Gabby to play. She was an accomplished musician and took her talent seriously. She had an ardent talent for playing piano, although she rarely performed for an audience. Gabby reserved this honor for her family and only a few strangers.

She sat in front of her favorite grand piano, the Bechstein, which had been transferred from their townhouse in London. It now sat as a focal point in the salon. Gabby was especially fond of this piano because of the silvery tone, an easy touch. She sat on the bench in front of the piano not moving for some time. Then her fingertips plunged onto the keyboard at once. She played the music of Frédéric Chopin. It was Sonata, op. 35 in B-flat Minor. Kare sat deep in the armchair, his arms on the console, a glass of wine in his hand. She played the first movement with such intensity, maelstrom, and desperation that Kare was paralyzed by the sound as he focused on her figure. She swayed back and forth, her blonde hair unraveling down her back. Gabby played the second movement like Beethoven Scherzo. The third movement contained the most famous funeral march ever written. A chill passed through his spine. *Why did she choose the funeral march? Can she foresee the future?* His hand shook, and he spilled some wine. Her hands glided over the keyboard. The last movement, she played with eerie shades, sweeping into unrecognized notes. Kare closed his eyes. Tears rolled down his cheeks, and then silence.

Kare gazed at her longingly. She looked exhausted with emotion, her face wild. Her hair was unraveled over her sweaty forehead. Gabby composed herself, and her angelic face smiled at Kare. He approached her and kissed her on the cheeks. He felt that tonight she had played from her heart with a grieving sense of emotion. Kare remembered that Gabby had once quoted Oscar Wilde after playing Chopin. She had said, "After playing Chopin, I feel as if I have been weeping over sins that I have never committed and mourning over tragedies that were not my own."

Uncle Andrew asked Kare to join him in his study for a chat. They sat on the couch. "Would you like a cigar?" his uncle asked.

"No thanks. Not today," Kare replied.

Uncle Andrew lit one for himself. "Brandy?" he offered.

"Yes, that would be nice," Kare said.

His uncle switched the radio to BBC news. The news from Europe was grim. The German forces were pushing into the Balkans and Greece. On June 22, the Germans launched the invasion of Russia. The German army had made astonishing advances. The Soviet forces were collapsing on all fronts. Andrew shut the radio off. "Bloody disaster," he said. "We are next. Norway will be their staging ground from the north, and France will be their staging ground from the south. We need America to enter this bloody war! Without the Americans, we will lose this fight!"

Kare thought about his mission. He was scared and wanted to be alone. He stood up. "Uncle Andrew, I would like to retire for the night."

"Of course, my chap, go rest, but before you go, I have something for you." Uncle Andrew went to his drawer cabinet and fetched a box. From inside, he retrieved a letter and two keys on a long chain. He handed them to Kare. "When you are in Berlin, go to this address. It is that of my former business associate. He will give you a safety deposit box once you present this long key, and inside is another box. The small key will open it. The contents inside that are yours to keep. This will be my war effort contribution. It will help you survive."

"What is in it?" Kare asked.

"It is for you to find out. Goodnight, my lad. Keep the letter safe, and wear the key around your neck."

It was just after ten o'clock, and the house was quiet. The ladies must have retired to their bedrooms. In his room, he removed his shirt. It was a warm night in June. Wearing his undershirt, he lay on the bed, gazing at the ceiling. He couldn't fall asleep. A million thoughts about the unknown that awaited him flew through his mind. Chopin's music played in his head. He was restless, and he needed some fresh air.

Kare sat on the porch gazing at the distant woods. The moonlight cast deep and mysterious shadows among the trees beyond. Tomorrow, he would leave his adopted family for the SOE. Kare hated the Nazi regime and was looking to get even. He wanted to avenge his parents' tormentors, although he had no ill feelings toward the ordinary Germans. The thought of war and killing people revolted him, and he hoped to never be in a situation that would force him to personally face violence.

In the distant sky, Kare heard the sound of plane engines. *Is that the Germans on their way to bomb London or is it the British defending their home sky?* Two searchlights played hide-and-seek in the distant, dark sky and then disappeared. Quiet fell on the night. The only sound he heard was the noise of forest animals foraging for food in the woods until the sudden sound of footsteps on wooden floorboards jolted Kare from his thoughts. He gazed in that direction. The silhouette of a woman was approaching. It was Gabby. She wore her French purple robe de chamber and matching slippers. She sat next to him on the bench and stared at the woods. Then she asked, "At what time will you be leaving us tomorrow?"

"At seven. The driver will pick me up."

"I couldn't fall asleep."

"Neither could I," he said in a hushed voice, not looking at her. "How unpredictable our lives are. We are not in control of our destiny."

"Are you scared to go?"

"Yes. Going into war is like rolling a dice. Some of us will come back, and some of us will die."

She looked at the walled garden. "Let's take a walk." Guided by the moonlight, they slowly strolled into the garden, passing a fountain of softly falling water. They passed their victory garden and walked toward the glass greenhouse.

Kare whispered, "I will miss the orchids in the greenhouse." They entered the warm greenhouse. This was Kare's "crystal palace." In his spare time, his passion was to tend to the orchids. They reminded him of creatures from outer space and were arranged neatly on wooden shelves. Kare gazed at Gabby and said, "Please take care of my orchids while I am away."

"I will make sure they are taken care of," she replied. They sat on a wooden bench, looking at the orchids. The flowers cast long, dark shadows brushed with a hint of color shining from the moonlight. It was mysteriously quiet. "Will you miss me?" Gabby said.

"I will miss you all."

"Will you miss me?" she repeated.

"Of course I will miss you. I will miss our walks in the woods and your sweet voice reading poetry. I will miss the sound of your piano playing and, most of all, I will miss our horseback riding in the countryside. Yes, I will miss you."

She replied in a low voice, "Promise me you'll come back."

"I will come back. God willing." It was the first time he had ever evoked God's name.

Gabby suddenly reached over, took Kare's hand in hers, and placed it on her breast. She looked into his eyes in a mysterious, sensual way. With her voice slightly trembling, she said, "Kare, I want you to make love to me."

Kare was taken aback by her unexpected request. He gazed at her face. She appeared to be serene and at peace. Her blue eyes sparkled. *Is the moon playing tricks on me?* he thought. He wanted to say something, but his mind went blank. His mouth dried, and a million thoughts buzzed through his mind, but lovemaking was not one of them. Gabby reached into her robe and Kare's hand over her warm breast. He felt her heart beating hard. *Is this the Gabby I have always known?* Then he imagined a rush of a stormy wind. He felt that the wind was lifting a veil from Gabby's face. He noticed a mature woman in front of him; Gabby, the girl, had vanished into thin air.

Kare composed himself, swallowed hard, and said, "It is not a good idea. I am leaving tomorrow. And another reason …" He did not get the chance to finish his words.

Gabby placed her fingers on his mouth and softly whispered into his ear, "Shhhh. Take me away."

She leaned over and kissed his lips. She whispered the Roman poet Virgil's line, "If your love is pleasing, yield yourself to love."

Their lips met again. Her mouth opened, and her wet tongue touched his. Kare felt a rush of carnal desire. It was a strange feeling of pleasure. He kissed her neck. The smell of her perfume intoxicated him. They kissed deeply, passionately, both gasping for air. Kare was lost in her arms. He touched her breast. Her nipples were hard, and she let out a low moan. Gabby opened her robe, exposing her breasts. Kare slowly kissed his way down and kissed them softly. She held him tight to her chest. Then he pulled back and looked into her eyes. Blonde hair spread over her shoulders, casting a blue hue on her skin. She was like Venus de Milo. He wanted her.

Breathing hard, Gabby slipped her underwear down, dropping them into a pool at her feet on the dark stone floor. Kare's heart pounded with desire, blood rushing to his pelvis. He pulled her close to him. His hands glided down her long ballerina legs. His fingers slowly caressed them and then moved in circles below her stomach. Her body trembled with excitement. Kare kissed her bare body, gliding his tongue on her firm stomach. She opened her legs and his hand rubbed her gently. He could feel that she was as aroused as he. Her body moved and curved with his touch. Her breathing was erratic as Kare explored her body. It was uncharted territory. She moaned, kissing him hard on his open mouth. "I want you to make love to me," she whispered.

Kare let go of her body. She stood up, eyeing him. He was sitting on the edge of the bench. He slowly unbuckled his belt, never letting his eyes leave Gabby's. He lifted off the bench briefly to let his trousers and underwear fall. He reached for his wallet. Being a young, virile man, he always kept a condom in there. He slipped it onto himself. In the dark, the white Durex stood like a lighthouse beacon, lighting Kare's way to a safe harbor. He embraced and held her round buttocks with his hands, lifting her and sliding her onto him. Gently, he let her body ease onto him; she took him all the way into her body, and they started to move in unison. She sat on him, wrapping her hands around his neck, kissing him passionately. She let out a sound of pleasure. They were one. Her eyes closed; her body tilted slightly away. They sat for a long moment. He felt her, resting himself in her sacred temple. Then she moved, thrusting herself onto him. She moved again, slowly, lifting and sinking, lifting and sinking. Kare closed his eyes, lost in a sea of pleasure. He let her take the lead.

It was not the first time he had made love. It was, however, the first time he felt this unknown burning, deep, passionate, emotional attachment. *Is it love?* he asked himself, tenderly kissing her open, wet mouth. She embraced him and kissed him passionately. Breathlessly, Gabby thrust and twisted her body faster with moans of pleasure. Like the experienced equestrian she was, she moved up and down as if she was riding her stallion, deeper and deeper. He lost all sense of time. He kissed her sweet neck. She moved faster and then stopped, squeezing her legs. Her torso trembled with spasms from her neck down to where their bodies met. Kare felt her climax. She let out a rush of air; then she galloped again faster and faster like a jockey rushing to the finish line. He could not wait anymore. Kare opened his gates and felt the unmistakable rush of pleasure erupt. He let out a cry. They were like two puzzle pieces, a perfect match. They kissed passionately and gasped for air, lifting and sliding, lifting and sliding. She climaxed again and let out a cry. Then it was over.

They sat together in each other's arms, embracing for a while, catching their breaths. Her head rested on his shoulder. Kare glided his hand up and down her bare back. It was wet with perspiration. "Wow," she whispered into his ear. "You are my first."

He paused for a moment and said, "I will treasure this moment forever."

She lifted her head and looked at him. Her blonde hair was like a wet curtain hanging over her face. Kare pushed a lock behind her ear. Their faces slowly leaned toward each other and they kissed. Her face and lips were wet and hot. He still felt himself inside her warm body. She whispered, "I will miss you." Then she rested her head against his shoulder. It was quiet, and they sat in silence. She spoke again, "It's getting late, and you need to wake up early. You have a long day ahead of you tomorrow." She moved, and Kare released his grip on her body. She slowly slid off of him, stood up, and fixed her hair. "Let's go to the house, darling." She extended her hand toward his.

Kare looked at her and said, "You go ahead, Gabby. I will be inside later. I would like to sit here for a while longer."

"Okay. Goodnight, my dear." She kissed him, put on her robe, closing it, and glided toward the entrance. Her silhouette paused for a moment at the doorframe. Then, like Cinderella, she vanished into the night.

Kare sat deep in thought. He tried to understand what had just happened. He couldn't sort his thoughts. He felt deep feelings for Gabby, but a guilty feeling swept over his heart. He felt guilty for violating her youthful innocence and for not being able to satiate his desires. The thoughts of lovemaking swept over him with pleasure. He told himself that it might be all right because, after all, they were consenting adults, and she was eighteen. His mind wondered, *Why did Gabby choose to play the Chopin funeral march? Perhaps it was a personal funeral for her innocent youth and the birth of her womanhood.* Kare glanced at his watch. It was already after midnight. He put his pants on and stood up. When he glanced down at the floor, he noticed that Gabby had forgotten her underwear. He picked them up, shoved them into his trouser pocket, and then walked toward the house.

In the morning, a car arrived from the SOE facility to pick Kare up. Andrew was outside with Sally and Laura waiting for him to come out of the house. Kare noticed with a sinking heart that Gabby was not there. He hugged and kissed Sally and Laura and shook hands with his uncle. Sally and Laura had tears on their cheeks. "Kare, take care of yourself," said Sally. "Be safe and write to us."

"Come back safe soon," Laura said.

"Good luck with your mission," Uncle Andrew whispered into Kare's ear.

"Thank you," Kare said. Then he asked, "Where's Gabby?"

Andrew replied, "She was bloody upset this morning. She took her horse and gallivanted away into the woods."

"I was hoping she would be here," Kare said in an anguished voice.

"She's bloody sensitive sometimes. I can't figure her out."

Kare scanned the surrounding woods. Gabby was nowhere to be seen. He felt ambivalent and ineffably depressed. *Is it because of last night?* Then he said, "Please say goodbye to Gabby for me. I need to go."

He climbed into the car. The driver cranked the engine. In a low gear, they drove on the rough pavement. Kare waved to his uncle and the ladies. Then they disappeared as the car went around the curve. As they drove on the long driveway, Kare scanned the woods on both sides of the road hoping to see Gabby. As they reached the next curve, Kare glanced in the car's passenger wing side mirror. An image of a galloping horse appeared. It got closer and closer. "Stop the car!" Kare yelled to the driver. The driver slammed on the brakes.

Kare jumped out of the car, hoping that the galloping figure was Gabby. It was! She was approaching him, riding on her favorite black stallion. He rushed toward her. She jumped off the saddle and ran toward him. They hugged and kissed for a long moment. Then she said, "I wanted to say good-bye to you in private." Tears flowed down her cheeks. Kare wiped them with his hands. She looked so beautiful this morning, wearing her red riding boots and a long-sleeved white shirt. Her blonde hair was neatly tucked under a kerchief, and her blue eyes sparkled.

He said, "Damn this war! Last night, when we were in each other's arms, I felt like I didn't want to go away; I wanted to be with for you forever."

"I felt the same, darling."

For a moment, he was ready to skip his mission. Then he remembered and put his hand into his trouser pocket and pulled out her white underwear. She looked at them and said, "Keep them, Kare, as a memory of me." Kare was surprised and slipped them back into his pocket. As her eyes overflowed with tears, she said, "Take care of yourself, dear." Then she put a small blue envelope into his jacket pocket. She kissed him gently for a long moment and looked into his eyes. He felt her love, and his heart melted. Then she turned around, mounted her stallion, and galloped away.

Kare watched her image get smaller and smaller until it finally vanished around the bend. He stood for a moment and then heard the driver shout, "Sir, we must go!"

Kare removed Gabby's envelope from his jacket pocket. It smelled of her perfume, the same smell that had enchanted him the previous evening. Kare closed his eyes, and his head flooded with the memories from that moment. He felt a flood of pleasure flowing through his body. He slowly tore the envelope open. Inside, there was a poem written in red ink.

Remember me by the words of Sara Teasdale:

I bid you awake at dawn and discover
I have gone my way and left you free.

Yours,
Gabriella

SOE Agent for Britain

Kare arrived at to the SOE training facility in Borehamwood. It was only a few miles from his uncle's estate. The Thatched Barn was located near BBC Studios, where Kare had last worked.

Kare's mission was to gather information about planned future movies in the United Film AG Babelsberg Studio near Potsdam, Germany. The studio was under the directorship of the Ministry of Propaganda, which was under the leadership of Joseph Goebbels. It was vital for Britain to know, in advance, what movies the Ministry of Propaganda was planning to release in the future. The movies were intended to sway the world's opinion. The SOE department wanted no surprises in the war of propaganda. Kare was seated in Major Stanley's office. The officer said, "Your mission consists of getting information and writing consistent reports. In your training, you will learn about methods of delivery and contact with local agents. Your drop-off location will be at Potsdam. No weapon or parachute training will be necessary. All of your communication with headquarters will be via written coded messages or BBC radio news and music programs that contain secret messages."

"How long will my training be?"

"I would say approximately two months. It all depends on how fast you learn." Major Stanley, however, did not divulge the precise details of Kare's mission.

Kare needed to give up all of his personal possessions: clothes, shoes, and Uncle Andrew's letter of instructions, along with the keys. He also had to give up his letter from Gabby. He was stripped bare and given new clothes. No outside contact would be permitted.

His movement and daily life would be supervised. He was under surveillance and segregated from other agents.

Major Stanley dropped a box of documentary films in Kare's lap. They were about the life of Amazonian Indians. Kare was asked to watch all of them and learn about the natives' lives in the jungle. He was taught basic phrases in Portuguese, such as greetings: *Oi* (Hello), *Bom dia* (Good day), *Bon noite* (Good night), *Como vai voce* (How are you), and so on.

Weeks later, he was given a box of books, articles, newspaper photos, and information pertaining to the sinking of the RMS *Titanic*. He was asked to learn and memorize events, personal stories of the passengers who survived the sinking, and the ship's layout: the dining room, the grand staircase, the captain's bridge, the Marconi communication room, and the ship's boiler rooms. He had a lot to learn, but studying was not difficult for him. Soon, he became an expert on the voyage and sinking of the *Titanic*, but Kare wondered why the information would be so crucial to him.

Three weeks later, Major Stanley revealed to Kare the details of the mission. He said, "There are rumors that a world-renowned movie director, Herbert Selpin, has received an assignment from Joseph Goebbels to produce a film about the sinking of the *Titanic*. This will be an epic movie production of German propaganda. Your mission is to approach Herbert Selpin and entice him to hire you as an expert on the story of the *Titanic*. It will be up to you to find the right moment and place to meet the director in Germany. In addition, we want to find out about other feature films in production—documentaries, newsreels, and German military training films. All are of great interest to us. Do you have questions?"

"Yes, sir. As I've been out of Germany for three and a half years, I need a cover story for my mission."

"We created one for you. As an independent movie producer, you traveled to Brazil to shoot a documentary about the indigenous people of the Amazon Jungle. You spent years there. Now you are on your way back to Germany to promote the documentary and find work as a cameraman."

"What about my school records in Berlin? They may expose my cover."

The major took a large photo out of a folder and handed it to Kare. It was an aerial photo of Berlin after bombing. "Do you recognize The Kino Academy location?"

"No, sir."

"You see this area?" He pointed with a pencil. "It was destroyed in a bombing because of its close proximity to the military storage facility." Now Kare recognized that all that was left of the school was rubble and bricks on the sidewalk.

Then Kare was given a stack of photographs of the original RMS *Titanic*'s interiors during its construction. The major said, "When you present these photos to Herr Director, he will hire you for sure. These photographs are the key to getting your foot in the door of Babelsberg UFA studios." The major also handed him two 35-millimeter show reel containers containing black-and-white documentaries of the Brazilian Amazon. These would be his cinema photography portfolio.

As for his parents' arrest, the major reaffirmed Uncle Andrew's findings that the Gestapo had not recorded his mother's arrest. Then he handed back Kare's uncle's letter of instructions and the keys along with some personal belongings.

Prior to leaving for his mission, Kare wrote three letters to his uncle's family. He wrote to his Uncle Andrew and Aunt Sally, thanking them for everything they had done for him. He thanked Sally for being a wonderful surrogate mother. He thanked Andrew for treating him like his own son and for his financial support. Kare wrote that he would not disappoint them and would make them proud of his services in the war. He also wrote a letter to Laura and thanked her for being a loyal friend. He was proud of her achievement of becoming a nurse. He encouraged her to become a doctor. One day, he wrote, he would beat her on the tennis court. Until then, he would cherish their time together. He was hoping to see her sometime in the near future. Last, he wrote a letter to Gabby. He expressed his deep friendship and love for her. He said he hoped she felt the same toward him. The poem she had left with him had touched his soul. She was right about the future. It cannot be foretold. Therefore, the chance of him not coming back was real. He would cherish the memories of being with her, and she should continue with her life and not plan her future based on his return.

The major promised to deliver the letters in person at the appropriate moment.

The life expectancy of an SOE agent in occupied Europe was just six weeks. Kare and his mission were given the code name, Blue Angel, and then he was transported to Helford Estuary in Cornwall. Major Stanley, standing at the boat dock, turned toward Kare and said, "Good luck, my chap." Then he saluted him.

"Thanks," Kare said. "Please give this sealed envelope to my uncle in the event that I do not come back."

"Have a positive outlook, my chap. You are coming back. I will keep this in a safe place" With that, the major shook his hand.

In the letter, Kare had written:

August 1941

Dear Aunt & Uncle,

This is my last wish. The money that I deposited in your bank, I wish to donate to your dearest cause, the Jewish Zionist Organization, for the settlement of the Jewish people in their homeland, Palestine.

Love,
Kare

The fishing boat was operated by the SOE organization. The plan was to transfer him onto a Portuguese merchant ship on the high seas. Portugal was a neutral country during the war. Some captains were on the SOE's payroll for the transportation of human agents and merchandise to the occupied countries and Germany.

It was a moonless night, and the sea was rough when Kare boarded the fishing boat. The captain and two boat mates greeted him. He stood on the captain's bridge as the boat left the pier. The noise and the smell of diesel fumes were in the air. Standing on the bridge deck, Kare watched the shoreline lights dim then vanish altogether from the horizon. He was struck with the reality that this was a point of no return. He looked at the sea. Across the ocean lay the unknown. Fear crept in; he felt it in his stomach. What if he did not succeed on this assignment? He couldn't bear the thought of disappointing Uncle Andrew. He looked up to him as a father figure for his hard-as-a-rock personality, one that Kare was able to lean on when he was in distress. He was leaving the safety of England and the comfort of daily life; he may never see his loved ones again. He was saddened that he might never see Gabby. For the past two months, he had been lying in bed alone in The Thatched Barn thinking of his feelings toward her. *Is it love?* he wondered. *Or is it a moment in my life when she filled the void of loneliness in my soul?* He must come back from this mission to find out.

In the howling wind, Kare heard the voice of the captain. "Sir, would you care for a sip of gin?"

"Yes, thanks. A sip of gin would be good." The drink warmed his heart. The sea was angry, and wind splashed salty water on his face.

"Sir, the sea is too rough. You will be more comfortable in the front cabin below deck."

"Much obliged," Kare answered. The boat rocked on the waves, and with unsteady footing, he descended below the deck.

He made himself comfortable in a corner, and the humming engine put him to sleep.

Kare was awakened by one of the mates. "Sir, we are approaching the transfer ship. Get ready!" he said.

Kare buttoned his jacket and put on a life preserver. He had two suitcases, one for his personal belongings and the other for the show reels. The fishing boat maneuvered in the darkness close to the ship. *It will be a difficult transfer*, Kare thought. The sea was rough. Although he had practiced the maneuver before, the water was angrier than it had been during his practice. Ropes were thrown from the Portuguese ship, and the fishing boat slowly attached itself to the side of the merchant ship. A rope ladder was lowered. Kare missed his grip on the ladder on his first attempt. On the second try, he grabbed the ladder and was helped by the seaman of the fishing boat to begin his climb. Waves splashed on him, and with all of his strength, he managed to climb to the top. Four strong hands whisked him onto the firm ship deck. A seaman threw a blanket over him, and a man rushed him into the ship's cabin. Someone thrust a towel into his hands. Kare sat on the bench, wiping his face. A dim light bulb was the only source of light in the cabin. A seaman handed him a cup of tea. Kare did not manage to get a look at him before he vanished from the cabin.

He sat for a while, and then the captain, dressed in raingear, came in holding Kare's suitcases. "Welcome aboard," he said in broken English with a hint of a Portuguese accent. "We should be in Rotterdam by noon. Keep your life preserver on at all times." He swiftly left the cabin.

A year ago, the Germans had occupied the Netherlands. Rotterdam was now a port for the German navy. The Dutch had resisted the German army, but they had been no match for the German blitz. The Dutch army had only one tank and a privately owned aircraft gun. Rotterdam had been bombed with ninety-seven tons of explosives. The Luftwaffe obliterated the city center, and the Germans overcame the Dutch resistance in two days.

Kare had been warned of the danger of the passage through the Strait of Dover. The Nazi subs were hunting merchant ships on their way to British ports.

Kare slept for a long time, and when he woke up, it was almost midday. The sun was out, and the sea was calm. He felt pain in his left palm. It was badly cut and bruised, probably from his nocturnal climb up the ladder. Kare walked to the bridge where the captain was standing scanning the horizon with binoculars. "All clear," he said. "We should arrive in Rotterdam by noon." He glanced at Kare's hand, then took him inside and bandaged it.

A German navy patrol boat approached the ship. The *Kriegsmarine* (Coast Guard) officials asked for identification and the type of cargo on board. The *Kriegsmarine* cleared the ship to proceed to Rotterdam. Kare was delighted to see the shores of the Netherlands. He went inside the cabin and changed into clean clothes—shirt, pants, and jacket. He disposed of the old clothes in the garbage. The ship docked at the pier. A Dutch customs agent boarded the ship. Then a Gestapo officer in civilian clothes, accompanied by an SS soldier, asked for his passport. The Gestapo officer flipped through Kare's Dutch passport issued by the SOE, which showed visas for his arrival to Brazil dated 1937 and his departure from Brazil in 1941. It was stamped with his arrival in Lisbon in August 1941. "From where are you coming?"

"Lisbon. I arrived on a ship from Brazil two days ago."

"How long were you in Brazil?"

"Two years."

"What was your purpose visiting Brazil?"

"Visiting my mother. She lives in Rio. And to film a documentary of the Amazonian region." Kare handed him a business card: Kare Hoffmann, cinematographer. Berlin.

"What is your destination now?"

"Berlin to promote my documentary."

"Are you German?"

"Yes."

"Your German ID, please. Why are you traveling with a Dutch passport?"

"My mother is Dutch. At that time, I did not have time to get my German Passport."

The custom official asked, "Do you have anything to declare?"

"No."

"Please open your suitcase."

Kare showed him the movie films and personal possessions. The Gestapo officer handed his documents back. "Next time, you travel with a German passport. Heil Hitler!"

With a sigh of relief, Kare found himself clear to disembark. The Rotterdam center showed the scars of last year's bombing by the Luftwaffe. There was rubble and destruction everywhere. Some building repairs and reconstructions were in progress. The Rotterdam Blaak railway station had been totally destroyed. The terminal was in midst of repairs. A temporary ticket office was nearby. Kare bought a ticket for the train to Amsterdam. He walked around the station and struck up a conversation with a local resident. "The bombing leveled around two point six square kilometers of the city," the man told him. "The Germans killed over a thousand people and made eighty-five thousand homeless." Kare still smelled burning oil in the air from the bombing.

Kare arrived in Amsterdam late at night. He headed to a safe house, a rooming hotel that was near the main terminal, and stayed there for the night.

Berlin, 1941

In the morning, Kare strolled on Albert Cuyp Street. There was an open market and no evidence of war. The bicycle and pedestrian traffic was as heavy as he remembered from the last time he was in Amsterdam. Within the crowds, there were SS uniformed soldiers minding their own business. Hearing some of them talk among themselves, Kare detected an Austrian-German accent. *They must be from Austria*, thought Kare. He stopped into a haberdashery and purchased a suit, a shirt, and a tie.

After dinner, he boarded a night train to Berlin. On the train, he shared a cabin with a German salesman who was returning to Berlin. Two SS soldiers entered the cabin, celebrating their leave with bottles of beer. They were already quite drunk and unsteady on their feet. They collapsed on the opposite bench, offering drinks to the salesman and Kare. The train began moving, and soon the soldiers were sleeping on each other's shoulders. Kare conversed with the salesman, who complained of the lack of raw materials and manpower in his small pharmaceutical company. All of the resources were diverted to military enterprises, leaving shortages for civilian businesses. The defeat against Britain and the invasion of Russia had left him with little enthusiasm for the war. Kare listened for a while, then excused himself and went to sleep.

Kare was awakened on the border of Holland and Germany. "Passports!" Kare handed his ID to the custom official, who was accompanied by a Gestapo man. He glanced at Kare and then moved on.

He arrived in Berlin and got off at Anhalter Bahnhof Station near Potsdamer Platz. It was the largest business center in Europe and shared the iconic status of Piccadilly Circus in London and

Times Square in New York City. There were many department stores, cafés, and beer-drinking places. It was a major hub for U-Bahns departing to various neighborhoods of Berlin. It was a paradigm for the modern metropolis.

Despite the war, the sidewalk cafés were bustling with soldiers and businesspeople dressed professionally—men in jackets and women wearing fashionable hats and white gloves. Kare joined them. He ordered *zanderfilet* (pan-fried pike perch) and a Berliner beer, enjoying the Sunday afternoon. He needed to find a hotel to settle in and decided on the Schloss Charlottenburg area. It was quiet and on the outskirts of Berlin, a residential neighborhood full of greenery and not too far from Queen Sophie Charlotte's palace, which was far away from Berlin Center and British nighttime bombers. Kare settled in the Hotel Charlotte on Bismarck Strasse conveniently close to the U- Bahn station.

The next day, Kare went to the office of his uncle's former business associates. They were located nearby the Potsdamer Platz. In the law office, he presented his uncle's business card to the secretary, who led him into the conference room. A middle-aged gentleman in a black suit walked in and introduced himself. "Herr Otto Bruch," he said, extending his hand.

"Kare Hoffmann." Kare shook the man's hand.

"Please, sit down." Otto read the letter of introduction from Uncle Andrew. "I see you are a nephew of Mr. Schonkoff."

"Yes, I received this letter in Brazil a month ago."

"I see. Were you there on holiday or business?"

"I was visiting my mother. She lives there."

Otto stood up. "Excuse me, Mr. Hoffmann. I will be back in a minute." He left the room, then came back and placed a white paper with four circles drawn on it on the table. Kare remembered his uncle's instructions. He took four cloves from his envelope and placed them on the circles. This was a secret code between Otto and Andrew. The cloves represented the symbol of myriad treasures carried by deities of God's fortune in Japan and China.

Otto asked, "May I have the key for the safe, please?" He took the long key, opened the safe, took out a metal box, and handed it to Kare. "Please, Mr. Hoffmann, sign this receipt." Then Otto returned the cloves to him, shook his hand, and wished him good luck.

Kare took a U-Bahn and got off at the Unter den Linden Boulevard stop. He walked to Number 77, a famous address of the Adlon Hotel, an imposing four-story brick building right in the heart of Berlin, steps away from the Brandenburg Gate. Between the two world wars, it hosted celebrities, including Tsar Nicholas II, John D. Rockefeller, US President Herbert Hoover, Charlie Chaplin, and the famous actress Marlene Dietrich. Now, it was where Herr Director, Herbert Selpin, stayed on the weekends.

Kare entered the opulent, huge lobby. It was lit with bright, large crystal chandeliers. The floor was carpeted, and the ceiling was held up by enormous square marble columns. The interior was decorated with a mix of neobaroque and Louis XVI style furnishings.

Kare approached the lobby concierge and said, "I am looking for Mr. Herbert Selpin."

"He is expected this weekend, sir."

"Thanks. Where can I have a drink?"

"May I recommend our oriental garden lounge?"

"Thank you." Kare walked toward the hotel garden, which was decorated in a Japanese motif. A large elephant fountain was the focal point in the room. He sat at the bar and ordered a beer. He needed to scout the lounge and the dining area because Major Stanley had indicated that this section was Selpin's favorite watering hole. This was where he made his royal court usually on the weekends at around eight in the evening.

Kare took the U-Bahn back to his hotel. He was curious to find out what was in Uncle Andrew's box. Safe in his room, he sat on his bed, took out the key, and opened the box. Inside was something rolled up in soft felt cloth. He unrolled the covering. To his amazement, gold coins, pound sterling banknotes, *reichsmarks*, and pieces of Art Deco jewelry tumbled onto the bed. He closed the curtains and placed a piece of chewing gum into the lock hole. This was a standard procedure taught to him during SOE "spy school." He spread the contents of the box neatly on the bedcover. He tallied up 5,000 pound sterling notes, 50,000 reichsmarks, forty Union Bank of Switzerland stamped pieces, 10 grams bullions of 24 karat gold, fifty $20 US liberty gold coins, forty $20 US 1933 double eagle gold coins, an Art Deco ruby and diamond ring, and an Art Deco gold bracelet. Kare sat on the bed in shock over his uncle's generosity.

Why did he give me this gift? Was it because he felt guilty for convincing me to go to the lion's den? Or was it for his survival and for the war effort? He thought that whatever his motive had been, financial independence would make the difference in accomplishing his mission, but he would need to hide it in a safe place. For the night, he put it with his clothes in the suitcase and locked it.

The next day, he took a U-Bahn to Potsdamer Platz, went to a department store, and purchased a small tool kit and a RCA Victor transportable 78-rpm record player with a lockable top. Back in his hotel room, he disassembled the record player and discarded the entire motor mechanism. He left only the turntable with the needle arm intact. He placed the treasure box inside the record player interior, placed the turntable on top, and locked the cover. No one would suspect that the RCA record player was a hiding place for his treasure. He placed it next to his suitcase in the room.

Dressed in his best, Kare went to meet Selpin in the Hotel Adlon. He arrived at 7:30 p.m. The hotel façade was draped with Nazi flags. Several black Mercedes were parked in front of the entry. On the sidewalk, there was a small crowd of beautifully dressed ladies and gentlemen. There were also some uniformed SS and Wehrmacht officers.

Kare entered the hotel and found a table in the oriental garden lounge area. He sat down and ordered a tall Berliner beer. Observing the bar area, he noticed at the far corner that two guests were seated reading the newspaper suspiciously observing the guests. *They must be Gestapo fellows,* Kare thought to himself. The bar area was full of ladies, uniformed officers sitting and standing with drinks in hand, and cigarette smokers who were conversing in loud voices. It was a lively place. Kare picked up a copy of *Signal* magazine, the propaganda magazine of the Third Reich, and sat deep in his chair reading.

At precisely 8:03 p.m., a noisy party entered the lounge. A tall man in his late thirties dressed in a black evening suit, puffing a cigar, walked toward the bar. Kare recognized him from photographs. It was the director, Herbert Selpin. Ladies and men followed him, talking loudly and laughing. Their behavior provoked whispers and stares from the seated lounge guests. Selpin ordered drinks, puffing on his cigar, and stood with his back to the bar.

Kare saw an opening. He waved to the waiter, who came over. Kare slipped one reichsmark and the envelope containing one of the *Titanic* photographs into the waiter's hand and asked him to give it to the director. Kare eyed the waiter as he gave the envelope to Selpin. The director asked whom it was from, and the waiter pointed to Kare seated at the table. Kare stood up and slightly bowed his head in acknowledgment. Herr Selpin opened the envelope and pulled out the contents. He looked at the photo of the grand staircase of the RMS *Titanic*. He puffed smoke, then looked toward Kare and waved him over. Kare approached the party and introduced himself. "Kare Hoffmann, cinematographer," he said as he handed Selpin a business card. He shook the director's hand.

Selpin asked, "Where did you get this photo?"

"Sir, I have a stack of photos of the RMS *Titanic*. I bought them at a flea market years ago."

"Why are you showing this to me?"

"Sir, there are rumors that you are planning to shoot a movie about the RMS *Titanic*, and I thought you should have this."

"The rumors are correct. Cinematographer?" the director questioned. "Are you in the movie business? I have never heard of you."

"Sir, I am an independent cameraman. I just spent three years in the Brazilian Amazon shooting a documentary."

"Interesting," Selpin said. "How much do you want for the photos?" He chewed on his cigar.

"Sir, I would like to give them to you at no cost."

"Why is that?"

"Sir, I am looking for employment in the movie industry. I have experience as a cinema photographer and as a cameraman, and when I was younger, I collected and read everything that was available on the ill-fated voyage of the RMS *Titanic*. I am sure you can use my knowledge for the filming of your production." Kare swallowed hard, looking at the director.

"Okay, fair enough," Selpin said. He turned toward a brunette dressed in a stylish black-and-white dress. "Fräulein Lizzel, what is my schedule for the next week?"

She pulled a black appointment book from her bag. Flipping through the pages, she said, "You have an opening on Wednesday afternoon from one to two."

Herr Selpin turned toward Kare and said, "Do you have show reels of your work?"

"Yes, Herr Selpin." He reached into his briefcase and pulled out two 35-millimeter/300-meter reels and handed them to Herr Selpin. "It would be my honor, sir, to have this opportunity for you to review my artistic work. One reel is marked London. It includes my cinema photography work in Technicolor, a ten-minute segment of daily life in the city of London. And the one marked Brazil is a ten-minute segment in black and white, edited from my one-hour documentary on the Amazon jungle of Brazil."

Herr Selpin handed the reels to Lizzel, then he turned to Kare and said, "Bring all of your photos of the *Titanic* to the Babelsberg UFA studio next Wednesday afternoon at one. Ask for my office when you get there."

Fräulein Kirsten Heiberg had been listening to the conversation. Kare recognized her. She was a very popular actress and singer in Germany. She said, "Herr Hoffmann, tell us about your documentary film."

Herr Selpin introduced Kare to his party. "They are all part of my cast for the *Titanic* movie, and Lizzel Luss is my personal assistant," Selpin said. He kissed her hand, looking into her eyes as she smiled at him.

Kare proceeded to tell them about his adventures in the jungles of the Amazon, filming the savages. He told them convincingly about his encounters with animals and the fight for his life with a ten-meter python. Soon, partygoers surrounded Kare, holding drinks, smoking, and asking questions. They listened intently to his stories. Suddenly, Kare realized that he had become the focal point of the party. He did not want to compete with Selpin for attention, so he stopped talking. He turned toward Selpin and said, "I apologize for interrupting your party. Thank you for your time. I will bring the rest of the photos for you next week. I have a dinner appointment." He turned toward the ladies, bowed slightly, kissed their hands, said, "Goodbye, and Heil Hitler." He left the hotel.

Outside, he took a deep breath. *Mission accomplished*, he said to himself.

Sanssouci Park

The following Wednesday, Kare checked out of the Hotel Charlotte, took his suitcases and the RCA record player, and boarded the train to Potsdam, which was an hour from Berlin. Potsdam was the city of the German Federation state Brandenburg and was situated on the Havel River twenty-four kilometers southwest of Berlin's city center. Potsdam had a claim to national and international nobility. In Germany, it had a status similar to that of Windsor in Britain. It was the residence of the Prussian kings and German kaisers. Potsdam was the site of royal palaces, and Sanssouci Park, which covered an area of 287 hectors. One of the most beautiful palace complexes in this park was Schloss Sanssouci, the summer palace of Frederick the Great. In the southeastern part of Potsdam was Babelsberg, where the major film production studio, UFA, was located adjacent to a historic park with significant landmarks, including the Babelsberg Palace and the Einstein Tower.

Kare arrived at Potsdam's main train station by noon. He stored his two suitcases at the station to be picked up later. Carrying his record player, he boarded a bus to the city center and got off at Friedrich-Ebert-Strasse. It was the main drag within the old city walls near the Nauener Tor Gates. Five walls had enclosed the city of Potsdam in 1772.

Before the war, Potsdam had attracted large crowds of tourists. Now it was deserted except for the locals and some uniformed military personnel. Kare sat outdoors enjoying a plate of *brandenburger landente* (stuffed duck with red cabbage and potato dumplings on the side) with a Berliner pilsner, his favorite beer. While eating lunch, he noticed a sign across the street on the second floor of a building offering rooms to rent. After lunch, he checked it out and rented a room for one week until he could find a place to make his permanent home.

Kare packed up the suit he'd bought in Amsterdam and set off to make another stop—this one at the prearranged drop-off location given to him by the SOE in London, the Old Dutch Center, a few blocks from where he was renting the room. The Dutch neighborhood was called Holländisches Viertel, built in 1734 to 1742 by Dutch artisans and craftsmen and lived in by Dutch descendants, now Germans. Kare remembered the address number, 6 Bankert Strasse. He found a post that read, "Jakob's Tailor Shop." The surrounding streets reminded him of typical streets in Amsterdam. Jakob's Tailor Shop was on the ground floor. There were two residential stories above. He entered the store. A white-haired, medium built proprietor greeted him, "Good day."

"Good day. I have a suit that needs alterations."

The tailor invited him behind the counter and had Kare put the suit on behind a stretched curtain. Standing on a small wooden platform, the tailor pinned Kare's cuffs. Kare dropped his business card on the floor. "Kare Hoffmann, cinematographer," the tailor read as he picked up the card. Then he stood up and gave it to Kare. "You dropped a card."

"Oh, thanks," Kare said. This was the prearranged secret code for contact. Jakob was the SOE drop location and an agent of Britain. He asked, "Are you working in Babelsberg studio?"

"Not yet. I have an appointment this Wednesday. Do you think the suit will be ready by Tuesday?"

"Do I have a choice?" the tailor asked with a smile.

Kare asked, "Do you still speak Dutch?"

The door to the store opened and a woman walked in. "I will be with you in a moment," Jakob said. Then, he turned toward Kare and said, "Yes." At the counter, he wrote a receipt and gave it to Kare. "Herr Hoffmann, have a nice day," he said. He shook Kare's hand. "My name is Jakob de Jager." Kare thanked him and left the store.

The next day, Kare noticed an old bicycle in the hallway at his rooming house. He asked the landlord, "Can I borrow it to tour the city?"

"Yes. When you come back, put it in the same place."

Kare decided to take a ride to Sanssouci Park, which was twenty minutes by bike. Schloss Sanssouci Palace was beautiful and the oldest complex in the park. In French, *sanssouci* means "without care"—a true reflection of the flamboyant character of this enchanting rococo palace built by Frederick the Great in 1745.

Kare left the bike near the ticket office and joined a small group of tourists for a tour of the palace. Before embarking upon the tour, they stopped to watch a large unit of German paratroopers descend onto the palace grounds to be photographed as a group on the terrace stairs. The men were dressed in camouflaged *Fallschirmjäger* (jump smocks) and yellow scarves. A small embroidered insignia on their breast pockets depicted a diving gold eagle gripping a swastika.

The tour of the rococo rooms was enchanting. Kare was taken aback by the glorious interiors designed by Knobelsdorff and Johann August Nahl. The king had wished to be buried in the palace area near the tomb of his beloved Italian greyhounds, but instead had been buried in the Garrison Church at Potsdam, Garnisonkirche.

After the tour of the interior, Kare explored the park grounds from one end to the other. A thought flashed in his mind: *What a good place to hide Uncle Andrew's treasures!* The park had no military value for the British, and the palaces were international historic treasures. It would be safe from RAF bombs, despite the fact that Hitler's Luftwaffe in 1940 had bombed and damaged London's landmark, St. Paul's Cathedral. Kare decided to scout for the best place to hide his treasures. As he was riding his bike away from the *Romische Bader* (roman baths), he saw an illustrious gilded pavilion in the woods. It was the *Chinesisches Teehaus* (Chinese tea house). It was a glistening, small, rounded pavilion surrounded by gilded columns on one side and windows on the other. He walked closer to investigate the structure. It would be a great location—in the woods and off the paths of the park, isolated from the main road. It was a hidden jewel. It looked deserted. He walked closer. In the back of the pavilion, away from *trompe loeil* porticos, were ornamental windows flanked by gilded life-size sculptures of Chinese gentlemen and ladies. The female sculptures were dressed in traditional Tang Dynasty clothing—short sleeves; long skirts, wide open; long scarves; and coned, pointed shoes. On their heads sat phoenix crowns. At the edge of the portico columns and near the first Chinese figure, a narrow strip of grass surrounded the building. He took a branch from the woods and poked the ground. Perfect for digging—soft earth with no obstructions or rocks. Kare made a mental note that this was the spot for his dig. He would come back from Okonomieweg-Sanssouci one evening to hide his treasure box.

It was early evening when Kare returned to his room. He remembered that he needed to pick his suit up from the tailor, for he had an important meeting the next day at UFA studios. He took the bike to the Dutch quarters. Jakob had the suit ready. Kare took it and left another jacket with Jakob to be cleaned.

Back in his room, Kare checked the suit. On the inside, next to the suit pocket, was a hidden compartment constructed by the tailor. The plan was that Kare would drop his clothes for cleaning once a week. Within the secret compartment in the jacket, he would deposit his reports to the SOE. Jakob would remove the reports and have them picked up by another courier. Then the reports would be broadcast by secret transmissions to London. If caught and interrogated by Gestapo, Kare could only reveal Jakob the tailor.

Babelsberg, 1941

The UFA grounds were at Alfred Hirchmeier Strasse, the site of the film studio where Germany's first films were produced in 1912. From 1917, this studio became Universal Film AG, which produced some of the most renowned films of the silent era, such as *Metropolis*. Now, the studio had been taken over by the Nazi Ministry of Propaganda and was personally supervised by Joseph Goebbels. After the takeover, considerable resources were given to the cinema and other media. Goebbels resisted the complete "Nazification" of the arts. He knew that the masses must be allowed some respite from slogans and propaganda. He assured that UFA at Babelsberg continued to produce a stream of comedies and light romances, which drew mass audiences to the cinema, where they also watched the propaganda newsreels and Nazi epics. He was known as Babelsberg Stud or Bock von Babelsberg. The Nazis produced more than 1,500 films, and there were nearly 400 cinemas in Berlin alone. The most talented film actors, producers, and directors had been Jews. The Nazis took the first steps to expel them from the industry. Many of those individuals had left for America. Marlene Dietrich opposed the Nazi regime and left for America, never to return during World War II despite the personal effort by Goebbels to convince her to return to Germany. Dietrich had spent many years in Hollywood. Her association with Jewish producers and actors made her "un-German" to the Nazis.

At 1:00 p.m., Kare arrived at the UFA studio gates, which were guarded by civilians and SS guards. Kare gave his name. A call was made to the office of Herr Selpin, and he was given a pass. There were three long, one-story buildings to the left of the gate. One was the office of Herr Selpin. The others were administrative and security offices and the studio infirmary. In the conference room, portraits of Goebbels and the Fuhrer were hanging on the wall. Herr Selpin walked in dressed in a white shirt and suspenders without a jacket. A cigar hung out of his mouth. He shook Kare's hand. "When did you arrive in town?" he asked.

"Two days ago. I wanted to see the famous sites in Potsdam," Kare replied. "Ah, beautiful Sanssouci Park."

"Where are you staying?"

"In the center of the old city."

"Good. Very convenient," Selpin said. He was all about business. "Let me see the photos."

Kare handed him more than thirty photos of the RMS *Titanic*. He spread them out on the table. Looking at them, chewing on his cigar, Selpin uttered the words, "Splendid, splendid," to himself. Then he turned to Kare and asked him about his professional experience in the movie industry. Kare told him about his work in the London studios before the war, then about his experience in the jungles of the Amazon. Herr Selpin told Kare that he remembered when he worked on movies in England before the war. "How do you like working with the English?" he asked.

"Okay, a little stiff. I prefer working with a German crew. They are more innovative," Kare answered.

"I agree," Herr Selpin said. "I reviewed your show reels with my chief of photography, Hans Lubner, and we both had a positive reaction to your artistic work; however, at this time, I do not have a position for a cinema photographer. Would you accept a position as a second cameraman?" He paused for a moment fiddling with his cigar, then said, "What is your answer to my offer?"

Kare was quick to reply, "Sir, it would be my privilege to be working with your team, and I accept your offer."

Herr Selpin extended his hand for a handshake and said, "I will also need your assistance in building movie sets for my upcoming film, *Titanic*. Let's see what your technical abilities are. Go see Hans Lubner in Studio D and he will check your camera abilities. Then call me tomorrow morning before eleven and I will let you know when you can start. We are currently short on manpower, and a good technical man is hard to come by these days. Good luck. See Lizzel. She will direct you to Studio D."

Kare found Hans Lubner testing shots on the set. He was shooting Selpin's latest propaganda movie, *Carl Peters*. Hans sat in a chair maneuvering a Bolex 35-millimeter camera that was mounted on an elevated crane. "Cut. Lights off." He lowered the camera boom, walked toward Kare, and introduced himself. Kare shook his hand. "Let's sit down," Hans said. They eased into folding chairs on the set. Hans shouted to the crew, "Twenty-minute break!" He turned to Kare and said, "Tell me what you know."

Kare proceeded to tell Hans about his technical abilities and his experience working in Denham Studios. He talked about his experience in the jungles of Brazil and his education at the Kino Academy in Berlin.

Hans listened and nodded his head while sipping a glass of water. He said, "I worked in London from nineteen thirty-three to thirty-four. It was a very good experience. I will set up another test shot on the set. Ja. You will have a chance to take control of the camera. Ja. Let's see what you can do." Hans went to talk to the stage director.

Kare said, "I'm ready."

"Lights on."

Kare took off his jacket and placed it on the chair. The actor walked onto the set in a khaki uniform and a brimmed hat and stood against a painted background of East Africa. He held a rifle in his hands. Looking through the viewfinder, Kare manipulated the camera boom and adjusted the level of the camera to the height of the actor on the stage. The stage director told the actor to deliberately switch his travel direction. Kare set the camera on the travel curve in front of the camera, right to left. The actor exited to the left; that would create a match cut of the moving actor, who was walking right to left. Kare knew how to maintain screen direction. It was important to maintain directional continuity in the shot.

Hans interjected, "I can see you have experience handling the continuous shot."

"Thanks," Kare said.

"I can use an assistant. We are shooting several films now, and it is hard to find good help."

"Herr Selpin asked me to call him tomorrow. I can start any day."

Hans replied, "I will speak to Herr Selpin. Are you staying in town?"

"Yes, I rented a room in Potsdam."

"Good," Hans said. "Well, until next time." He shook Kare's hand.

Kare stopped at the administration office and filled out an application for employment. The next day, he called Herr Selpin's office. Lizzel told him that he had gotten the job and that he would start on the following Monday. He felt a great sense of relief.

Longing for Father

"*Ich komme nach Leipzig, an den Ort, wo man die ganze Welt im Kleinen sehen kann.* (I am coming to Leipzig, to the place where one can see the whole world in miniature.)" Kare remembered the quote by the German poet, Gotthold Ephraim Lessing.

He had the urge to see his father in Leipzig. He hadn't seen him in seven years. Kare had a burning desire to hug him and tell him how much he and his mom loved him. He needed his father to know that his mother had never betrayed him. It had been his own brother, Peter, who loved the Nazis more than he loved his brother's family.

Kare's heart cried out for revenge. He mustered all of his courage and decided that the truth of Lila's whereabouts must be told; this would be his way of serving justice. Fear crept into Kare's thoughts. The truth might make his father believe he had been lied to. *What will be his response?* Kare remembered his father saying, "Integrity, honesty, and telling the truth are noble virtues."

He would travel to Leipzig to see his father. He took the train to Berlin, and then continued to Leipzig, one of the two largest cities, along with Dresden, in the state of Saxony. Kare had visited the city with his father many times before to see his uncle, Peter. His mother, Lila, did not get along with her brother-in-law and had always avoided visiting his family.

On the train, as he looked through the window, Kare's thoughts drifted to the times when he and his father had visited the City Academy of Visual Arts, enjoying the art and sculpture exhibits. He loved the Sunday-night recitals at the University of Music and Theater. He thought about how he had enjoyed those evenings being with his father after stopping at the café for ice cream or cake.

Kare arrived at the main train station, an old terminal built in 1915. Now, it was draped with Nazi flags. A large crowd of civilians, *Wehrmacht* uniformed men, and SS soldiers were boarding various trains in these early morning hours.

Prior to boarding a trolley, Kare checked into a room in a small hotel in the vicinity of the train station. He planned to stay for one night. Riding the trolley, he remembered that, once a month, on the third Friday, Uncle Peter had a crew of gardeners come to tend his property. Kare wondered if today was the Friday and if he would find the gardeners on the grounds of the Hoffmann estate. He got off the trolley in the vicinity of the main courthouse; it was a short walk to the estate on Wachter Strasse. The three-story Italian Tuscan residence was situated on a triangular block between Beethoven, Wachter, and Ferdinand Rhode-Strasse. It was a quiet residential neighborhood, once the suburbs of the city. Now, it was Leipzig's cultural and local governmental center.

Kare reached the estate and stood across the street. Sweet, happy thoughts of when he had spent time with the Hoffmann's filled his mind. Looking past the property fence enclosing the estate, he gazed at the porch. There he noticed a man sitting in a chair, reading a newspaper. *That must be my father,* he said to himself. Eric was a creature of habit. When in Leipzig for a visit, each morning he would sit on the semi-circular porch and read the newspaper.

An urge filled Kare and he wanted to call out Eric's name, but he restrained himself. He needed to be discreet and thought about how to approach and get his father's attention without exposing himself to the rest of his uncle's family. Kare walked around the edge of the property. There, he noticed the gardener in blue overalls, clipping the hedges near the fence. A plan hatched in his mind. Kare took a piece of paper and a pencil from his pocket and wrote a message to his father. Approaching the gardener, he said, "Good morning."

"Good morning," the gardener replied.

"What a nice day," Kare said.

Looking at Kare, the gardener removed his hat and wiped his forehead. "Yes, it is a nice day. Do I know you?"

"No."

"You look familiar."

Kare remembered the man from a long time ago. He had seen the gardener on the property before. He hoped that the worker would not recognize him. "You're probably mistaking me for someone else," Kare replied. "Can you do me a favor? You see that man sitting on the porch? Please give him this note." Along with the note, he handed one reichsmark to the gardener, who was surprised by the sudden request.

Holding the piece of paper and looking at the money, the gardener said, "It is not necessary."

Kare interrupted him, "It is for you. Have a beer on me."

The gardener hesitated, but put the reichsmark into his pocket. Then he turned and walked toward the porch to deliver the note.

On the Beethoven Strasse side of the street, there was a service gate. The gate key hung on the adjacent tree. Kare tried the gate, which was unlocked. A barking German shepherd ran toward him. It was Fritz! The dog recognized Kare, jumped up against him, and licked his hands. Kare was happy to greet Fritz, then sent him away. In the note to his father, Kare had instructed him to meet him inside the gardening shed at the far corner of the secluded area of the property. Filled with great anticipation, Kare entered the dark, earth-scented building and awaited his father. Suddenly, the door swung open and a bright light blinded Kare's eyes. The silhouette of a man appeared in the doorframe. An excited voice called, "Kare, are you here?"

Kare was standing at the far corner of the shed next to the hanging gardening tools. As he rushed toward his father, a spade fell from the wall and crashed to the floor with a loud bang. They embraced and kissed each other. His father looked older, now bearded. His hair was all white. "What are you doing here hiding in the shed?" asked Eric.

"Come inside and close the door," Kare said. He let his eyes adjust to the dark, then said, "Dad, no one must know that I am here."

"Why?" Eric said. "Are you in trouble with the law?"

"No. Sit here on the box. Let's talk." They sat facing each other, holding hands.

His father said, "You are so grown up. It must be three years since I saw you last."

Kare swallowed hard, "We need to talk. I do not have much time."

The small windows at each end of the shed cast streaks of sunlight onto the floor. As Kare held his father's hands, he looked straight into his eyes and proceeded to tell him what Uncle Andrew had told him in London about his mother's arrest. Listening to the revelations of his wife's arrest, Eric froze in disbelief. His hands got cold and trembled. He exclaimed, "What a fool I was!" Tears ran down his face. "How can it be? Peter, my own flesh and blood, betraying me like this!"

Kare told his father that Lila was in a concentration camp—Bergen-Belsen he thought. Eric placed his two hands on his face, shaking and sobbing. Kare hugged him and said, "Father, there is nothing we can do now. Let's pray that we will survive this war." A tear rolled down his cheek. Then he told his father that, in case the UFA Studio security personnel contacted him, he should affirm that Lila was in Brazil and that Kare had spent years in the Brazilian Jungle shooting documentaries.

Eric, who was only half listening, nodded in agreement. "How can I look in my brother's eyes? It is entirely my fault! Forgive me, my son."

"Dad, I am proud of you for saying what you did in front of the students. You are my hero. Some other professors in your university kept quiet and did not resist. You are a true patriot, and I love you for it," They hugged again, and Kare said, "We need to part now. I hope we see each other soon." Then he left the shelter of the shed. As he closed the door, he heard Eric utter the words, "*Sie ist geurteilt verurteilt!* (She is condemned!)" Kare said to himself, *Why is he quoting Goethe's* Faust*?* Kare snuck off the property grounds. He had not told his father why he was back in Germany.

Going back to the hotel, Kare was elated to have seen his father and felt as if a heavy stone had been lifted from his chest. Uncle Andrew had been right; Father had not known of his wife's arrest. Kare and his father had always shared their thoughts and feelings in the past, and he hoped the revelation of the truth would force Peter to never inflict such injury upon his brother again.

In the evening, Kare went to the local restaurant and ordered *Leipziger Allerlei* (vegetable stew) with crayfish. He finished dinner with his favorite pastry, the Leipzig Lark, a short crust dish filled with crushed almonds, nuts, and strawberry jam. Feeling emotionally drained from the meeting with his father, he returned to his hotel room.

Early in the morning, he took the train back to Berlin. On the way, he grabbed a cup of tea and a pastry at the train station. A newspaper boy passed by shouting, "A tragedy in Leipzig!"

Kare bought the morning news, tucked it under his arm, and boarded the train. When he was settled, he opened the newspaper, and to his horror, he couldn't believe what he read: "Two blood-drenched corpses belonging to those of a prominent Leipzig family, the Hoffman's, have been found. Eric Hoffmann had accidentally discharged a hunting rifle and killed his brother, Peter. He then turned the rifle on himself. Two brothers dead."

Kare stopped reading and slumped into the train seat, covering his face with the newspaper. He felt remorse. *Had it been injudicious and imprudent on my part for telling my father the truth?* His revenge had dug two graves—one for his father and one for his uncle. Tears streamed down his face as his mind raced. *Why did I have to tell him the truth? Father had known right from wrong; he was a lawyer after all. What made him act in such desperation? There is no greater tragedy than having one sibling murder another. Was it uncontrolled revenge?*

"No vengeful murder shall be justified," his father had told him once.

Was it self defense? Had they argued? Had Peter lost the argument, forcing Eric to become the judge and the executioner? Kare knew that his father couldn't have gotten away with this murder. He must have judged himself, placed the rifle on his chest, and taken the quarrel to the grave.

"There is neither justice nor judge in the world." Kare thought of Uncle Andrew's quote.

The train to Berlin became a funeral ride. He grieved the loss of his father and his Uncle Peter. When he arrived at the station in Berlin, he composed himself and concluded that his father had been true to himself until the very end. Eric had solved Faust's *Gretchenfrage* (Gretchen question) He had made a difficult decision: The guilty must be punished.

Meant to Be

Kare was in no mood to start his job at the UFA Studios. He made a call to Lizzel and postponed the start of his employment. He spent days alone, locked away in his room, mourning his father's death. This senseless tragedy plummeted him into utter hopelessness. Remembering his meeting with father, Kare saw himself as "bad"—acting out of self-interest and revenge without regard for consequences. Now, he felt guilty. A "bad shadow" hung over him. He searched his soul, trying to come to terms with the tragic loss.

After a few days, he heard a knock on his door. It was his landlady, Frau Pauline. Behind her stood Hans Lubner from UFA Studios.

Surprised, Kare said, "Please come in. I apologize for my appearance. Please sit down."

"I brought you some cabbage soup," the landlady said as she placed it on the table.

"*Danke schön*, Frau Pauline, for the soup."

"*Bitte schön* (You're welcome). I will leave you two alone." She closed the door.

Sitting in front of Kare, Hans said, "I am very sorry for your loss. It is a real tragedy. How are you coping with it?"

"Not too well. I am depressed and haunted by recent events."

"It is natural to feel depressed, but you have to start thinking positively about your life. Get rid of this black cloud that hangs over you. Don't be crushed by it; otherwise, there will be no peace for you."

"It is hard to get rid of these negative thoughts."

"You know, Kare, life must go on. You need to get busy. I need you on the movie set. What do you say? Start working on Monday."

"*Danke*. I need more time to think and to clear my mind. I need to gain back my positive energy."

"Well, you know, Kare, may I suggest you start by shaving, Ja? Put on clean clothes, Ja, and go for a long walk to be among people. You can't be cooped up in the room feeling sorry for yourself for the rest of your life. Fresh air will do you good."

"I appreciate your advice, and thank you for your visit."

The next day, Kare took a long walk in the woods of Sanssouci Park. The sap of life started flowing though his veins again. He bade his sorrow farewell and, once again, was full of life.

Kare decided to look for a permanent place to live in Potsdam. It was also time for him to write his first report to London. After it was finished, he placed the report in the secret compartment of his jacket and dropped it off at Jakob's tailor shop. While he conversed with the tailor, Kare asked if he knew of a vacant room in the neighborhood.

Jakob answered, "Yes! One of my customers told me of a vacancy in his building." Jakob gave Kare the address—69 Gottenberg Strasse.

Kare went to the address and met the landlord, a Dutch German named Ard van Waar who was glad to rent a flat to another German Dutchman. The flat needed some repairs. It consisted of age-worn rooms with paint peeling from the walls. There was a small salon, a bedroom, a kitchen alcove with a small table, and a bathroom suitable for washing a dog, not fit for human hygiene; however, he decided he would take the place anyway since he had the money to renovate it. He had a new coat of off-white paint put on the walls and had the bathroom renovated with new ceramic tiles on the walls and floor. On the bathroom wall, over the refurbished sink, behind the mirror, he built himself a secret hideaway wall cabinet. The landlord was surprised to see his upper flat clean and looking brand new. Kare needed a means of transportation, so he bought a used bike. He also bought a shovel and a small handsaw.

Potsdam was in the vicinity of Berlin. The German Luftwaffe bombed Brittan's industrial facilities. In the spring of 1940, the British were given permission to bomb industrial targets in Berlin.

They bombed Tempelhof and Siemensstadt, Berlin. The flashes of exploding bombs were seen and heard in Potsdam. The city instituted a nightly blackout. The war was close to home. Then a month later, the attacks became less frequent, and nightlife returned to normal. Potsdam had no military value, so bombs weren't aimed there.

Kare decided that it was now time to hide his uncle's treasure. He modified the shovel by cutting it to the exact length of sixty centimeters. He removed the treasure box from the record player, and then placed the gold coins and bullions in a water resistant storage bag, which his tailor had made to his specifications, but he kept the reichsmarks, pound sterling banknotes, and the Art Deco jewelry. Kare put the storage bag back into the metal box, wrapped it in an old blanket, took the shovel and the treasure box, and rode off on his bike to the Chinese pavilion in Sanssouci Park. His plan was to hang around until dark when he could safely bury the treasure.

It was a moonless night. The Chinese pavilion was near the edge of the park's periphery road. It was deserted. Kare left his bike in the woods and walked toward the gilded Chinese figures at the edge of the pavilion portico, carrying his shovel, the treasure, and the blankets. Along the way he found and picked up a flat stone suitable for his purpose. He placed the end of the shovel by the edge of the portico and, using it as a measuring stick, made a mark with a stick. Then he measured from the Chinese sculpture and marked the spot for the dig. He spread the old blankets on the ground then dug up the layer of grass that covered the earth, placing the sod on the blankets. He dug a square hole sixty centimeters in length, width, and depth. He carefully placed the soil on the blanket. When he reached the right depth, he placed the box at the bottom and put the stone on top. He put the displaced soil back into the hole, packing it with his feet. Then he covered the top with sod. He tossed the excess soil into the woods. When he was satisfied that his task could not be detected, Kare rode away on his bike back to his flat.

Kare arrived at work early on Monday morning to start his work at the film studio. Lizzel was already in her office. "Good morning, Kare. I am sorry to hear about your loss."

"Good morning, Fräulein Lizzel. Thank you for your sympathy."

"Hans Lubner would like you to see him at studio D, but before you go there, stop next door at the security office for your employment ID."

The security office was under the jurisdiction of *Sicherheitspolizei*, the SS Security Police. The UFA Studios were part of the Ministry of Propaganda. All of the workers had to be background checked and had to pledge their allegiance to the Nazis. Jews were not allowed to work in the UFA Film Studio.

Kare was invited to sit down in the office of the chief of security. On the wall were portraits of Der Fuhrer, Adolf Hitler; SS-Reichsführer, Heinrich Himmler; Third Reich minister of propaganda, Joseph Goebbels; and SS-Gruppenführer, Henrich Muller. Kare's interviewer was none other than the chief of security, SS-Sturmhauptführer Ulrich Herwarth. He was dressed in a black *Totenkopfverbände* (skull unit) uniform. The SS captain was blonde, blue-eyed, and had a scar running across his left cheek. Kare later found out that this scar was a result of a drunken brawl a few years prior in a Potsdam beer hall. A broken bottle to his cheek had forever decorated his face. Ulrich as seated at the table holding a cigarette in one hand, and holding Kare's employment application in the other. A folder with Kare's name on it was on the table. The captain said, "I am very sorry for your loss. It was a true tragic accident."

"*Danke*," Kare said, lowering his eyes.

"Herr Hoffmann, you came from a well-known family in Leipzig. It is a real loss to the Reich. Such a dedicated industrialist like your Uncle Peter, a real Nazi. I read the obituary in the newspaper," the captain said as he waited for Kare's reaction.

Kare mournfully replied, "I will miss them both."

"I need to ask you a few questions. When and how long were you in England?"

"From nineteen thirty-seven to thirty-eight. I worked at Durham London studios."

"What did you do there?"

"I was an intern—number-one assistant cameraman."

"What movies did you work on?"

"*The Citadel* and *Goodbye, Mr. Chips*."

"Ah yes, I saw *The Citadel*. It was very interesting. *Mr. Chips* was a British propaganda movie. I hated it."

"I am an artist and a cinematographer. I do not write the plots. For me, it was an opportunity to work with great directors and actors. I film movies artistically. I do not get myself involved with politics."

The captain lit another cigarette, put the match in the ashtray, and continued. "You listed your mother's address as Rio, Brazil."

"Yes, she has lived there for some time. She came to visit me in nineteen thirty-eight, missed Brazil, and went back."

"Her name is listed here as Abigail Hoffmann. For some reason, we could not find her records in Berlin's ministry."

"It is possible that they were misplaced."

"What was her maiden name?"

"Abigail Karsten. She was Dutch."

The SS captain wrote on a piece of paper. "Are you or any of your family Jews?"

"No, I am Roman Catholic," Kare answered.

"Do you belong to the Communist party?"

"No."

"Do you belong to the NSDAP (Nazi Party)?"

"No, but I did belong to Hitler's Youth Movement."

"We cannot locate your Kino Academy records for some reason."

"The school was destroyed by bombing."

Ulrich did not respond to Kare's statement. "Herr Selpin has asked me to hire you right away. He needs you as a historical expert for his movie, so I am obliged to fulfill his needs; however, I am still missing information on your background. Is there anything you want to add to it?"

"No."

"Herr Hoffmann, you are clear to work in the studio, but you are still under investigation," the captain said. "Good luck. Pick up your ID at the front office, and I will see you around the studio. If you have any problems, do not hesitate to see me. You will find that I personally know all of the employees on the UFA grounds." Then he saluted and said, "Heil Hitler."

Kare replied, "Heil Hitler," and left the office.

Upon leaving, he felt a great sense of relief that the interview had gone well. He had falsified his mother's name on the employment application and had also listed his parents' marriage place as Berlin; they had actually been married in Leipzig in 1922 in the law offices of his father's friend, Judge Gustav. Kare hoped the SS captain would stop digging into his family records. He relied on the good standing of the Hoffmann's Leipzig family. They had a good relationship with the Nazi regime.

In the UFA studio, Herr Director Selpin and his assistant writer, Walter Zerlett-Olfenius, were planning a major epic movie, *Titanic,* to be filmed starting in mid 1942. Kare was given a preliminary plot of the movie and its script. Selpin wanted Kare to plan the required camera shots, camera angles, and camera position for each scene and record them on the script. Kare was also hired as a historical expert on the *Titanic*. He knew the ship's physical features and interiors well. The movie script was constantly being changed, and Kare had to update the positions and angles of the cameras.

In the meantime, Kare was assigned to the filming of the movie, *Geheimakte WBI (Geheimakte WBI Secret File W8 1).* It was a German propaganda movie about Sergeant Wilhelm Bauer, the inventor of the U-boat, and his successful blockade of the port of Schleswig Holstein in Denmark. Kare's experience was in filming static shots. It was hard to shoot the interior of a submarine, especially intercutting shots in front of the submarine's dials. Kare worked hard with the editing crew on the final cuts of the submarine interiors. Hans Lubner commended him on the final results. After only a month of working in the studio, Kare had gained the respect of the crew for his technical abilities. His experience at Dunham studios in London had paid off.

While shooting a scene of *Geheimakte*, the camera, positioned on a moving dolly, cut Kare's right hand. It was bleeding heavily, so he wrapped his hand in a towel and went to the studio infirmary. The receptionist sat him in the exam cubicle. She closed the curtain, and the doctor came to examine his wound. The doctor said that there was no need to stitch the cut. He would send a nurse to dress Kare's hand. Then he left the cubicle.

A few minutes later, a curtain opened and a nurse wearing a crisp white uniform walked in. "Herr Hoffmann, let me see your hand," she said sweetly.

Kare looked at her, and for some reason, she reminded him of someone he had known in the past. He searched his memory, trying to recall the image of this nurse's face. Then it came to him like an electric shock. *Could this be Monika?* Now, he was staring at her blue eyes, blonde hair, and enchanting face. He remembered that he had been infatuated with her image at the Hitler Youth Rally six years before. His heart jolted. *This must be the same girl I filmed at that rally. It must be*, he thought to himself. The nurse noticed his intense gaze. Their eyes met momentarily. She smiled, then lowered her eyes and continued to clean his wound with alcohol. Kare said, "Fräulein, have we met before?"

She looked at him with a surprised expression on her face and replied, "I don't think so, Herr Hoffmann."

"Pardon me. Is your name Monika?"

She looked at him with raised eyebrows and eyes wide open.

Kare's heart melted. "I knew it! I met you in nineteen thirty-five or six at Hitler's Youth Rally in Berlin. I was the boy filming movies with my camera. Do you remember me?"

Monika put his hand down and took a step back, trying to collect her memories. "No, I do not remember you."

Kare's heart collapsed from discouragement. Then he stood up, opened his wallet, and took a black-and-white photo from it. He handed the photo to Monika who took it and looked at the picture in amazement. With a smile on her face, she said, "Where did you get this photo of me? I must be no older than fourteen here!"

"I made a print from the movie of the rally that I attended."

"Why?"

Kare was quick to answer, "I was an admirer of yours."

She blushed and handed the photo back to Kare saying, "Thanks for your compliment."

Kare gave the photo back to her. "This is for you. You can have it."

"Thanks," she said, putting it in the pocket of her uniform. "Now, let's finish bandaging that hand."

Kare noticed her breathtaking beauty and the fact that she was now a woman. Her body bent over his injured hand, so close that he could smell her perfume. With his heart racing, he forgot his love for Gabby; now, he was in love with Monika. She finished bandaging his hand. Standing with scissors and bandages in her hands, she said, "Now, you are as good as new."

"*Danke*," Kare said, eyeing her. He extended his "good" hand. "I would like to formally introduce myself. My name is Kare Hoffmann, cinematographer."

She held out her warm hand to meet his. "Fräulein Monika Freude Daecher."

"May I ask if we could go for a beer or coffee?"

She smiled and paused, and for a moment, their eyes met. Then she said, "Would you like to join my friends and I this Saturday? We meet each week at the beer hall in Potsdam."

Kare's heart came to life. "Yes! I am new in town, and I would love to meet your friends." He let go of her hand. "Where?"

"*Bierstuben*," she replied. "It is in the open market next to the church in the center of the old city. We usually meet at eight in the evening and sit in the back rows."

"I will be there."

She then said her goodbyes and left the cubicle. She walked slowly, turned around and glanced once more at Kare, a tiny smile overcoming her lips. He was elated. *What are the chances of meeting someone from the past like this? One in a million! Was it luck or was it meant to be?*

Friendship

On Saturday evening, Kare walked toward Brandenburg Strasse in the old town center. He found *Bierstuben*-Kammern-Sanssouci Hall. It was a place full of people. There were dark wood-paneled walls lined with tables, and a large bar. The beer hall was noisy and filled with cigarette smoke. A waitress in a traditional German folk dress ran around, passing *beer vom fass* in tall glasses to the customers. It took Kare a few minutes to get oriented to the place. He walked to the rear of the hall, and then he saw a beautiful woman in a purple dress waving at him. It was Monika. He headed toward her table, which was full of people. She pointed to an empty seat opposite her that she had saved. Monika introduced him to her friends. "Herr Kare Hoffmann, the newest employee at the studio."

Her friends nodded in acknowledgment. He recognized the faces of some of her friends, whom he had seen at the film studio. Sitting next to her was SS Captain Herwarth. Monika introduced Kare to him. He extended his hand to Kare, and with a cigarette hanging from his mouth, he said, "We met a few days ago. Herr director insisted that I should approve his application right away before my completion of his background check. Herr Hoffmann, do you have anything to add to your interview?" His question was sarcastic. He puffed smoke toward Kare. The captain looked annoyed and grumpy.

He probably dislikes my presence next to Monika, Kare thought. Ulrich's facial scar seemed to be more pronounced in the dim light of the beer hall. He looked sinister.

Monika placed her hand on the captain's arm and said, "Be nice, Ulrich. You are not working right now."

Kare ignored Ulrich's invidious remarks. A sudden tap on his shoulder made Kare turn around. Standing in front of him was a uniformed Wehrmacht officer wearing glasses and holding a beer glass in one hand. He asked, "Kare, do you recognize me?"

Kare looked at him trying to recall his memory. "Yes!" he said, his eyes lighting up. "Hugo Dodtt." Kare stood up, hugging him. "For a moment, I did not recognize you. It has been almost ten years since I last saw you! You look splendid!" Kare remembered Hugo from grade school when he was a chubby-looking boy. They had shared a desk in the classroom. "What are you doing in Potsdam?" Kare asked.

"I am only here for one day with my officers' group for a visit to Sanssouci Park to take a traditional photograph in front of the beautiful terraced vineyards. What are you doing here?" he asked.

"I just started working at the UFA Film Studio."

Hugo smiled, faced Kare's table, and with his loud voice said, "I always knew that Kare would be a cinematographer! I remember him running and filming anything that moved or did not move during our school years."

"*Danke*," Kare said. "Would you like to sit with us?"

"No." Beer glass in hand, Hugo pointed to the table swarming with Wehrmacht officers drinking, smoking, and talking noisily. "That is my party, but we need to get together someday."

"I would like that."

Hugo took a paper from his pocket and wrote down a phone number in Berlin. "Call me if you are in town. Ask for Captain Dodtt at the offices of Hauptmann Rittmeister Logistics." Hugo hugged Kare and said, "Good luck with the new job, and do not forget to call me!"

Kare returned to the table. Monika smiled, looking at Kare. "An old friend?" Monika asked.

"Yes, I have known him since fifth grade."

"A friend from OKH, Army Group Command. He must have some connections," Ulrich said.

Kare had not noticed Hugo's insignia on his uniform. Kare replied, "His father made a military career in the Wehrmacht. He was at the rank of general if I remember correctly."

Kare had hoped that he could have a one-on-one talk with Monika, but it was impossible. The conversation turned to the work in the studio, the escalating prices of food, and the scarcity of women's shoes and cosmetics. When Ulrich stepped out to excuse himself to the washroom, Kare took this opportunity to speak to Monika. Looking at her, he asked, "Would you like to go to a park Sunday?"

She was surprised at Kare's direct request. "On Sundays, I go to church."

"Which one?"

"Sankt Peter und Paul Kirche am Bassingplatz. It is a Catholic church. It's right down the street from where I live. Are you a churchgoer?"

"No, but my father was a Catholic."

Her blue eyes opened wide. "Then join me at the church!" she said with excitement.

Kare could not remember the last time he had been to church, and definitely not for Sunday services. He had been brought up as a nonbeliever. Kare disregarded his atheism and replied, "I will be there."

"Great, I will see you at morning services."

Ulrich came back, looking at the two of them with a quizzical expression on his face. Kare turned the conversation to something else and drank his beer. He knew Ulrich was guarding Monika's attention. Kare wanted to ask Monika if Ulrich was her boyfriend or just an admirer of hers. *Will Monika come to the church by herself?* he wondered.

At midnight, the party broke up. Monika said goodnight to Kare, not mentioning the church service. Captain Herwarth gave her and her roommate, Heidi, a ride back to Babelsberg. Kare walked to his flat. *She did not mention church in front of Ulrich. Maybe she did not want him to know about our meeting.* He would find out tomorrow. *I don't know what to do in a church. Do I pray? Do I make the sign of the cross? Am I Jewish? What would a Jewish boy do in a church?* However, he figured that it would be a good cover for him since he had said that he was Roman Catholic on his application.

On Sunday, Kare dressed in his black suit, white shirt, brown diagonal-stripe necktie, and a black wool felt fedora. He looked forward to seeing Monika again. He left his flat on Holländisches Viertel, then crossed the street and made a short cut through Bassinplatz Park. It was a beautiful day; autumn leaves were spread at his feet as he walked. Morning sun bathed the trees, casting long shadows on the ground. Worshippers, dressed in their finest, walked toward the neo-Romanesque Sankt Peter und Paul Kirche. He hoped that this time, he would have some privacy with Monika, so that they could talk without interference.

The Nazis tolerated the Christian religion. Martin Bormann had exclaimed, "National socialism and Christianity are irreconcilable."

Hitler supported that view, stating, "One day, we want to be in a position where only complete idiots stand in the pulpit and preach to old women."

The Nazis viewed Christianity as a faith tainted by Jews. The Nazi who still wanted a spiritual home was offered a faith called *Gottglaubig*, God Be Livery, as an alternative to established churches.

Kare was a nonbeliever, although he reconciled with himself that he had been born a Jew. Now, he needed to keep that a secret.

The church was magnificent—yellow brick with an Italian-style campanile. It was sixty meters in height and had been built in 1867 with Byzantine-Roman stylistic elements. There were three famous paintings in the church by the artist, Antoine Pesne, in baroque rococo style. One of the paintings at the church alter was named *Christ Fears No Death.*

The service started. Kare stood at the rear of the church, searching for Monika. He finally found her in the back row, dressed in a smart black-and white-suit, white gloves. A stylish *film noir*–style chapeau was perched low on her forehead, accentuating her blonde hair. She waved for him to sit next to her. She had come with her roommate, Heidi. "*Guten Morgen,*" Kare said in a hushed tone.

The priest entered the church carrying the cross. He opened the service with a prayer. Then they were all seated. Kare and Monika exchanged glances. She smiled at him. Kare thought to himself, *She reminds me of the painting I saw in Uncle Andrew's art catalogues by Tamara de Lempicka. The girl with gloves, wavy blonde hair, large, sensual blue eyes, aristocratic nose and plump lips*—La Belle Blonde. Kare felt her warm body next to him. He tingled with excitement. They listened to the priest reading a verse from Psalm 121:

> *I will lift up mine eyes unto the hills, from whence cometh my help. My help cometh from the Lord, which made heaven and earth. He will not suffer thy foot to be moved: he that keepeth thee will not slumber. Behold, he that keepeth Israel shall neither slumber nor sleep. The Lord is thy keeper: the Lord is thy shade upon thy right hand. The sun shall not smite thee by day, nor the moon by night. The Lord shall preserve thee from all evil: he shall preserve thy soul. The Lord shall preserve thy going out and thy coming in from this time forth, and even for evermore.*

It was strange that the Psalm mentioned Israel. The Nazis had banished the Jews. Kare followed the service with interest, standing and listening in silence. It was the first time he had heard Monika sing—"Hallelujah." Her voice was clear and sweet. It was like heavenly angels singing to him. They sat down, and the service continued with a homily. The altar boys, wearing white, passed around the collection basket. Kare put five reichsmarks into it, a generous donation. He noticed Monika's gaze of approval. Monika's hands touched his, and a chill passed through his spine. He gently pressed her hand. She responded with her own light squeeze, glancing quickly at him. During the Lord's Prayer, Monika knelt. Then she went to receive communion. The priest closed the service with a prayer for the soldiers' safe return and a prayer for peace. He reminded the congregation of upcoming events and charity collections for the needy and soldiers at war. The service was over. The church was loud with the chatter of congregants walking slowly toward the exit. Kare followed Monika and Heidi to the street. It was just last night that they had been near the church at the beer hall. Now, they were parishioners. The street looked different than it had in the dark.

Heidi parted for an appointment in the city. Then Kare asked Monika, "Would you enjoy taking a walk in the old square?" She pleasantly agreed.

Tucking her purse under her arm, Monika asked, "Did you like the services?"

"Yes. I am not a churchgoer, but I enjoyed the services today."

"I am a believer in prayers, and I attend services every Sunday."

"What were you praying for?"

"I prayed for peace and the end of the war. My brother, Jorgen, is serving in the war."

"What do you hear from him?"

"Not much. It had been a month since we last heard from him, and my mother is worried."

"Where's your brother serving?"

"In the Wehrmacht on the Russian front. I don't have a good feeling about the war."

Kare did not want to have a depressing conversation about war on their first date together. As they passed a small café, he asked, "Would you like to sit down for coffee and a pastry?"

"Yes, that would be nice."

They ordered coffee and cake. "How long have you been working in the studio?" he asked.

"Since I finished nursing school last year. How about you?" She held the spoon in her mouth for a moment, and Kare's heart melted.

"I just started working there. I was in the Brazilian jungle for four years filming the Amazon for a documentary movie."

She took another bite of her cake and said, "How interesting. And before that?"

"Before that, I worked in Denham Studios in London."

"I always wanted to see London. Is it as interesting as they say?"

"Very different than it is here."

The waitress came over and asked if they wanted anything else. "A glass of water," Monika said.

He ordered another cup of coffee and turned back to Monika. "Is Ulrich your boyfriend?"

Monika seemed surprised by his direct question once again. Her face grew serious and she said, "No, he is just a friend. He is very helpful. I am not dating anyone right now."

Kare's heart raced, and he decided to take the plunge. "Monika, it would be my pleasure to ask you for another date. Perhaps dinner?"

She smiled and said, "I can see that you are very persistent and direct. I hardly know you."

"You're right, but I feel like I've known you for a long time."

Looking at him, she lowered her head sideways. "You seem like a nice fellow. I accept. We have a date."

Kare's face lit up, and he nervously shifted his body on the chair. "Great," he said. He moved closer to the table, looking at her. "Is next Saturday okay?"

She nodded her head. "It's a date." She then excused herself and went to the powder room.

Kare was left sitting alone, elated, staring at Monika's glass of water. She had left traces of her red lipstick on the edge of the glass. He thought, *How lucky for the glass to have touched her lips.* He wished that it had been his lips kissing hers. Kare was lost in his thoughts when Monika returned.

She said, "I have an appointment with Heidi in town."

Kare paid the bill before they left. Standing in front of the café, Monika extended her hand and said, "It was a pleasure spending time with you." Kare held her hand a little bit longer, gazing into her blue eyes. Then he gave her a French hug, kissing both cheeks. The smell of her perfume made him dizzy. She seemed surprised by the embrace and blushed. Kare walked down the street, daydreaming.

The next day, Kare stopped by the infirmary to change his bandages. To Kare's disappointment, Monika was not there, but the receptionist told him that Heidi would take care of him. "*Guten Morgen,* Herr Hoffmann. Let me see your wound."

"Please, call me Kare."

Heidi was a nurse like Monika. They were also roommates on Jagersteig Strasse in Babelsberg. It was a short walking distance from the studio grounds.

Kare asked, "Where is Monika today?"

"She is in Berlin today, seeing her mother." Heidi cleaned his wound and started to wrap new bandages around his hand. She was a woman of medium height, with nice facial features and brown eyes. She kept her brown hair short. As she leaned close to Kare, she said in a low voice, "Kare, my advice to you is to keep a low profile with your dating Monika." He was taken aback By Heidi's words. Then she said, "Herr Herwarth, the captain, is a very jealous man. Anyone who approaches Monika makes him upset. He can be a nasty, mean person. I have seen him when he gets into a rage."

Kare asked in a hushed tone, "Does Monika date him?"

"No. She refuses his advances. She doesn't really like him. Monika told me last night that she likes you and that you have a date on Saturday. It is not my business, but Monika can sometimes be a little naïve and does not see through people. Take her to dinner in Berlin, not Potsdam."

Kare realized that Heidi was a street-smart woman and was thankful for her advice. He asked Heidi to tell Monika to meet him at the train station on Saturday at noon.

Heidi nodded her head and said, "Ulrich has spies everywhere. Be careful what you say." Then she said in a louder voice, "You are all set."

"Thanks," Kare said and left the room.

He was working on the move set when Selpin called him into his office. "Kare, the script for *Titanic* is finished, and we are scheduled to start filming in May of next year. I want you to work with the stage designers to draw scenes and build the stage of the Titanic's interior based on your photos."

On Saturday, Kare waited at the Potsdam train station for Monika. He hadn't seen her all week. He stood across from the ticket booth, waiting, looking at his watch. It was past twelve. The next train to Berlin was at one. At 12:30, a crowd rushed to the train from the bus station. In the crowd was Monika. She wore the same black-and-white suit that she had worn to church on Sunday. She wore a different hat this time—a small black "doll" hat with a white feather. Monika looked smart with her matching black-and-white high heels. She carried a light coat over her arm. Kare greeted her with another French hug. This time, she was not surprised. She smiled, out of breath, and huffed, "I rushed up the stairs. The bus was late. Sorry it took me longer to get here. Have you been waiting long?"

"No, let's go," he said. He handed the conductor their tickets.

Monika asked Kare "Where are we heading?"

"To Charlottenburg," he replied. "I know a nice quiet Italian restaurant, Maria and Angelo's. I have eaten there before. Do you know the place?"

"No, I do not go to restaurants a lot. It is too expensive, and with what I make in salary, I help my mother as well."

"Is your mother all right?"

"She's fine. Mother was the breadwinner in my family. My father was a drunk and abused us. He died a few years ago from liver disease. I came from a poor family. I struggled with life most of the time." Her face clouded with sadness. "Why am I even telling you this? Let's talk about you."

Kare told her of his life growing up in a middle-class family in Berlin. It seemed to be the opposite of Monika's dysfunctional family life. Kare said, "You did all right. You went to school and became a nurse."

"Yes, I was lucky. My mother worked as a maid for a prominent SS general named Heinrich Zeig. He worked for Joseph Goebbels' propaganda ministry. Thanks to him, I was able to join the women's Red Cross League. My life was entrusted to Frau Scholtz-Klink, deputy leader of the *Nationalsozialistische Frauenschaft* [National Socialist Women's League]. They helped me through nursing school. There, I met my best friend and roommate, Heidi. Do you know she's from Potsdam?"

"No," Kare said.

"I arranged for her to get a job at UFA Studios through my mother's contact."

"You're lucky to have a friend like her. She warned me about Captain Herwarth's personality."

The train arrived at the Charlottenburg train station, muffling Kare's voice. When they got off, it was still early for dinner. Kare had planned to have a stroll in the beautiful Schloss Charlottenburg Park, the former residence of Queen Sophie Charlotte. The grounds of the park were some of the most picturesque places in Berlin. They walked along tidy gravel paths, passing baroque-style gardens arranged in geometric patterns. The sun gave a golden glow to the orange trees arranged around the water fountain. They strolled on the path along the Spree River, admiring vibrant ornate shrubs and flowers. It was a truly romantic spot. Kare took Monika's coat and placed it over his shoulder. As they walked, they talked about each other's goals and aspirations. Kare felt as if he was floating on a bubble; he was infatuated with Monika.

He remembered the time he had felt this way with Gabby. That seemed to have happened a long time ago. Six months had passed now, and the substantial truth was that it had left Kare with just a silhouette of pleasant thoughts. Now, he was in love with Monika.

He got hold of Monika's fingers, and she responded by holding his hand like an innocent child. She gazed at him, smiling.

Kare had a burning question to ask Monika and decided that now was the right time. "Monika, Heidi suggested that we keep our friendship discreet, hidden away from the prying eyes of Captain Herwarth."

"Oh, him! Ever since I started working at the studios, he has been chasing me and asking for a date. I do not like him and do not know how to avoid him. Heidi knows how to say no. I should learn from her. You know, the captain is quite vain and pretentious. He was the chief of detectives for the police department in Potsdam before he became the chief of security at the studios. When I moved, he helped me. He has a car, and when I need a ride, he gives me one. But, he has a dark side. He can be cruel, mean, rapacious, and selfish. He is also very frugal. When we go out as a group in town, he's always trying to avoid paying his share. He thinks the German woman is to be cute and full of curves—a naïve little thing—tender, sweet, and stupid. All women should stay at home and bear children to the Reich. He thinks that all SS men have the right to choose their ideal Aryan woman, and the women should oblige. I am a little naïve, but I am not stupid."

"I don't find you stupid. On the contrary, I was happy to have this conversation with you."

Monika seemed to relax and open up to him, and they were enjoying their time together. They walked to the restaurant. It was a magnificent place and a wonderful way to sample the cooking and wine of the Mediterranean cuisine prepared by the chef, Angelo.

The ride back to Potsdam was silent. Monika fell asleep on Kare's shoulders. At the train station, he got a taxi and took Monika home. She got out of the taxi and said, "Goodnight. I had the best time tonight!" Her blue eyes sparkled in the moonlight. He promised to be at church the next morning and watched her walk slowly into her house.

In Love with Monika

Titanic was ready to be filmed. Director Herbert Selpin and Walter Zerlett-Olfenius had written the movie plot. Kare was given final camera positions and angles to be incorporated into the movie script. The film used the sinking of the RMS *Titanic* as a setting for an attempt to discredit British and American capitalist dealings and glorify the bravery and selflessness of German men. Kare wrote his first report to London:

> *The* Titanic *movie is based on the ill-fated maiden voyage. The movie script is full of hate of big business and corporate board room dealings on Wall Street and Bond Street. They changed the fate of the White Star stock value and put the* Titanic *against a direct collision with the iceberg. It reflects the Nazi ideology, which dictates that Jews are behind capitalism in America. The script glorifies the selflessness of a brave German officer on board, who predicts the collision and relentlessly asks the ship captain to slow down. The epilogue shows that the capitalistic economy and the quest for profits override the safety of the* Titanic *passengers. The movie script was personally approved by Nazi propaganda minister Joseph Goebbels.*

Kare continued dating Monika, which they tried to keep secret, but Potsdam was too small a place. Although they avoided seeing each other on the studio grounds, people could see when two people are in love. Rumors circulated around the studio that Monika had a boyfriend. Captain Ulrich Herwarth was not happy.

One day, Captain Herwarth encountered Kare in the studio parking lot. He said, in an insidious voice, “Herr Hoffmann, you know I am still checking your background. Don't get too cozy with Fräulein Monika." Then he rolled up the car window and drove away. Kare grumbled to Hans Lubner, his superior, "Ulrich is poking his nose into my personal life."

"Don't pay attention to him. He is physically menacing, like a Nordic blond beast. He does it to all of us. He tries to keep us off balance. He holds undue high regard for his position as chief of security, but in reality, he is a spy for the Gestapo. The women in the studio dislike him. Be careful. He is a snake; don't get him cornered, or he will bite you."

A month later, Kare called Hugo Dodtt. He made a date to have lunch with him in Berlin. They sat on the terrace of Kranzkers Café in Unter den Linden, having a few beers and sandwiches. They discussed one another's past and present. After lunch, they strolled along Unter den Linden. It was a nice, breezy Saturday.

Kare said, "Hugo, you know, a lot of people are not enthusiastic about the prospect of fighting the Soviet Union."

"Kare, enthusiasm is not the point, but when one is ordered to fight, the Wehrmacht does it extremely well! We do our damn duty!"

"You are a military transport logistic officer. You provide combat service support. From your point of view, do you see a fast victory?"

"So far, Operation Barbarossa has hit the Russians like a hurricane. The Wehrmacht has made astonishing advances. We are at the gates of Moscow."

"The German forces are getting further and further into Russian territory. Remember Napoleon's Grand Army and the Russian winter of 1812?"

Hugo was silent for a long minute. Then he stopped walking and lit a cigarette. He took a deep drag, looked at Kare, his face serious. He said, "I see you did not forget your history. I remember in school, you were always excellent in history class." Then he said, pointing the cigarette toward the horizon, swinging his hand in an arc, "As you know, the army prepared for the quick summer campaign to achieve victory over the Soviet Union. I hope we can do it. If we can't, I will start worrying. Our supply lines are stretched to a breaking point. Can you imagine, in this day and age, we are still using horses for transport? I have not seen a plane for contingency to fight or supply for winter weather."

They walked for a while in silence until Kare said, "I would like to meet your fiancée. Monika and I, and maybe Heidi and her boyfriend, all of us could go to a concert or dinner. What do you think?"

Hugo smiled and his face lit up. "Great idea! I can get tickets for the concert. It is on me. You buy us dinner."

"It is a deal!" They promised to see each other soon.

The mood in the fall of 1941 was depressing. People on the street worried about domestic economic politics. They were annoyed and frustrated. They could still buy food in the market, but luxuries were slowly vanishing from stores. An underground black market developed. The war in the east was causing people to become heavily concerned. Germans anticipated heavy losses.

Kare started attending Sunday church services with Monika. She told him his company gave her a great deal of spiritual uplifting. She was worried for the well-being of her brother on the Russian front. Monika and Kare mostly spent time together on the weekends. During the week, he was busy on the studio grounds, preparing for the filming of *Titanic.* He traveled with the film crew to scout for filming locations in the Baltic Sea area. The studio was also planning a Christmas party, and this would be Kare's first.

After church services, Kare and Monika visited the small coffee shop down the street. They made it a habit to have their coffee and cake at the place where they'd had their first date.

This Sunday, they waited for Heidi. She arrived, accompanied by her boyfriend, and introduced him to Kare. "This is Theodore Klinger." He was a broad-shouldered lad in his early thirties, tall with black hair. He held a cane in his hand. The four of them ordered tea and cake.

Kare asked, "Where are you from, Herr Klinger?"

"You can call me Theodore. I am from Potsdam." Kare could tell they were holding hands under the table. "We have known each other since grade school. We met in our neighborhood."

Monika interrupted by saying, "But they didn't start dating until last year."

"Interesting," Kare said.

Heidi, now interrupting, said, "Theodore was serving in the Panzer division in the African Corps in Libya. His leg and stomach were badly wounded. I met him in the rehab center in Potsdam."

Kare asked politely, "How is your leg wound?"

"Much better now that Heidi makes sure I exercise it. We walk together a lot." He smiled at Heidi. Theodore had been discharged from the Wehrmacht. He was teaching in an all-boys' public school that specialized in math and science. Heidi was a Catholic, and Theodore was a member of the Protestant church, and like most Germans, both Catholics and Protestants, they were indifferent to the all-embracing Nazi ideology.

However, in 1941, cracks started to appear in the blind German belief in Nazi ideology. Kare remembered reading a quote by Pastor Martin Niemoller, one of the few Germans willing to speak out against the Nazis: "First, the Nazi went after the Jews. But, I was not a Jew, so I did not object. Then they went after the Catholics, but I was not a Catholic, so I did not object. Then they went after the trade unionists, but I was not a trade unionist, so I did not object. Then they came after me, and there was no one left to object." Kare observed that, as long as citizens went to worship in the churches and did not protest against the regime, the Nazis left them alone.

Monika told Kare about her life. She had come from an unstable home. Her father was a bricklayer, but seldom worked. He was drunk most of the time. They moved a lot because they were always behind on the rent. Monika's negative views of the Jews were developed during this period. Some of their landlords had been Jews, several of whom had evicted her and her family. Anti-Semitism had run rampant throughout her working-class neighborhood. She, too, was infected with "brown demons"—the Nazi ideologies.

The prevailing German view held that Jews were not just a collection of individuals but a group acting in concert as if with one will, especially because of their particular talent for economic infiltration, which would eventually accrue and give power to them through economic domination. That's what the ordinary German believed. The facts were that 50 percent of all of Berlin's doctors had been Jews, and 50 percent of Berlin's lawyers had also been Jews—before the Nazis banished them from their professions. The anti-Semitic mindset of the Nazis had spawned this thinking about Jews that had become integrated into German political and social culture.

Once, Kare and Monika had a serious discussion about the "Jewish Problem." "Do you have any good views of the Jews?" asked Kare.

She thought for a while and then said, "My brother was very sick as a young boy and almost died. We had no money to pay a doctor. Mother called Dr. Klein, a Jewish doctor. He came to our apartment, treated my brother, gave him medicine, and never charged for his services. My mother was very upset when he was forced to close his office. You know, Kare, I heard voices from the pulpit of my church. It was criticism for the open violence against the Jews. Now, it is only silence. I hate politics and war. One day, the Jews will retaliate against the Germans, but now, let's talk about something else."

In November 1941, Kare made arrangements with Hugo to meet for a concert and dinner in Berlin. Kare, Monika, Heidi, and Theodore met Hugo and his fiancée, Kristin. She was a good-looking woman and a music teacher. The concert began twenty minutes late. The program began with the works of Mozart, *Eine Kleine Nachtmusik* (A Little Night Music), then a performance of Piano Sonata no. 8, K. 310. Mozart had written this sonata in Paris about his mother's death. It was among the finest pieces of work from the classical period. Kare closed his eyes toward the end, listening to the slow, restrained movement. After intermission, works of Beethoven were performed, beginning with Symphony no. 6, op. 68, *Pastoral*–five scenes inspired by Beethoven's love of nature including a vivid storm. The concert concluded with a piano sonata in F minor, *Appassionato*, op. 57.

After the performance, Kare asked Kristin what she thought of the conductor's performance.

She said, "Wilhelm Furtwangler is a man of iron will, and it showed in his conducting tonight. When Mozart wrote "Allegro," how fast is fast? Is it a pace? A trot on a gallop? Wilhelm got it right. He followed his instincts. He oriented the orchestra to sound more bass, more tempo, not following the printed score. He had his own idea. Tonight's performance of the orchestra had the most gorgeous arabesque sound. Wilhelm presents a glorious school of German conducting. He was at his best tonight. *Sans peur et sans reproche!* (Without fear and without reproach!)"

Kare replied, "You should be a music critic."

"She is the best!" Hugo said. "You should hear her perform at the piano."

They entered the French Bistro, Le Train Bleu. It was a replica of a famous train dining car on the line between Leons, Marseille, and Monte Carlo. It was decorated with mahogany paneled walls, beveled glass mirrors, and green tufted seating. Victorian chandeliers hung throughout the dining room, and palm trees added ambience. All of the waiters wore typical French uniforms and carried white towels over their arms. It was a classic French eatery. Monika whispered to Kare, "I have never been in such a classy restaurant. I am sure it is expensive."

Kare tapped her hand and said, "I can afford it." He ordered a bottle of 1937 Vintage Pommery champagne.

"What is the occasion?" Hugo asked.

"To our friendship!" he replied. Then he presented a small box wrapped in gold paper to Monika.

She was surprised. "For me? What is the occasion?"

"Yes, it's for you!"

All eyed Monika. She fumbled with the box, trying to guess what was inside.

Heidi smiled and said, "Monika, open it!"

In silence, Monika unwrapped the box. "Wow!" the ladies exclaimed.

Monika's hands were shaking slightly. She looked in the box in disbelief. Inside was a magnificent Art Deco ruby and diamond ring. Kare held her hand and broke the silence. Looking at her, he said, "This is for our friendship. Will you accept this ring as our engagement and commitment to each other?"

Her face glowed. A tear rolled from her blue eyes. "I will! No one has ever given me such a perfect present, no one!"

They kissed as everyone watched them. Kare placed the ring on her finger. The ruby and diamond sparkled on her hand. Monika admired the ring and showed it off to the other ladies.

Heidi proposed a toast, raising her glass, "To the most beautiful couple, and to my best friend, Monika. I wish you both the best. You deserve each other." She emptied the glass into her mouth and kissed Monika.

Kare asked Hugo, "How long have you been engaged?"

"Now, it will be eight months. We are planning to get married next year."

Kare noticed some tension in his voice. Hugo was normally quite a loquacious man, but today he was tight lipped and deep in his own thoughts. When Hugo excused himself and went to the washroom, Kare followed him. At the basin, as they washed their hands, Kare looked in the mirror to make sure no one else was in the room. Turning to Hugo, he said, "Hey, Hugo, what's bothering you? You are too quiet today."

He said, "I have a lot of pressure on me from my job. In fact, this is a good opportunity to talk. Let's go outside for a cigarette."

They stood on the sidewalk next to the bistro door. No one was nearby. Hugo said solemnly, "I do not want to disappoint Kristin, but I received orders to move my staff closer to the eastern front after the New Year. This is the end game. The Soviets are now counter attacking and have started to resist. The Wehrmacht has had terrific losses in the thousands. This represents 15 percent of the army's strength. If we do not overcome the Soviet army, we are doomed." He tossed the cigarette butt into the street. "Don't say anything to anyone," he said as he put his arms around Kare's shoulders. "Let's drink for the coming New Year and a quick end to the war."

Christmas

In late November, winter arrived. It was a cold 1941. The studio planned to close from December 7 until January 7. On December 6, the studio invited the employees and their families to a traditional St. Nicholas Day children's party. A large Christmas tree stood on the studio stage. It was decorated with *raeuchermaennchen* (traditional wooden figurines), toys, and lit candles. Branches of dark green pine and fir needles tied with red ribbons were strung on the walls. Over 300 people were invited to the party. Monika served food and sweets to the kids at the long table. St. Nicholas sat on the stage, dressed in red, white, and green. He had a long white beard. Next to him stood Knecht Ruprecht (servant Rupert) dressed in black clothes with a devil-like tail and a red tongue. In one hand, he held a stick, and in the other, a small whip. His duty was to punish the small children who had not behaved well. Kids lined up to sit on St. Nicholas' lap, sing songs, or recite poems before receiving a gift. St. Nicholas would ask the child if he or she had behaved throughout the year. They all said yes to avoid the sinister black Ruprecht. It was a noisy, beautiful celebration. For a few hours, they were all able to forget the war. Kare had helped with the decorations the day before. With a glass of punch in his hand, he admired the children. Each wore a costume and held a stick with a silver star on the end. He hoped that, one day, he and Monika would have their own children. The party lasted until five in the afternoon.

At nine in the evening, there was a party for the employees and their spouses. Another stage was set up, and a jazz band played dance music. Kare, dressed in a black suit, met up with Monika, who was dressed in a long black gown with a short white jacket, white gloves, and black high-heeled shoes, which Kare had given her for this occasion. They sat at a round table covered with a dark-green cloth. A lantern with candles sat in the center of the table decorated with pine branches and artificial red and yellow apples. The smell of fresh pine needles was in the air. Kare fetched drinks from the open bar. Heidi and Theodore joined them at the table, drinking and talking. Heidi turned to Kare and said, "What are your plans for Christmas eve?"

"Nothing special."

"Then you and Monika are invited to my parents' house for dinner."

Kare looked at Monika for her approval. She said, "Today, Heidi invited me and my mother for dinner."

He smiled and said, "Then I will go, too." Kare asked Heidi what he should bring for the dinner.

"Bring yourself," she said with a sly smile.

Kare turned to Monika and said, "What should I bring?"

Monika put her hand over Kare's and said, "Later. Let's dance now."

The orchestra played a slow tune. Monika and Kare joined others on the dance floor. As he held her body tight, she placed her head against his shoulder. Her golden hair brushed his cheek. The smell of her perfume ignited his passion. He came closer to her, and they moved and glided on the dance floor as one. Listening to the orchestra, Kare kept thinking about how lucky he was to have met his girl, Monika.

When they returned to the table, Kare asked Monika, "When is your mother coming?"

"On the twenty-second," she said. "I want you to meet her."

"Yes, of course."

"I am going to Berlin tomorrow to visit her for a few days."

"I need to go to Berlin, too, to do some shopping. Let's meet at the train station tomorrow."

Her eyes lit up. "Great!"

Just then, Kristen Heiberg, "the new Marlene Dietrich," a beautiful Norwegian actress and singer who made her home in Nazi Germany, took center stage. She was dressed in white and wore a

Venetian masquerade mask over her eyes. She sang her 1938 hit song, "La Margarita."

Kare asked Heidi for a dance. She gladly stood up, holding his hand, and they moved to the tune of the foxtrot. Theodore was still limping and preferred not to dance. The movements gave him pains in his legs. Heidi and Kare were on the dance floor, talking and dancing. Then Heidi said, "Kare, look. Ulrich is annoying Monika."

Kare glanced toward their table. Ulrich, dressed in a black suit, was pestering Monika. Then he grabbed her hand and pulled her onto the dance floor. Monika appeared to be quite unhappy. Ulrich seemed to be trying to dance to the tune of the orchestra, but he was unsteady on his feet; he was drunk. Kare watched Ulrich try to get closer to Monika in a repugnant way. She rolled her head back to position herself further away and slightly pushed him with her hand. Ulrich lost his balance, stumbled, and fell to the floor. Monika stood there apprehensively, not knowing what to do. Ulrich tried to stand up but tumbled down again. His SS buddies rushed to him from their table, picked him up, and quickly ushered him away from the dance floor. Kare stopped dancing and rushed toward Monika. Heidi was there to comfort her as well. All eyes were on Monika. Kristen Heiberg stopped singing, but the orchestra continued playing. Kare sat Monika down and sat next to her. She was distressed. "What happened?" Kare questioned.

She replied, "Ulrich was drunk. I told him that I would not dance with him in that state, but he insisted. Then he fumbled onto the dance floor and fell. He is a real boozehound!" She started to cry.

Heidi took Monika's hands. "Let's go to the powder room," she said.

Theodore stood next to Kare. He said, "Kare, take Monika home. The party is over for you. There are too many people staring at us."

One of the SS police guards came over to Kare's table and apologized for Ulrich's behavior. Kare dismissed him with a nod. Many thoughts ran through his mind. It was a bad omen; the snake had been cornered, and he would bite.

Kare took Monika to her flat. Sitting on the bed next to her, he tried to comfort her. She sobbed. Her body shook. "It reminded me of my father's drunkenness and abusive behavior toward my mother," she said between sobs.

Kare calmed her down, wiping her tears with a handkerchief. "Darling, I am very sorry for what happened tonight. Damn Ulrich, spoiling your holiday evening. Go to bed, darling. Tomorrow, you will feel better. I will meet you at the train station." He kissed her goodnight and left the house.

As he walked along the street, the cold wind blew on his damp forehead. A chill passed through his body. He hoped that, in a month's time, this whole episode would be forgotten.

The next day, Kare met Monika at the train station. She was still shaken about last night's episode, but she looked more composed. They boarded the train to Berlin. She rested her head on his shoulder. Holding each other's hand, they rode the train in silence.

In Potsdam Plaza, Monika parted his company with a kiss and took the U-Bahn to visit her mother.

Kare went shopping. The city was decorated with holiday displays. In Potsdam Plaza, he wandered through Christmas booths, watching toymakers, goldsmiths, and wood carvers. There were musicians, dancers, jugglers, and acrobats entertaining children. A tall Christmas tree decorated the Plaza area. Despite the war and daily hardship, the shopping area was full of people who sought diversions to keep their morale up. On the black market, Kare bought Monika rayon stockings and a pair of black high-heeled court shoes with ankle straps. He also bought a few bottles of French perfume. Then he took the train back to Potsdam.

He wrote his weekly report to London, dated it December 7, 1941, dropped it at the tailor's shop, and returned to his flat. Kare retrieved his short-wave Volksempfänger VE 301 DYN radio, now considered illegal by the Nazis, from the attic and listened to the latest BBC news. The headlines read: "Japan bombed Pearl Harbor on December 7, 1941." America had declared war on Japan. Kare was glued to the news. It became clear to him that the implications of the event were enormous.

On December 11, Hitler declared war on the United States of America. The upcoming New Year of 1942 looked bleak and depressing.

On December 24, Christmas Eve, Kare went to Heidi's parents' house in Potsdam for a traditional holiday meal. It was his first time meeting Heidi's parents, Ludwig and Krista. They were in their early fifties; they had married late, and Heidi was their only child. Heidi's father had a small repair garage in town that also sold gasoline. Her mother was a homemaker.

Ludwig and Kare struck up a conversation. Kare was looking to buy a used 1937 Opel Olympia CL two-door car from a coworker. Now, he was interested to know what price he should offer. Ludwig suggested he bring the car to the garage for a condition check.

Kare also finally got to meet Monika's mother, Ingrid. She was in her late forties. A slim, blonde woman with nice features, she resembled Monika. She looked older than her age. Her blue eyes appeared tired and lacked the sparkle of life.

They sat down for a traditional Christmas Eve dinner of fish, potatoes, and cucumber salad with lemons. Kare had been able to buy a goose on the black market, and it was served with red cabbage.

The conversation at the table turned to the war with America and the decline in living standards. Ludwig used the word *swindle* again and again. "Some are getting fat from this war while others starve. The civil servants and especially the army officers continue their comfortable lives of idleness just as before the war. And we, the rubbish, are worse off than we were during World War I."

Krista tried to lighten the conversation. "Are you all going to the midnight mass?"

Monika looked at Kare. "Yes, I will be going," he said.

Ingrid replied in a concerned, motherly voice, "I haven't heard from Jorgen in over two months from the Eastern Front."

Kare suggested that he could call Hugo and find out how Jorgen's unit was doing. "I will let you know," he assured her.

Monika gazed at Kare and said, "*Danke*. It will soothe us to know how he's doing."

After dinner, they returned to the salon. Kare had brought presents for all. To Krista and Ingrid, he gave French perfume. To Heidi and Monika, he gave rayon stockings. Kare also gave Monika an additional present. He asked her to open it later in her flat. Inside were the black high-heels with a smaller box tucked into the toe of one of the shoes. In the smaller box was a gold Art Deco bracelet. It was from Uncle Andrew's treasure box. He was thankful for all of these riches that had been bequeathed to him. To Ludwig, he gave a bottle of French brandy.

Heidi said, "Kare, these presents cost a lot of money. You're crazy for doing this."

Kare said, "I made a lot of money selling my documentary about the Brazilian Amazon to National Geographic. How much money does one need? The notion that money buys happiness is false. I feel a sense of happiness when I spend more on others than on myself. In the spirit of the holiday, it makes me happier that you are all happy to receive my gifts."

"Well said!" said Monika, sitting next to Kare. She hugged him and kissed him on his lips.

Ludwig, smiling, said, "Let's open the brandy to celebrate love."

Monika gave Kare a small box wrapped in green paper. "Open it!" she insisted. It was a beautiful, small, silver-plated medallion with the image of Madonna and a child. Looking at Kare, she said, "I hope you like it."

"I love it," Kare replied.

"Keep it for good luck. She will keep you safe." Kare put it in his pocket and kissed Monika.

New Year, 1942

Kare and Monika decided to celebrate the upcoming New Year alone in a small restaurant in Potsdam. Monika held Kare's moving body as they shared a slow dance, listening to a jazz tune coming from the airwaves. It was the Tommy Dorsey Orchestra playing "I am Getting Sentimental over You." Monika silently placed her golden head on Kare's shoulder. There were only a few dancers on the floor in this small restaurant, celebrating the New Year. Kare kissed her neck and embraced her tightly as they glided over the dance floor. He imagined that they were alone, dancing somewhere like a café on an exotic beach with the blue ocean shining from the blue moon. He turned and looked into Monika's eyes. They were as blue as sapphires. She glanced at him, smiling. It is said that one can see another's soul in a person's eyes. He saw in Monika's eyes a leaping flame, a sacred fire named Desire. He placed his head against her golden locks. Her perfume and shampoo smelled like fire, exciting his senses. He whispered, "Darling Monika, will you spend the night with me?"

She did not hesitate and whispered in his ear, "I am yours tonight and all other nights." Her body slightly trembled with excitement. Kare's heart, beating eighty beats per minute, jolted.

It was months ago that he had last seen Gabby. He recalled the details and setting of their lovemaking in the greenhouse, but now, he was madly in love with Monika. He felt regret. If he could only see Gabby, what would he tell her—that he loved someone else? It would hurt her. He realized his feelings toward Gabby were only feelings of friendship; she filled a void in his life. He would tell her, "Forgive me. You deserve better."

They left the restaurant and went outside. Snowflakes had begun to fall on the deserted street, making it all white. A silent night. Hugging each other for warmth, they trod against the swirling, windy, frosty night in silence, each one in the other's thoughts.

Kare's flat was nearby. They rushed up the stairs and removed their snowy shoes and coats. They embraced, leaning against the entry door, kissing. The flat was chilly, so Kare placed coals into the small cast iron *Balcke-Dürr* heater standing in the corner. He lit a newspaper. The flame ignited, spreading a mysterious glow on Monika's face. She sat on the edge of the bed, glancing at him. He sat next to her and kissed her red lips. Her mouth opened, their tongues touched, kindling their carnal desires. As they kissed passionately, their lungs gasped for air. Monika stood up and removed her stockings and girdle, placing them neatly on the bed. Kare whispered, "Dear Monika." Looking into her eyes, he said, "I love you."

Her eyes were half closed, her mouth slightly open as she whispered, "I love you, too."

Their mouths kissed again. It was not the first time they had kissed, but this time it was like drinking old port—sweet and mysterious. Kare's hand slid between her legs. He felt her legs relax and move apart. His fingers probed her underwear. She was wet with the desire of love. Kissing her, he rested his fingers on her firm belly, then slid into her underwear, touching her golden temple. Monika let out a slight sound of pleasure; it was all new to her. With her head close to his, she said in a trembling voice, "Kare, do you have a robe?"

Kare stopped exploring her body, withdrew his hand from her underwear and said, "No, I don't. Would you like pajamas?"

She nodded her golden head, smiling in approval. Kare handed her his blue plaid flannel pajamas. She said, "Just the top." Then she stood up, took her night bag and ambled to the washroom.

Sitting on the bed, he felt his underwear wet with the anticipation of lovemaking. Chilled air filled the room. He raked the glowing coals in his heater. A rush of warm air filled the room. The only sources of light were two candles on a small table. The flickering candles cast wavering shadows on the wall and ceiling. It was a wintery night, and wind whistled through window cracks.

It was snowing and dark outside. Kare took a record and placed it on his new record player. It was his favorite symphony—Mahler's Symphony no. 5 in C-sharp Minor. It started off quietly, hardly a noise. Then the sound of the orchestra filled the room. Kare kept the volume level low to keep from waking his landlord a floor below. He removed his clothes, except for his underwear, and sat on the bed. He listened to the music in the dim light, his erect hardness pushing against his white underwear. The light in the washroom shut off. Monika walked into the bedroom. The orchestra played wild, mysterious, passionate notes. He looked at Monika coming toward him slowly. She was so beautiful, so pure. Her golden hair unraveled over his blue pajama top. Her long legs were bare. She came to his arms. Her lips were red like berries. They embraced and kissed. He wanted her. They kissed gently to slow musical movements, then passionately to the tunes that included a rising crescendo of the symphony. Kissing, open mouthed, gasping for air, their tongues united. These were pure, wild kisses. Kare's unsteady hands unbuttoned her top and slid inside, exposing her round porcelain shoulders. He kissed her sweet neck, thinking, *Is this all a dream?* Her warm body assured him that it was not. The girl in his arms was, in fact, Monika. Indescribable pleasure filled his body. The sound of strings and wild instruments playing was a haunting sound of the mysterious and wild Mahler's Fifth. The image of her in the woods, lying on the ground, surrounded by ferns, excited him. He wanted to explore her untouched, curvaceous body. He removed her top, and as she let it slip onto the bed, he laid his hand on her breast. She embraced him hard, kissing him with her warm mouth. Kare kissed her pink pearl-shaped breast, touching her nipples with his tongue. Monika trembled with desire. He let her lie down on the bed as he removed her black underwear, exposing her golden triangle. He kissed it, and she placed her hand on his back, holding him tight. Kare moved slowly over her body. She lay on the bed, her golden hair spread on the white pillow. She was like a magical goddess awaiting her lover. Kare was deliberately slowing his lovemaking. It was their first time. Their warm bodies lay embraced for a long time as they kissed, kissing in a grip of love.

Kare whispered in a hushed voice, "Monika, darling, I need to put on a condom."

"It is okay. I am in a safe period. Don't stop." She was ready for him.

His hard erection found her open door, and he slowly entered it. Their eyes gazed at each other as they breathed hard in anticipation of the unknown. Then Monika gravitated into him, slowly and firmly. He felt himself sliding deeper and deeper. She trembled and let out a rush of air from her open mouth. Her eyes closed, and she hugged him tight, spreading her legs wide open. Then he entered all the way, and they were one. For a while, he felt her inner walls pounding with her pulse. They moved together. The music of Mahler's Fifth played in a slow tempo. Slowly, their bare bodies were now one, lifting and sinking. Kare slid his hand behind her round, firm buttocks. She responded by lifting her legs and placing them on his behind. They moved again in unison, breathing ecstatically. He kissed her neck and moved deeper into her.

Kare's mind wandered with the pleasure of lovemaking. He wanted it to last forever. One of the candles flickered out, and the room became a bit darker. Monika's low cries of pleasure echoed throughout the dim room with each thrust into her warm body. Monika moved faster. Kare responded to her thrusts. He looked at her in the dark, her face glowing wet with perspiration. Her eyes were closed, and she was lost in her paradise. Gripping his body tightly, she moved faster and faster. She exploded with a rush of movements as Kare thrust hard into her. She trembled and let out a loud cry of joy. Kare placed his mouth on hers to muffle the sound. She kissed him passionately, moaning into his mouth. Squeezing her legs as they moved and thrust into each other, she found her release again. Her body curved and twisted. Kare felt her body exploding with pleasure. He withdrew from her. She opened her eyes, looking at him. He maneuvered her body on top of him. Sitting, Monika got hold of his erection and slid it into her. She was still. He felt himself getting harder in her temple. She looked wild, her wheat-colored locks covering her face like a blanket. They took hold of each other's hands, gripping fingers tight. Then she moved on top of him, slower then faster. Strange sounds came out of her mouth from each movement. Kare lost himself in her and came suddenly and unexpectedly. He let out a loud cry, continuing to move in her. Monika looked at him, breathing hard and still moving on him.

Then she slowed down, sitting on him. A smile appeared on her glowing face. *She looks so different,* he thought. He loved her, and he always had. Exhausted, she collapsed on his chest. Her hair covered Kare's face. The smell of her sweat mixed with her perfume excited him. He could still feel his hardness inside her.

"I love you," she said, kissing his neck. "I never knew that this kind of pleasure existed."

"I love you, too," Kare said. They lay together, listening to each other's heartbeats. The music stopped, and the sound of the record player's needle scratching the record echoed. *Scratch, scratch, scratch.* Monika fell asleep in his arms. He gently lifted her off of him and laid her next to him. She opened her eyes briefly and smiled. Then she fell asleep again. He covered her and reached to pull out the cord of the record player. Silence filled the room. He looked at the watch, and saw that it was after two. It was a new year, 1942. He gripped Monika's bare body and fell asleep.

Kare opened his eyes, and it was morning. Monika propped her elbow up on the bed and rested her face in her hand, grinning and looking at Kare, gliding her fingers over his brown hair. Kare pulled her to his chest and they kissed.

"When did you wake up?" he asked, gazing at her lovely face.

Her hair was neatly combed. Her lips were red, and the aroma of fresh scented soap and perfume came from her bare body. "Nine o'clock. I did not want to wake you up."

"What time is it anyway?" Kare asked, looking at the watch on the nightstand. It was after ten.

The room was chilly, so Kare jumped from the warm bed and stuffed more coal into the stove. Warm air soon filled the room. It was still snowing outside. Back in bed, Kare wrapped himself in the blanket. He lay next to Monika, and she gazed at him sensually, gliding her hand over his chest, resting on his awakened hard one. Her mouth kissed his. He kissed her neck and then her cherry nipples. The scent of sweet perfume filled his senses. He was awakened. Monika wanted him again. Kare, moving his tongue over her body, caused a pleasurable moan to come from her mouth. He rested his head between her legs. A scent of soap filled his nostrils. *She must have washed herself this morning.* A waft of Je Reviens perfume came from her golden triangle. It excited him now. Hard, breathing erratically, his tongue slowly reached her wet, open temple, exploring it, licking it like sweet ice cream. His hand rested under her firm buttocks. Monika held his head under the blanket, moving her lower body up and down over his warm wet tongue. Kare explored her inner walls, probing with his fingers. Her pleasurable moans echoed. Twisting and moving, breathing heavily, she moved her hips up and down. Then she moved faster, squeezing and relaxing, holding Kare's head, her fingers entwined in his brown hair. She pressed his face between her legs. Trembling, her legs moved up and down and then relaxed. She climaxed with a loud cry. It was filled with lust and gentle spasms. She put her legs on his shoulders. Kare slid into her. He did not feel the chill when the blanket fell from his bare body. She was ready, gyrating her buttocks, pushing against him. He rested in her golden temple. With Monika's hands on his shoulders, they moved slowly, then faster. Then they climaxed together. He lay on her, kissing her mouth.

Clear blue eyes open, she said, "What a night!"

"It was paradise," he said. "I wish I could enter this Garden of Eden again." He kissed her round lips. Now, he felt drained and deeply in love. They propped themselves on pillows to sit. Kare asked, "Would you like a Brazilian coffee?"

"Yes."

The smell of brewing coffee filled the room. Kare placed Mozart's Adagio in B Minor, K. 540 on the record player. Sitting on the bed, they drank hot coffee, the liquid warming their hands.

Monika said, "Kare, you travel a lot. Tell me about the land called Brazil."

"Oh, exciting Rio."

"Yes, yes, tell me now!" she said excitedly.

Kare reached toward Monika, placing her coffee cup on the night table. He said, "Now, relax," and he closed her eyelids with his fingers. "Come close to me." Her body lay against his warm chest. "Now, Monika, imagine this. We are awakened in the morning in a beautiful hotel room. We are in Rio. The sunrays streak through wooden slatted shades, casting shadows on the stone floor. We lie hand in hand." He grabbed her hand under the blanket. "I get up and open the veranda doors, and the sun and a cool breeze fill the room. You join me and we stand next to each other, topless. In front of us is a cinematic beach. Palm trees slowly sway in the cool breeze over the white sand. A turquoise-colored ocean stretches to the horizon. Gentle waves crash on the beach, inviting us to come. Embracing each other, we walk toward the beach. The sun is high, casting warmth on our half-naked bodies. We walk on the sand barefoot. The sound of a mysterious samba comes from a distant beach café. The Cariocas in skimpy bikinis (*fio dental*), some naked on the beach, are sunning or playing ball. A red, blue, and green parrot flies by and then lands on your hand. You feed him a peanut, and then he flies away. I cut a red-and-orange-colored wild hibiscus flower and place it in your golden hair. Your hair, scented with coconut, shines in the light. Your lips are red, the color of guarana berries. I kiss your mouth." Kare bent down and kissed her lips. Monika's eyes remained closed; a smile graced her face. She was in an exotic beach dream. Mozart's music was still playing. Kare continued to tell her of their adventure. "We are standing on the famous beach, the Ipanema. We walk to the nearest open beach bar, and I order a *caipirinha*, a traditional alcoholic drink made with lime and sugar, for each of us. We sit on chairs, sipping the exotic potion, looking into each other's eyes. The drink transports us to an uninhabited world. We shed the rest of our clothes. We run, hand in hand, toward the open, crashing waves. We lay on the sand making love."

Monika opened her eyes, smiling. "Please, Kare, take me to this exotic place. Promise me, promise me!"

"I promise I will take you to this enchanting place someday. Tomorrow, I will take you to visit Corcovado. I will take you on a cog train to the top of the mountain for the stunning views of Rio de Janeiro under the arms of *Cristo Redentor*. God is Brazilian (*Deus e Brasileiro*)." Monika's eyes and mouth were wide open as she said, "Kare, you are lucky to have visited those exotic lands. I have been nowhere. Can we visit Rio?"

"Yes," he said. "We will dance the samba at the carnival someday." Kare had created a fantasy in Monika's mind. He had taken her away to the Land of Oz.

The German Titanic

1942 began with a bustle of activity on the movie studio grounds. Kare was busy with the stage crew, constructing large sets of the *Titanic*. The largest and most elaborate set was the main dining hall with the cascading grand staircase. The set included balconies overlooking the main dining hall. Carpenters worked a furious schedule to meet deadlines for shooting in May. It was winter, and as soon as the weather permitted, the film crew was to shoot on the SS *Cap Arcona*, a German navy troop transporter ship. Her silhouette resembled that of the British RMS *Titanic*.

Herbert Selpin, the director, was busy in a meeting with Joseph Goebbels regarding the appropriation of finances for this ambitious movie epic. He was constantly bickering with Goebbels because he needed more funds to finance the most expensive movie enterprise ever taken on by UFA Studios as of that time. Nevertheless, the movie screenplay was completed.

In February, Kare's friend, Hugo, before departing to the Eastern front, called Kare. "Sorry for the bad news. Jurgen and his entire unit were listed as missing in action. I think they were taken as prisoners by the Soviets."

When Kare relayed the news, Monika was devastated. Distraught and depressed, she withdrew from others for a long month. Now, she went to church more often, praying for her brother's safe return. Kare, busy on the *Titanic* sets, saw Monika seldom that month.

In March, RAF bombers appeared in the skies, bombing targets around the clock. In the Babelsberg studio, a bomb shelter was under construction to accommodate 400 people. The war was coming home. Nightly, the noise of bombs echoed throughout Potsdam, and a blackout was enforced.

After one of those nightly bombings, Kare said, "Dear Monika, we are safe from the British bombers here in my flat. The center of the city of Potsdam is a historical monument. I don't think it will be bombed. I want you to move from your flat, which is too close to the studio grounds. The RAF bombardiers may have it in their crosshairs." Monika agreed.

In a few weeks, Kare was scheduled to start shooting *Titanic* on the Bay of Lübeck in the Baltic Sea. Traveling over land in Germany was now dangerous. RAF and American planes appeared out of nowhere, bombing and strafing railroads and convoys on the roads.

One evening, Kare sat Monika down for a talk. He said, "Dear, I don't want to distress you, but we are at war, and anything can happened to me. I want you to have this envelope." He handed her a blue wax-sealed envelope.

She was surprised. "Why are you saying this?"

"We have to be realistic. I will be traveling a lot with the film crew. Anything can happen on the roads."

"I cannot bear the thought of losing you." She started sobbing; he tried to comfort her, but they sat in silence in each other's arms. Outside, the exploding bombs echoed in the far distance.

Kare handed her a chain with two small keys strung on it. "Dear, take this chain and place it around your neck. Keep this safe. Now follow me."

In the bathroom, he removed the mirror from the hook. Behind it was a flat panel with a lock. One of the keys on her chain opened it. There was a built-in hidden safe in the wall. There, he kept his reichsmarks and other valuables. "Now, let's put this envelope in a safe place."

She placed the envelope inside the safe. Then he asked Monika to lock the door and placed the mirror back on the wall.

He said, "Open the envelope if I do not come back. There are instructions for you. It is my last wish. Everything that is in the safe is yours." Now she was crying. Kare kissed her and wiped her tears with his hand.

On Sunday after church at the café, Theodore and Heidi had good news. They had decided to get married in June. Heidi turned to Kare and said, "When are you getting married?"

Monika looked at Kare smiling. He replied, "We have not decided yet." Then he took Monika's hand and asked, "Monika, will you marry me?"

It was so spontaneous that Monika was caught off guard.

She looked serious and said, "No." Kare's heart stopped for a second. Then she smiled and said, "Of course I will marry you, you fool! What took you so long to ask me? Yes, yes, and a thousand times yes." She hugged Kare hard.

Heidi and Theodore yelled, "Congratulations! Let's have a double wedding."

Monika looked to Kare for an answer. He said, "I think we should marry after the completion of the shooting of the *Titanic*. It will probably be late summer. Then I would like to have a wedding in Holland."

"Holland?" Monika said in a surprised voice.

"Yes, it is my family tradition. I need to discuss it with you." Kare was hatching a secret plan. After the filming of the *Titanic*, he was planning to take Monika to Holland and find a way, through smugglers, to the shores of Britain.

That evening, he wrote his latest report to London. He recorded his observations on the Wehrmacht movements on the roads, not mentioning his marriage proposal to Monika.

In late May, the film crew left the studio for the Port of Lübeck. A large gray ship, the *Kriegsmarine* SS *Cap Arcona*, flying the Third Reich insignia, was anchored in the bay. The ship was used as a German troop transport. The SS *Cap Arcona* resembled the doomed *Titanic* in size and look. It would be used in the filming of the German version of the most famous maritime disaster.

Kare boarded the ship with the film crew, surveying the scene locations based on the script. He was assigned to be in charge of the filming on a barge at water level. Then he traveled over land to the nearest fishing villages to recruit accessory boats. They would need them during the shooting of the water rescue scenes. All was set for the actual filming in July.

Kare returned to his flat in Potsdam. As he was climbing the stairs, the landlord called him to his apartment.

"What's up?" Kare said.

The old man said, in a serious, low voice, "A policeman in civilian clothes came one day when no one was in the flat. He showed me his detective ID and asked me to open the door to your flat. He spent half an hour there and then left. He warned me not to say anything to anyone. Is everything okay?"

Kare asked, "Did the detective have a scar on his face?"

"Yes!" the landlord said.

"I know who is behind it." He thanked the landlord and rushed to the flat. Monika was still in the studio infirmary working. Kare went to the bathroom to check his safe. Nothing had been touched. He looked around and found nothing amiss. Then he noticed that, in his desk drawer, the postcards from Brazil were not in the same order. Someone had touched them. When Monika came home, happy to see him, he asked if she had looked through his mother's postcards from Brazil. She said, "No. Why are you asking?"

"Oh, I am just wondering," he said.

Kare had been receiving postcards from Brazil addressed by his mother. It was all a front arranged by the SOE in London. Kare knew it had been Ulrich Ulrich rummaging and looking for something. Ulrich was now consumed with jealousy. He had told Heidi that he knew Monika was living with Kare and he couldn't bear it.

Later that day, Monika asked, "Kare, have you seen my peach-colored underwear?"

"No."

She never found them. Then Kare realized that Ulrich had a little secret. He had a panty fetish. He remembered that, one time, Heidi had mentioned that she had seen Ulrich touching Monika's panties on the wash line outside their flat. He couldn't have Monika, so he stole her underwear. He had deviant sexual fantasies and a psychiatric disorder, so he gratified himself with Monika's clothing. It made Kare uneasy and angry. Ulrich had violated his and Monika's privacy. There was nothing Kare could do about it. Ulrich was the "Nazi law." On the other hand, Kare had come to the realization that Ulrich needed Monika around. He needed to have his fantasies.

Kare was careful as an agent. His never left his jackets with the secret compartments in his flat. The one he wasn't wearing was in the tailor shop for cleaning at all times. He would place the weekly reports and return the jacket to the tailor's the same day. He would only take it to place another report. However, Ulrich was an experienced detective. Kare thought that the officer suspected something but probably could not place what it was. He had searched, hoping to find something to incriminate Kare, who decided that it was getting too dangerous. After the filming of *Titanic*, he would quit the studio and take Monika with him to Holland.

In July, the entire film crew, the actors and their wardrobes, the lighting and camera equipment, and the extras, all left for Lübeck for filming on the SS *Cap Arcona.* The director planned to shoot all the easy scenes first. The captain's bridge, the ship's deck, and the passenger scenes were all filmed by mid July. Now, they were ready to film the difficult scenes—the night shots on the *Titanic*, the panic of the passengers on board, and the lowering of lifeboats into the water. The weather did not cooperate; high winds, rough seas, and rainy skies prevented filming the water scenes. Selpin was behind schedule, retaking shots again and again. To save money, they used some of the German seamen and their officers as extras. They were not professional actors and needed numerous rehearsals. The director and film crew were not satisfied with the results. Lifeboats fell into the water, and the lowering mechanism jammed during filming.

The director then took personal charge of the filming. After shooting night after night, they hoped for the right shot but without satisfaction or success. He was a perfectionist. This film was supposed to be his legacy. Now, he was short tempered. Selpin blamed the flop on the actors, the crew, and the navy officers on board the ship. He called for a general meeting. Kare was on shore and not present at the time.

The director denounced the captain and the officers by saying that they were jackasses. As far he was concerned, the captain and his *Kriegsmarine* officers only qualified to command paper ships in a bathtub, and their only interest was getting into bed with his actors. A shouting matched ensued between the director, the captain, and Selpin's personal friend, screenwriter Walter Zerlett-Olfenius. Selpin accused Olfenius for being incompetent like the rest of the ship's crew. Then Selpin stormed out of the meeting room. Subsequently, the director was recalled to explain his behavior to Joseph Goebbels and asked to retract his statements. He stubbornly refused. On July 31, 1942, he was arrested. Herbert Selpin was found dead in his cell a day later. He was hung with his suspenders.

Shock, bewilderment and disbelief hit the film crew. A rumor circulated that the Gestapo had killed him. The filming stopped. The entire production returned to Babelsberg.

During the trip back from the Bay of Lübeck to UFA Studios, the *Titanic* actors, Otto Wernicke (*Titanic* captain), Hans Nielseu (first officer), Ef Furbringer (Sir Bruce Ismay), and Charlotte Thiele (Lady Astor), were agitated and angry. They knew Herbert Selpin on a personal basis. He was their friend. Selpin's outburst and criticism of the *Cap Arcona*'s officers had been just. The officers had not behaved as gentlemen on board; they had molested the actors on the ship. The director had the right to sack and lecture the ship's crew. Now, his criticism gone evil, Goebbels had silenced him ruthlessly by hanging him. The film crew talked of a protest and a strike in the studio. Kare realized that Goebbels had used Selpin's death as a warning: Do as I say or pay the price! The actors and film crew drafted a petition of protest against Goebbels. They elected Kare to deliver it to the general manager of the studio.

Kare was called to the security office. Ulrich, dressed in his black SS uniform, looked more sinister than ever. He shouted to Kare, "Tell the ungrateful, spoiled actors if they do not cooperate with the replacement director, Herr Warren, their careers in the movie business will be caput, finished!" He banged his fist on the table. Then he moved closer to Kare, looking him in the face. "There will be no revolt in the studio under my watch!" He poked his finger into Kare's chest, emphasizing his authority. "As for you, Kare, your days in this studio are numbered. I am gathering evidence on you, and when I am finished, I will put you away for years." The edges of his mouth foamed and his face twisted with anger.

Kare took a few steps back and said, "Ulrich, if you have anything on me, spit it out now. You have nothing on me."

"In due time! In due time, I will banish you from here. You know I can send you to the Eastern front now. Your deferment from the military service is only because of your benefactor, Herr Selpin. Now he's gone. You are not needed here anymore." He put his hands in Kare's face. "I will squeeze you slowly." He twisted his hands. It was obvious he enjoyed threatening Kare; he was a sadist, the incarnation of the image of the Devil. Then he waved Kare off with his hand. The meeting was over. "Heil Hitler," he shouted.

Kare did not say a word and walked away.

Shattered Dreams

Kare heard a cry and woke up. Monika was sleeping next to him, her body tossing and twitching. Kare put his hand on her shoulder. She stopped moving. *She is just dreaming,* he thought. He looked at his watch. Three in the morning. He tucked his body against hers and fell asleep.

At breakfast, Monika drank tea and crunched on toast. Putting down the newspaper from the previous day, she said, "I had a bad dream last night."

Kare replied, "I know. You fought someone and then you cried."

"Did I?"

"How bad was the dream?"

"Awful. It felt so real. You and I were standing on top of a cliff. For some reason, you slipped and fell. You were holding the rock with one hand, and you reached out your other hand toward me. I lay on the ground holding your hand, trying to pull you up. Your hands were slipping. Then I woke up. It was awful."

"It was a bad dream. It was only a dream."

"But why do I still feel that feeling?"

"I'm sorry to see you upset over a bad dream. Shall I drive you to work?"

"No, I forgot to tell you. I have an appointment with the doctor in town today."

"Anything wrong?"

"No, it is just routine. It is my yearly checkup with the gynecologist."

"Well, then I shall see you tonight."

Later that night, Monika read a book in bed. *She is quiet today,* Kare thought. He asked, "Is everything okay?"

She continued reading and said, "Everything is fine."

At the studio, Kare prepared the camera for the morning shoot. Today, they would film the corridors of the *Titanic* with the passengers rushing to the ship's deck. The stage was ready for filming when a messenger came to the studio. He was looking for Kare. "You are urgently needed at the security office," he said.

What now? Kare said to himself, cleaning his hands with a towel. He walked to the security annex.

Ulrich was waiting for Kare in his office under the portrait on the wall of the Gestapo leader, Heydrich, draped in black. Jewish partisans in Czechoslovakia had assassinated him the previous May. Ulrich, in his black SS-Totenkopfverband uniform, legs spread, hands resting behind his back, said, "Heil Hitler."

Kare replied in a low voice, "Heil Hitler. You wanted to see me?"

Ulrich looked at him for a minute and then screamed, "You think I am stupid? I knew you were hiding something from me! You dirty Jew! A rat! Scum of the earth!" The words spat out of his mouth like a machine gun.

"What are you talking about?"

Ulrich had a stick behind his back. He whipped it around and hit it on his desk with a loud bang. "Shut up!" he shouted at Kare. "You rat! You swine! You are a dirty Jew hiding behind an innocent persona. I had a feeling all along that you were a Jew!"

"You know I am not a Jew. I am a churchgoing Catholic."

"Ja?" he shouted. "*Wer Jude ist, bestimme ich.* (Who is a Jew, that I decide)," Ulrich said, lifting a folder from his desk. "Do you know what I have here?" He opened the folder, took out one paper and waved it in Kare's face along with "venomous halitosis." "It is a sworn statement from Geli, your Uncle Peter's wife. She states that your mother, Lila, was a Jew. Do you know the meaning of the word, *Rassenschande* (Race defilement)? Do you know what Nuremburg's law states? No Aryan should have sex with a Jew. Your father married a Jew. You are a swine, a filthy Jew!"

Kare swallowed hard and said, "Prove it, Ulrich!"

"I do not have to prove anything. I just need to turn you over to the Gestapo. They will get a confession from your guts. I will be nice to you. Confess to me and spare yourself the pain of torture."

"Let me see the document."

Ulrich threw it in his face and it fell on the floor. Kare picked it up and looked at the deposition. It was notarized and stamped by a judge in Leipzig. It looked authentic. He had been trapped by "Mephistopheles." He was cornered by Ulrich.

"I am dismissing you from your employment, Kare. No Jews may work in our studio. Wait until Monika finds out you are a Jew. Swine! Seducing a defenseless, pure, Aryan woman! You should be shot!" he screamed.

"I would like to have a word with Monika."

Ulrich hesitated at Kare's sudden request. Then he pointed the stick at the confession paper on the desk. He said, "First, you sign these documents or you will never see Monika again."

Kare's mind raced. He had no choice. It would be better to be arrested on an accusation of being a Jew than to be interrogated by the Gestapo, because they might find out that he was an agent of Britain. Either way, it was a death sentence. One would be a slow death, the other a bullet in his head, a quick death. He chose his punishment—a slow death. He took the pen, but did not read the *Schutzhaftbefehl*, a document through which the signer requested his own imprisonment. He signed it and sealed his fate. He was to be arrested under the same Nazi laws called "protective custody" that his father had spoken out in protest against at Humboldt University. Eric had called it an illegal and shameful law. The Gestapo had carte blanche to arrest anyone. They operated without judicial oversight.

Ulrich said, "You can see Monika. I will give you ten minutes. You are lucky, Kare. I am doing it for Monika's sake. Otherwise…" he pointed the stick at his throat and mimicked the motion of cutting his throat, his face twisting into a sadistic grin.

Kare rushed to the infirmary next door, a million thoughts clouding his mind. Monika and Heidi were in the supply room unpacking medical supplies and stocking the shelves. Monika was surprised by Kare's sudden outburst into the room. He shut the door. His face was lifeless. Monika detected that something was wrong. Kare remembered her premonition of bad news—the dream!

Kare stood, looking at her, searching for words. He said, "My dear Monika, I have to go away for a while."

She said, "Where?" in a concerned voice. Heidi stopped stocking the shelves behind Monika.

"I was arrested," he said.

"Arrested? For what? What did you do?" she asked. "It must be Ulrich." Her face turned serious. "That devil, Ulrich!" she repeated.

"Ulrich found out that my mother is a Jew. He accused me of being a Jew."

Now Monika became hysterical. Her hands in fists, she lowered her body, screaming, "Damn Ulrich! Damn Ulrich!" She was crying. "Why did you do this to me, Kare?" Now, she raised her voice, "I'm dead! I'm dead!" And she hit his chest with her fists, her face distorted in agony. "You are my world! Why would you do this to me?" Kare tried to hold her shoulders. She pushed him away. "I am carrying your child!" she screamed. "Now you damned me and our child. We are finished!"

The words hit him like a bolt of lightning. He fell on his knees and collapsed on the floor. Tears streamed down his face. His body shook as he tried to hold on to Monika's legs in an embrace. She allowed it for a moment and then pushed him away. *What have I done to my Monika?*

Crying, Monika bent her body over his, removed her Art Deco engagement ring, and threw it into his lap. She raised her voice and said, "I don't want to see you ever again! I am dead to you!" Then she ran from the room.

On his knees, Kare sobbed. Her words, "I am dead to you," stabbed his heart like a sharp knife. It was worse than the Torture of Tantalus. *Will Ulrich arrest Monika, too, for sleeping with the enemy, a Jew?* She could be stripped of her citizenship, or worse, sent to a concentration camp. He was filled with remorse. He felt guilty and wanted to die.

Two hands touched him. He looked up and saw Heidi. Standing above him, she lifted him from the floor, hugging him tight. Her face was wet with tears. Kare took hold of her hand and placed the Art Deco ring into her palm. He said, "Heidi, give this ring back to Monika. If she refuses, I want you to have it."

She replied, "Monika loves you. She will never love someone else. She didn't mean what she said. I know her. I don't care who you are. You will always be my dear friend. Let me talk to Ulrich."

"Don't!" Kare said. "He will hurt you."

"I am not afraid of him," she said as she walked outside.

"Ulrich, for God's sake, you can't do this to Monika. For once, can you not look the other way?" Kare heard her arguing in a loud voice.

Ulrich shouted back, "Heidi, stay out of my way! This is my order! Don't interfere with my official duty, and stop defending this *schwein* Jew. I know what is good for the Reich, and what is good for the Reich is good for Monika."

Then silence. She came back with a defeated look on her face. "It is no use," she said as she hugged Kare. "Go. Go where you have to go. I will take care of Monika. I will pray for your safe return."

Kare hugged Heidi and whispered into her ear, "Please tell Monika that I truly love her. Oh, my dear, I never intended to hurt her. My heart bleeds. Ask her for my forgiveness. Oh, Monika, within a depth of my heart, I swear I shall come back."

"I will tell her," she said. She kissed him on his cheek. "Go now, Kare. Ulrich is waiting for you," Tears welled up in her eyes.

Kare sat between two SS guards in the backseat of the car. Kare looked at the studio gates of Babelsberg for the last time.

Dante's Inferno

Kare was driven to the Gestapo's Potsdam *Sicherheitspolizei* by security police. He was thrown into a prison cell. Sitting on the concrete bed in the cell, he tried to dial back and understand what had happened. Despair set in. The unknown awaited him. He dreaded losing Monika. The words she'd spoken in the infirmary still reverberated in his mind: "You are dead to me!" The words were like a gaping wound in his heart. He knew what awaited him in the labor camp. He didn't know what awaited Monika.

The propaganda movies he had seen in the editing room at Babelsberg Studios had taught him the real truth. The labor camps were death camps. Prisoners were human slaves in holding pens, and the camps were Nazi killing zones. He remembered Uncle Andrew's words, "Your mother is in Bergen-Belsen." Now, he would be a slave too. Then the quote of Churchill surfaced in his mind, "If you are going through hell, keep going." Sitting in a fetal position, burying his hand between his legs, he fell into a restless sleep.

A guard calling his name awakened him. Handcuffed, Kare was pushed into a room and made to stand in front of a desk. A Gestapo *kriminalkommissar* (interrogator) came in holding a folder. He was all business. He questioned Kare's background, making notations on a paper. He sat behind his desk. A Nazi flag hung behind him on the wall. After a while, Kare realized from the questioning that the Gestapo were only after his Jewishness. They were in the dark about the fact that he was an agent for Britain. Kare stopped denying that he was a Jew. He hastened the interrogation to satisfy Ulrich's uncovering of his undocumented Judaism amidst the Aryans.

Kare remembered that his Aunt Geli had stated in the affidavit that Eric, his father, had been married to Lila, and that she was a Jew. Had she made this statement to avenge Peter's death, or had she just mentioned it casually during her interview with Ulrich? She had never mentioned his father's family in London or Apeldoorn. Was it coincidence or was it deliberate?

The Gestapo interrogator concluded the questioning. He stamped Kare's ID card with a big red *J*. He declared Kare guilty of racial inferiority as described in the Nuremberg Laws. Kare would be sent to a labor camp—his guilt: being born to a Jewish parent.

Returning to his cell, he found two drunken men sleeping on the concrete floor in a pool of vomit. The smell of urine and vomit made sleep impossible. Kare lay down on the concrete bed, turned himself against the cell wall and covered his face with his jacket. He finally fell asleep.

In the morning, he was awakened by a commotion in the cell. A guard was showering the drunks on the floor with a water hose. The men sprang up, cursing loudly. The guard let the two drunkards out of the cell. They disappeared, cursing, down a long corridor. The cell door slammed, and Kare was left alone. Then the guard returned. He hosed the cell floor clean and exited. Kare, sitting on the bench, disheveled and depressed, remembered his SOE instructors training him how to survive in prison. They had told him that despair would be his enemy in prison; hope and clinging to life would keep him going. He pulled a handkerchief from his pocket. He slowly unraveled it. There was the gift from Monika, a silver medallion of Madonna and Child. Kare stared at it for a long time. He imagined the image of Monika and their child in her arms. The blood started flowing in his veins. He felt a sudden strength in his body. All despair vanished.

The door slammed and the SS guard in a grey uniform walked in pushing a cart that held containers of food. He placed a metal plate and an aluminum cup on the cell floor. Kare stood to pick it up. They looked at each other for a moment. Then the guard said, "Do I know you?"

Kare replied, "You do look familiar. I met you in the beer hall. Now I remember. Your name is Frick, and you are Heidi's neighbor."

The guard came close to the cell bars. "What are you doing here?"

Kare hesitated to say the reason for his confinement. Then he thought that the guard would be able to find out anyway by looking at the arrest booking. "I have been accused of being an undesirable."

Frick said in a serious voice, "Oh, it is too bad. Does Heidi know about this?"

"Yes, she knows."

The SS guard shrugged and continued walking, pushing the cart and distributing food to the other cells in the corridor. Kare sat down to eat his chow. It was disgusting—plain porridge, a piece of *Graubrot* (rye bread), and hot water with a hint of tea, which was tasteless. He remembered again his instructors in London. They had told him, "You must eat whatever they give to you or you will perish." The food tasted exactly like the sample that he had been given to taste at the SOE training grounds in London.

The next night, he shared the cell with an accused burglar. Of course, the man denied the charge. At least he was not drunk. This was not his first time in the lockup. He knew all the policemen by their first names.

In the morning, Frick appeared with the cart. He removed the burglar from the cell and put him into the adjacent cell. Then he returned to Kare. He pushed the food and a blanket on the floor. He whispered, "Take it fast!" pointing to the blanket rolled with a cord. Kare quickly grabbed the blanket into his cell and took his food. Sitting on the concrete bed, he unrolled the blanket. There was a loaf of Berliner Lundbrut bread and a *Tburinger* German sausage wrapped in a newspaper. Wrapped around the sausage was a note from Heidi:

> *Thanks to F, I am able to write this to you. I hope you are in good spirits. I saw Monika yesterday. She is still angry and would not accept your ring back. She is talking about leaving Potsdam permanently. She is still staying in your flat. I know that she will come to her senses. In the meantime, the savior angel, Gabriel, should be with you. I believe in angels, and I am praying for your safety. Be strong. Monika and your child need you.*
> *Your friends,*

Heidi and Theodore

How strange mentioning angels, he thought, referring to his code name.

At 3:00 p.m., Frick came to Kare's cell. He told him, "Take your blanket. I will be driving you to the train station."

Handcuffed, blanket under his arm, he was driven to the Potsdam train platform to await the prison train. Standing on the platform, Frick asked Kare, "Do you want a cigarette?"

Kare had stopped smoking when he started working in Denham Studios in London. It was dangerous to smoke around celluloid film, which was extremely flammable. Now he had the urge to smoke. Frick stuffed the cigarette into Kare's mouth, lighting it. "*Danke*, Frick. I appreciate what you have done for me."

"It is not because of you. I have known Heidi since we were kids. I am doing it for her." He puffed his smoke into the air, looking at his watch. It was 4:00 p.m. A few freight trains loudly passed the station. Frick said, "The train should arrive at four twenty."

Kare looked at his watch, and then said, "Frick, please unbuckle my watch from my hand."

Frick put his cigarette into his mouth and unstrapped Kare's watch. Then Kare said, "Frick, it is yours to keep. It will be stolen from me anyway. I want you to have it."

Frick, taken aback, stood with a surprised look on his face, holding Kare's watch. He looked at the dial, *Doxa*.

"It is an expensive watch," Frick said.

"It will be of no use to me," replied Kare. Frick eyed the watch and then put it into his pocket. The train arrived at 4:20 with six cattle cars in the rear. Prisoners' hands and faces stared through barred windows. It shook Kare's heart with fear of what was to be expected. SS guards with machine guns jumped from the train, surrounding the prison wagons. An SS officer walked toward Frick. They exchanged words, and Frick handed him a folder. *It must be my arrest documents,* Kare thought. Frick removed Kare's handcuffs. Kare asked, "Where am I heading?"

"Buchenwald," he replied in a low voice, avoiding eye contact with Kare, who was walked to the last wagon. He climbed into it through the open sliding door. Then the door shut. It was dark inside, and it took a moment for his eyes to adjust. There were a dozen men sitting and standing in the front portion of the wagon. In the back were large wooden carts. Kare sat in the nearest available space. The train jolted and then started moving with a whistle. Kare sat looking at the dark faces next to him. Only the whites of their eyes were visible in the dark. No one spoke. Kare sat in a half-somnolent state for a while, listening to the *clickity clack* of the train wheels. Then he fell asleep. He was awakened by a jolt of the train. The train stopped, and it was dark outside. Kare asked the person next to him, "What time is it?"

The young man, unshaven, with a beard and long hair, said, "It is nighttime. Eight fifteen."

I slept for three hours, Kare thought. He introduced himself to the young man and said, "What is your name?"

"Abraham."

"Where are you from?"

"Berlin."

"What have you been accused of?"

"Being a Jew."

Kare unrolled his blanket, broke off a piece of bread and gave it to Abraham. The man took it quickly, shoving it into his mouth. *He must be very hungry,* Kare thought. Now, he broke off a piece of sausage and gave it to Abraham. The smell of the sausage awakened the other men on the train. They all looked at Kare and Abraham. Kare broke the bread and the sausage into small pieces, stood up and divided his meager food among them. They hadn't eaten in twenty-four hours. They all thanked Kare for sharing his food with them.

Kare struck up a conversation with Abraham, who told him his story. "For the past four months, I have been hiding in the outskirts of the Berlin forest in an abandoned hunter's hut, trying to survive. One day, mushroom foragers encountered me in the hut. They called the police, and I was arrested. My ID card was stamped with a red J for Jew."

Kare asked, "What is your occupation, Abraham?"

"I am a tailor, and I worked for Meyer's clothing store, making alterations. One day, Herr Meyer disappeared, abandoning the store. Without employment, I survived for a while. Then the Gestapo started rounding up every Jew in the city. I took a train to the outskirts and hid in a nearby forest."

"What about your family?"

"My parents and my sister were picked up by the Gestapo and shipped to a concentration camp. I do not know where because I was not home at the time of the roundup."

Kare sat in silence and covered his head with the blanket. He thought, *One day, you are untouchable and live in another world. The next, you are hunted like an animal and put in a cage. All of this because your ID card is stamped with the letter* J.

Kare knew nothing about Buchenwald concentration camp. In German, it meant "beech forest." It was one of the first and largest concentration camps in Germany. Ironically, it was near the city of Weimar, where his mother Lila had visited in the 1920s to study art. It had also been home to the famous literary figure, Johann Wolfgang von Goethe.

The train arrived at Bahnhof Buchenwald the next day. It was a short distance by foot to the camp. All prisoners were lined up and marched to the SS camp headquarters then through the gatehouse. There was a slogan on the outside of the main gate: *Jedem das seine.* Literally, it meant "to each his own," but truly it meant "everyone gets what he deserves." Kare stood in the large yard, facing the gatehouse. The south side of the camp, where Kare was standing, was called the Bunker. It was surrounded by an electrified fence, watchtowers, and chains of sentries outfitted with automatic machine guns. The group of prisoners was divided by name. Then they all marched to the main camp at the north side of the concentration camp. Kare was stripped of all of his belongings. His head was sheared to make him more of an undistinguishable person in the camp, part of the camp mess. He put Monika's medallion into his mouth, hiding it under his tongue. He was given a pajama-type uniform—white with black stripes running vertically—and a matching beret. The uniform bore a triangle with the camp's name. No one bothered to learn his name or the names of the other inmates. There were no Jacobs, Ivans, or Radaslows, but only prisoners with numbers. It was the first step toward turning them into subhumans. He was given an ID number: 629174. It was sewn onto his uniform. Then he was marched by the guards into a one-story wooden barrack, number 52A. It was hell. The smell of human bodies and the stench of sweat and rotting meat were in the air. On both sides, against the wall, were three levels of sleeping platforms, three people per cubicle, barely sixty centimeters in height. There were no mattresses, only bare, stinking wooden planks.

Kare stood, looking at rows and rows of inmates lying or standing—skeletons of people. Two inmates approached him, speaking in Russian and broken German. Kare said to himself, *They must be Soviet prisoners of war.* The tall one, Misha, unshaven with bad teeth, approached Kare. He pushed Kare against the wall, holding his hands against the planks. His mouth opened, sarcastically smiling. The awful, rotten smell engulfed Kare's face, taking his breath away. *What now*? Kare thought to himself. *If I resist, I may hurt myself.* It would be like a death sentence without proper medical care. He stood with a stolid expression on his face, not resisting. The other inmate, Sacha, pushed his hands into his pocket, taking the only thing he was allowed to have, a comb and a handkerchief with the Madonna and Child medallion wrapped in it. Misha released Kare from his grip, smiling, not saying anything, standing there. Sacha gave Misha the comb and the medallion. He examined the religious coin and put it in between his rotten teeth, testing the bending of the metal. It was not precious. He spat on the floor. Then, taking Kare's comb, he ran it over his unshaven head. He smiled at Kare, then placed the comb in his pocket. Kare reached his hand toward the medallion. "Give it to me!" he said in German.

"Not so fast!" Misha replied in Russian, moving his hand, chuckling and holding the medallion out of Kare's reach. He flipped the medallion into the air. Kare instinctively leapt, reaching for the falling medallion. He put it into his palm. Holding it tight, he landed on the floor.

Laughter erupted in the barracks and someone shouted, "Bravo!"

Kare, lying on the floor with his only possession, held it tight in his hand. Misha placed a leg on his torso just for a moment, then stepped back, extending his hand toward Kare. Kare hesitated and then grabbed his hand. Misha lifted him from the floor. Everyone in the barracks was chuckling. The show was over. Misha had showed who the boss was in the barracks. He assigned Kare to the top of the sleeping platform. Clutching his blanket, Kare climbed to the top, near the wooden ceiling rafter, between another Russian and a Czech. He covered himself with the blanket from head to toe and lay on the bare wood. He opened his palm, looking at the Madonna and Child. The image of Monika leapt from it. He closed his eyes, and tears rolled down his cheek. He imagined kissing Monika.

In the morning, all prisoners filed out of the barracks, standing for daily roll call. Kare noticed that behind the fence in front of him was a manmade stone structure—a zoo, a home for two black bears. They were there for the enjoyment of the SS guards and their families. *What a creepy place!* Kare thought to himself. His name was called out. He was assigned to work in the Gutslof Armament Factory. It was adjacent to the concentration camp barracks. His job was to load the finished artillery shells into wooden storage compartments.

It was a strange scene, a noisy factory. The smell of burning oil and metal shavings was coming from the factory floor. Men in striped pajamas labored like ants on the floor. The SS guard moved around, shouting, pushing and beating slackers with horsewhips. Some of the prisoners looked like shadows of themselves, skeletons shuffling around on their feet, holding heavy loads of metal. In Nazi concentration camps, slaves were socially dead people who, as in most slave societies, and were not thought of as human and had utilitarian value. In Nazi Germany, Jews were seen as evil and destructive to the moral and social order. They were supposed to suffer and die. Kare said to himself, *This place is a death camp. The masters have no interest in the well-being of the prisoners.*

At lunchtime, workers were fed a piece of bread, a bit of potato, and some fat from meat. *Starvation diet,* Kare said to himself. Prisoners were purposely starved so that they would weaken and die. Each was just a number. When one slave died, another slave replaced him. There was an endless number of slaves in the camp.

At evening roll call, Kare's name came up. A guard by the name of Gerhardt shouted obscenities at him and called him to come forward and stand in front of the prison roll call. He started cursing Kare and hitting him with a whip on his head and back. Kare instinctively tried to protect his face and head. The beating became brutal. Kare could not raise his hand in self-defense, which was the rule for the prisoners. It confirmed to the SS guards how devoid of dignity he was, how removed he was from being a human worthy of respect and moral consideration. A kick in his groin landed him on his knees. Then a hard blow struck Kare on his head with exploding pain. The beating continued. Blood came from his mouth. He saw the end, welcomed death, and blacked out.

Gerhardt was a sadist. He was active, not with a gun, but with a whip, and he frequently beat prisoners so terribly that they died of the effects. He appeared abnormal compared to other SS guards. Sometimes, he made the prisoner undress and kneel down. Then he would sexually defile him with his whip. It was obvious that it was to his own sexual gratification that he beat prisoners on their bare bodies. Kare learned later that this was the way the guards treated new prisoners. It was his bad luck to be an example about who was the boss in the camp. He was lucky to be beaten. Some prisoners were bitten by dogs or just shot on the spot. Sometimes, the SS guards hung a bearded Jew from the Goethe Oak Tree. Ironically, it had been a favorite spot for the poet, Johann Wolfgang von Goethe. When he lived nearby in Weimar, the Ettersberg Hill was a wilderness area. This spot afforded an overlook on Airois, the valley to the north. The tree was located beside the prison laundry complex.

Kare lay on the ground until dark. Then Misha and three other Russians sprang from the barracks and dragged him inside by his feet. They laid him on the floor and cleaned his face with a wet cloth. Someone stuck a small bottle into his mouth. The taste of bad alcohol woke Kare from his slumber. He started coughing, lying in pain on the floor, eyes open and looking at the many faces above him. Then he realized these guys had saved him from possible death. He closed his eyes and felt several hands lifting him from the ground and placing him on the wooden platform. Kare slipped into unconsciousness.

He dreamt of holding Monika's hand, the two of them running on a sandy beach in Rio toward the blue ocean, the hot sand burning their feet, and the cool ocean receding. He was exhausted from running; pain etched in his feet. Thirsty, he collapsed on the sand and could not move anymore. Monika urged him to continue to run. She grabbed his hand, pulling him, but he could not move.

Kare opened his eyes. It was daytime, and the barracks were empty. He touched his face. It was swollen, and his left eye was puffy. He could barely see. One of his teeth was broken, and his lip was swollen. He felt pain in his legs, and when he touched them, he felt that they were swollen from the beating. He lay motionless, thinking, *Is this the end of the road? Why did I go back to Germany? Was I walking with my head backwards unable to see what was ahead? Is this the fulfillment of a destiny freely chosen by my soul?* He would need to go through Hell before reaching the Promise Land. *Am I being tested to be worthy of Monika's love?* He recalled the journey of Dante through hell guided by the Roman poet, Virgil. Now, he was searching for the meaning of being in Buchenwald. He felt something next to his head and touched it. It was his comb.

After four months in the camp, Kare had learned how to survive. One day, while working in the armament factory, he was called by a guard to follow him. He was brought out to the main SS compound. There was a small theater for the entertainment of the camp's SS personnel. He was questioned by SS Officer Obersturmführer. "Do you know how to operate a movie projector?"

Kare recognized it as a standard 16-millimeter Bell & Howell movie projector. He said, "Yes."

"I thought so," the SS Obersturmführer said. "How long did you work at Babelsberg Studios?"

"About a year."

SS Officer Rudolph then said, "Once a week, you are assigned to the projection room."

On Saturdays, Kare was exempt from working in the factory. He was now the camp's movie projectionist. He was happy being around movies again. After showing one, sometimes two, movies, he was allowed to collect cigarette butts from the floor. This was his reward. He used the tobacco as barter to exchange for extra food and other items in the camp. Sometimes he would find leftover food or drinks after the movie showing. His handler allowed him to eat it but forbade him to take it into the barracks.

Kare sat at the projection booth, watching the movies and observing the SS guards and officers sitting and caressing females. Some of them were prisoners forced into prostitution for the enjoyment of the SS personnel. A brothel was running with the approval of the wife of Karl Otto Koch, the camp boss. She was called The Witch of Buchenwald, *Die Hexe von Buchenwald.*

One day, all Soviet prisoners from barrack 52A were roll called and marched into a secluded area of the camp by SS officers with dogs and Gestapo personnel. The firing was heard throughout the day. Word spread quickly throughout the camp that the visiting Gestapo from Dresden had executed the Soviet prisoners of war. Misha and Sacha were among the dead. They were shot in the back of the neck in the famous *Genickschuss* execution style. Kare was saddened and shocked by their deaths, a clear violation of the Geneva Convention and a war crime. Misha had come from a small village, Bykovo, in the Volgogradskaya region. Sasha, a Russian peasant, had come from Dyutyuli, the Respublika Tatarstan. Simple people with good hearts, they reminded Kare of the Russian peasants so vividly described by the Russian author, Anton Chekov. Now, barrack 52A was empty except for Kare and four other inmates. By evening, fresh new slaves filled the barracks, all Jews from France. The horror of the day—the deaths of 1,000 prisoners—was the conversation of the night.

After hearing of the deaths of the Soviet prisoners, someone suggested that a prayer should be said for the dead. A heated debate erupted among the group of Jews. The question was: *Can one say Kaddish for a non-Jew?* The bearded rabbi by the name of Bal Shem Tov said, "If a non-Jew was slain and did not die due to natural causes, it is the Jewish outlook of humanity that one can ask God to bind the soul of the dead with his ancestors."

The sage, Soloman Eiger, son of Akiva, said, "If the deceased apostate has no other mourners, then the one mourning should say Kaddish. There certainly can be no prohibition to utter this praise to the All Mighty at the Kaddish."

Bal Shem Tov settled the question. The group said Kaddish in the corner of the barracks. The rabbi asked Kare to utter the names of the deceased Soviet prisoners. In grief, uttering the names of Misha and Sacha, Kare felt the victims' pain. The souls of the dying men briefly left their bodies, broke their bounds, and inhabited his own. For Kare, it was a funeral pyre.

In 1943, Kare was transferred to a barrack that housed newly imprisoned Norwegian university students. Now, the SS guard Rudolph, who was a photographer, arranged better accommodations. He was in charge of light entertainment for the SS guards. Kare was granted charge of stage lighting during live performances for the SS camp personnel. He trained one of the Norwegian theater students named Bjork as his assistant.

After a few weeks, the Norwegian students, who were treated differently by the guards and allowed to wear regular clothes, revolted and resisted the SS guards for treating them as prisoners of war. The SS crushed the rebellion. The SS threatened to send them to the eastern front and march them into minefields as cannon fodder. Kare was caught in the mess of the resistance. SS guard Rudolph was enraged, lecturing Kare about not being grateful for his treatment. SS Rudolph would punish him. He threatened to put him to work in the infamous quarry, where thousands of prisoners were worked to death; however, he changed his mind when he got to know Kare on a personal basis. Suddenly, Kare was more than a number. He was as much flesh and blood and human as Rudolph.

A request came from the Mittelbau-Dora Camp for slaves to begin the construction of a large industrial complex. Kare's name came up at roll call. He was shipped with hundreds of other young slaves from Buchenwald to Harz Mountain north of the town of Nordhausen.

Kare was relieved to leave this evil place called Buchenwald, a slave camp of living and dying with prisoners from all over Europe—Russians, Jews, non-Jews, Poles, Slavs, and religious and political prisoners.

Sweet Revenge

The air raids by the Allies on the suburbs of Berlin became a daily occurrence. The noise of the falling and exploding bombs echoed in the UFA Studios in Babelsberg, yet, despite all that, the work at the studio continued, except for the brief periods when air raid sirens wailed and employees hurried to the bomb shelter. On those occasions, Monika and Heidi sat on a wooden bench and held hands, listening to the exploding bombs in the far-away distance. Monika would start praying. She was in her seventh month of pregnancy and planned to quit working. When the bombing stopped, the all-clear would be announced, and they would return to the infirmary, where work was their distraction from war.

On one occasion, when air raid sirens wailed on the studio grounds, the sound of anti-aircraft guns exploded in the sky. Then aircraft bombs started falling on a nearby military depot. Within a minute, a stray bomb fell on an adjacent housing complex; then another bomb exploded near the road close to the infirmary. The sound of the blast and wave of the explosion threw Monika off her feet. A cubicle partition collapsed on her, and bits of ceiling plaster fell down like snowflakes. Heidi, rushing in from the nearby room dazed and disheveled, called Monika's name aloud. "Monika, are you all right?"

Monika tried to free herself, but the large cloth made it difficult for her to stand up. Heidi frantically started removing the plaster with her bare hands, reaching Monika in seconds. She grabbed Monika's hand and yanked her from the rubble. "Are you hurt?" she asked, checking Monika's body with her hands.

"I'm okay," Monika replied in a shaking voice.

The smell of smoke and fire came through the broken glass windows. "Hurry up! We need to go to the air raid shelter!" Heidi screamed, pulling Monika by the hand toward the door.

Outside the infirmary, the area was full of smoke, debris, and wreckage. The smell of burning tires lingered in the air. They ran toward the air raid shelter nearby. As they passed the studio security complex, Monika glanced at the one-story building. It was now destroyed. The roof had collapsed and was on fire. As they passed it, Monika heard a cry. It came from the burning building. "Monika, help me!"

She froze. Heidi urged her to continue running. Then Monika heard a cry again. "Monika, help me!"

She peered through the black smoke toward the sound. Her eyes focused on a person lying on the ground with rubble covering his dark body. She instinctively came closer. It was Ulrich lying on the ground. His legs were caught between two large wooden beams. He was unable to free himself. His face was scorched and covered with black soot. His black SS uniform was torn and shredded. His eyes betrayed that he was gripped in fear, his face twisted as he expected death. The heat of the burning building was unbearable. His hand stretched toward Monika, as he begged her to remove him from the misery. As Monika looked at his outstretched hand, she saw the skeleton ring on his hand. Ruby eyes glowed; the fire reflected in the facets. It looked alive. Not feeling the intense heat anymore, she stood there for a moment, looking at him. She spit into his hand. "Burn in hell!" she cried. Then she turned around and ran toward the shelter.

As she reached the corner, explosions shook the ground and almost swept her off her feet. She turned around and looked at the security building. It was now engulfed in a fireball. Ulrich was not to be seen.

Ulrich had been stealing fuel from the studio and keeping it in cans in a storage room next to his office. He had been selling it on the black market. Now, all the fuel caught fire and exploded. No one survived in the security office that day. It was Monika's "Tosca's kiss."

In the air raid shelter, Monika and Heidi hugged each other, shaking from fear but glad to be alive. Monika said to Heidi, "I have gotten my revenge. My prayers came true. I thank the Lord that the evil one burned. He got what he deserved. This is justice." Then she asked, "Heidi, can I have my engagement ring back?"

Mittelbau-Dora

Kare was transported with hundreds of slave laborers to Mittelbau-Dora camp at Hertz Mountainon the outskirts of Nordhausen, east of Germany. He was one of the early arrivals from Buchenwald to Dora and was put with other inmates in tents near the entrance to tunnel B. The main entry to the camp was secured by barbwire, electrified fencing, and sentries outfitted with automatic machine guns. On the west side of the camp was a large, open lot used as a staging area for the prisoners' daily roll call before they marched to nearby construction sites and underground weapon development workshops. At the south side of the camp were prisoner barracks, and on the north side were the notorious crematoria.

Kare was put into the construction brigade of prisoners who were building permanent camp barracks, which was already in various completion stages. The camp planned to house over 16,000 slaves. Like the Buchenwald model, the SS Sturmbannführer, Otto Forschner, the camp commander, relied on political German prisoners in non-SS administrative positions. Kare's boss was Albert Kuntz, a communist. He was the camp construction supervisor.

Kare worked twelve-hour shifts, digging drainage trenches and hauling construction material on site. Two weeks into his new job, he encountered a film crew shooting high angles from the top of a truck, documenting the camp construction progress. Kare noticed the film crew again two weeks later at the same location. He decided that the next time, he would work closer to the film crew. Perhaps, he could strike up a conversation, and maybe he could tell them about his experience as a cameraman. The day the film crew was scheduled to be on site, Kare purposely loaded his wheelbarrow with cement bags that were to be hauled in the direction of the filming location. "Stop wandering from the work area!" the SS guard shouted at him.

Just then, the film crew appeared, placing the tripod on site. They started filming. Kare was watching their actions as he worked. He noticed that they were having a problem with the camera. Instinctively, he steered his wheelbarrow to the film location. When he was close to them, he shouted, "I can fix your camera!" The film crew turned around and looked at Kare in a kind of surprised way.

The SS guard ran after him with a stick in hand, shouting and landing blows on Kare's shoulder. "Get in line, swine! No talking!" Kare picked up a bag of cement and tried to use it to deflect the guard's blows.

One of the film crew members approached Kare. The SS guard rushed toward Kare again, ready to strike him, but the cameraman lifted his hand and said, "Hold on. I want to speak to this prisoner." He turned to Kare and said, "You shouted, 'I can fix your camera.' What do you know about this camera?"

Kare replied, "A lot. This particular spring wound Bolex Super 16-millimeter camera has a hand-wound mechanism that sometimes breaks down. The problem is in the spring pin device."

"How do you know so much about cameras?"

"I worked in Babelsberg Studio as a cinema photographer."

"Okay, then fix my camera."

The SS guard followed Kare to the camera on the tripod. Kare knew this particular movie camera had a pin in the winding mechanism. If it was not well oiled, it jammed and needed to be reset. He asked for a screwdriver, opened the cover, and unscrewed the winding mechanism. The pin holding the spring was detached as he had suspected. With two motions of the screwdriver, he reset the pin in the proper location. Then he closed the cover and wound the camera handle. It worked perfectly. The members of the camera crew watched him handle the equipment and were impressed. The cameraman took out a pen and his notebook and wrote down Kare's ID number, saying nothing. Then he waved him back to work.

The SS guard pushed him with the stick. "Hurry up! Get to work!" the guard shouted, pushing the stick into Kare's back. Then he struck him on the shoulder. "No talking on the job site without my permission!" Kare was conditioned to the pain. He had been struck so many times that it had become quite routine. He had black-and-blue marks all over his body.

Two weeks after his encounter with the film crew, at roll call, Kare's name was called and he was ordered to step forward. *Oh, bad news. What now?* Kare thought to himself. The SS guard said, "Follow me."

They walked toward the wooden barracks near the entrance to tunnel B. There were construction trailers for the civilian personnel working for WVHA- Altersgruppen C. Construction Company. They were in charge of the tunnel digging. They stopped in front of the trailer that had a sign on the door: Film Crew and Laboratory. No Entry—authorized personnel only! With his stick, the guard banged on the door. The man whom Kare had encountered two weeks previously appeared. He waved the guards off and said to Kare, "Come inside." Kare saw offices for the film crew, a laboratory, and storage area. "Wait here."

Kare's eyes wandered toward the wall where there were plans of the campsite and tunnels marked in various colored pencils. Hitler's portrait hung on the wall, looking at Kare in a sinister way straight into his eyes. The door opened, and a tall, young, good-looking uniformed SS *Untersturmführer* lieutenant walked in. "Six-two-nine-one-seven-four, I understand you are an experienced cameraman."

"Yes," Kare replied.

"Tell me more."

Kare proceeded to tell him more about his work experience.

"Impressive," said the officer in a cold, serious voice. "My chief of the film crew, Heinrich, said that he could use you. So, as of today, you work for me. Now let me tell you my rules. You do as I say, follow my orders, never answer back, complete your assignment as given to you, and never speak to other prisoners about your work or what you see. Any deviation from my instructions and I will personally put a bullet between your eyes." His words were like frost on buds. "You will find me cold as ice. If you try to break the ice, you will find cold water. Do not try to be cute with me. You sleep in your barracks but report here every morning at seven sharp. Not a minute late! Seven sharp! Understand?"

Kare nodded and said, "Yes sir." His heart rose with excitement. *Some angel is looking after me,* he said to himself, holding Monika's medallion in his hand inside his pocket.

He found out later that he was the most experienced in cinematography within the entire film crew. The lieutenant had no experience in filming. He held only an administrative position overseeing the film crew. The civilians in the film crew worked under contract for the WVHAA- Altersgruppen construction company. Their job was to record the progress of the construction on site. Then a documentary film of the progresses of construction would be shown to the top brass in Berlin. It needed to be of a high quality for professional presentation. They relied on Kare's experience to produce such high-quality films.

Kare followed the film crew in various tunnel construction sites, advising on lens use, lighting, and positioning of the camera. Walking through the tunnels, Kare encountered the horrible work conditions. Most of the workers were Soviet prisoners. Constant blast noises, dust, and harmful fumes invaded the tunnels. Drinking water was in short supply. The sanitary conditions were inhuman. Prisoners had to relieve themselves in the tunnel or into 200-liter steel drums cut in half with a board set on top. The odor of urine and raw sewage was unbearable. Tuberculosis and pneumonia was rampant. The twelve-hour, back-breaking labor and poor sanitary conditions combined with meager food and lack of clean water caused the spread of typhoid and dysentery among prisoners. Death occurred daily in the camp due to accidents, disease, and exhaustion.

By the end of the year, the population of the camp reached 12,682, and about 10,000 toiled and lived in tunnels. Most of the prisoners were non-Jews, Russian, Polish, French, German, Belgian, political activists, and a small group of Italians.

After each taping and development of the film, Kare was in charge of editing. He cut out the portions of the film showing the prisoners' conditions in the tunnels. Sometimes, he removed segments of scenes showing people and stored these clippings in a glass jar.

Lieutenant Willy Schmidt received compliments from Berlin on the high quality film presentation. He was asked if he was capable of filming rocket engine testing in the tunnels. After a consultation with Kare, he replied to his superior, "He is ready to take the challenge."

Now, Kare's life in the camp was tolerable. They let him wear civilian clothes on top of his prison uniform. The film crew supplemented his diet with food left over from the meals from the camp canteen. He was not going hungry any longer.

The condition of other inmates became worse as the war progressed. Their living conditions were atrocious. The tunnels were ready for the mass assembly of 'Weapons of Retaliation,' known as V-2 rockets, and jet engines. The best qualified people working on the assembly lines were from Western Europe; most of the 5,000 V-2 rocket assembly workers were Czech, French, and German civilians, and they worked for twelve hours a day, six days a week. Some of them held administrative positions in the factory. The assembly factory had the look of an updated high-tech enterprise, but in reality, it was run by forced labor. To the workers, it was a backbreaking production site. The beating and stabbing of prisoners were common occurrences. It was a cesspool of violence, cold, hunger, and production sabotage by non-German prisoners. The final assembly of the V-2 rocket began in the winter of 1944, and the result was of poor quality.

The film crew observed frequent failures of the V-2s, which were riddled with technical problems. They still successfully produced progressive documentaries and story films of assembly V-2 tests and the firing of engines. The montage sequence planned by Kare presented an impression rather than a representation of actual events. He had to tell a story for the viewers in Berlin. They also filmed slow motion events of the missile engine firing tests that the engineers could use to analyze the failures and successes of the engines. As the tunnels' construction was completed and the plant went into operation, thousands of Jewish prisoners from various countries were brought to Mittelbau-Dora. They were treated with great brutality and were assigned the most physically demanding jobs. Their mortality rate was higher than that of any other group of prisoners. Jewish prisoners who were exhausted and could not keep pace with the work were sent to Auschwitz in special transports to be killed.

The news from the warfront was bad for the Germans. Kare heard on the radio that on June 6, 1944, Allied forces had landed in Normandy. The invasion of Europe had begun. In December, twenty million Germans became homeless after Allied bombings. Kare predicted that the Allied victory was near. He needed to survive the brutality of the camp. His superior now allowed Kare to sleep in their offices. They moved the trailers into one of the tunnels away from Allied bombers.

In late January 1945, Kare noticed an increase of brutality in the camp. Execution of prisoners by firing or hanging increased on a daily basis. In April 1945, RAF bombers appeared over Mittelbau camp at Nordhausen and bombed it for two days. Evacuation proceeded. Thousands of prisoners were forced to march to other camps, some on foot, others by train. Some of the surviving inmates ended up in Bergen-Belsen and were exterminated by the thousands.

The film crew was ordered to evacuate the camp. Kare helped pack all of their equipment for shipment. He wondered what would happen to him. In the far distance, bombing noises of the advancing American 104 Timberwolf Army Infantry Division could be heard. They were not too far from the camp. On April 5, Willi, the SS Lieutenant, assembled the film crew for the last time. They were to depart the next day.

In the early morning, the lieutenant placed Kare on the trucks bearing the symbol of the Red Cross. The passengers of those trucks were driven to the Bay of Lübeck to be put on Swedish ships to freedom.

The Last Storm

It was a cool, sunny April day in 1945. Kare was now twenty-four years old and had survived the brutal prison camps of Buchenwald and Dora. Sitting on the track, elated and in a good mood, he sensed that freedom was within reach. The transport was full of French prisoners. Kare *comprendre un peu le Francais* (understood a little French), so he sat quietly, listening to the prisoners' conversation. Holding Monika's medallion tightly in his hand, he allowed his thoughts to wander. *Where is Monika now? Does she still love me? What about the child? Did she go through with her pregnancy or did she abort it? Did she open the sealed envelope I gave her?* In it, he had instructed her to dig up his treasure box buried in Sanssouci Park. He was anxiously looking forward to finding out the answers to all of his questions. His mind drifted to his uncle's family in London. *What happened to Gabby? Is she still waiting for my return?* His heart dropped at the thought of telling Gabby about his love for Monika. *How and when will I have to tell her?* His mind was occupied when the SS guard shouted for them to disembark. The rear cover of the truck was lifted. Kare saw that several truckloads of prisoners were lined up in the parking lot. It was late afternoon. He looked around. They were in the Bay of Lübeck on the Baltic Sea. He knew the area well, for it had been the location of the filming of the epic *Titanic*.

There, in the distance, Kare recognized the SS *Cap Arcona*. Adjacent to it were smaller vessels, the SS *Deutschland*, the SS *Thielbek* and the SS *Athens*. There were two even smaller vessels flying Swedish flags. They were painted white and emblazoned with a red cross on each side. The SS guards divided the group. All the French prisoners marched out toward the Swedish ships. Kare, with the rest of the prisoners, mostly Jews, marched toward the port quay. Sitting on the concrete pavement surrounded with SS guards and dogs, they waited for the SS *Athens* to transfer them to the larger ships in the bay. The smell of seawater and the light, salty breeze reenergized Kare. He took a deep breath. There were rumors that after a transfer to larger ships, they would be on their way to Sweden.

In April 1945, the captains of the SS *Cap Arcona* and the SS *Thielbek* had been informed that they were to prepare for a "special operation,"' and the following day, John Jacobsen, the Captain of the SS *Thielbek*, was summoned to a conference by the Gestapo along with Captain Bertram of the SS *Cap Arcona.* The captains were ordered to take concentration camp prisoners on board. Both captains refused and were relieved of their commands.

Kare noticed that besides the *Kriegsmarine* and SS guards, Swedish civilians with Red Cross bands on their arms were also present. One Red Cross worker came to the group with a notebook, making notations and taking a head count. Another took photos of the group of prisoners. After a few hours passed, the SS *Athens* docked portside. Kare and the rest of the group were transferred to the larger ship. All prisoners were put into the cargo hole. The dark hole had only a few large hatches that opened to the sky. Prisoners sat on the steel floor, waiting to be transferred to SS *Cap Arcona.* The smell of diesel fuel was in the air. SS Guards showed up on the deck of the ship with loaves of bread. They threw the loaves down through the hatch to the prisoners. Like hungry animals, the prisoners scrambled to grab some of some of the bread. Kare was strong and fit compared to the other skeletons, who were only shadows of themselves. They had no strength and hardly moved. Kare got hold of two loaves. He shared them with others. Some inmates fought with each other, holding bread, punching and brawling. The sound of sadistic laughter came from the SS guards as they watched the fighting through the hatch. Kare found a corner, sat there with his head between his legs, and fell asleep.

The engine's noise woke him. A streak of sunlight came through the hatch. It was early morning. The ship was moving, and then stopped. A fire hose was lowered, and empty cans were thrown through the hatch. A trickle of water came from the hose. Prisoners lined up to fill the cans with drinking water. When the cans were barely full, the hose was hoisted back up. Then the ship did not move for another three days. At the bow of the ship, conditions became unbearable. It was steaming hot. There was minimal fresh air during the day. The smell of urine and excrement filled the air, and prisoners shivered during the nights. With a meager diet, Kare's hope dashed away, and the thought of freedom evaporated into thin air. *It must be the chief of Gestapo, Heinrich Müller's, trick! They are planning to have us all die in this metal hole and then dispose us into the sea.* Kare kept thinking, *Where is the Swedish Red Cross? Maybe it was all theatrics, not to panic the prisoners.*

In the past two days, six prisoners had died and had to be hauled away and disposed of at sea. Then the order came: "Climb the ladder to the deck, *schnell!*" All scrambled to be first; the strong ones pushed the weak. Kare did not want to be the first one on the deck. He was still suspicious. When he did not hear gunshots, he ascended the ladder from the bow of the ship. His journey reminded him of the biblical story of Jonah's escape to freedom as he was spit out of the Leviathan's mouth.

The fresh air on deck changed his mood. He looked around. They were docked next to the SS *Cap Arcona*. Now, it looked unkempt, rusted, dilapidated—not the way he remembered it. A wooden bridge had been secured between the two ships. SS guards shouted orders for them to disembark and transfer to the SS *Cap Arcona*. It was all done in the presence of the Swedish Red Cross. The rest of the prisoners were transported not too far from the SS *Cap Arcona* to the SS *Thielbek*. Kare was familiar with the layout of the SS *Cap Arcona*. It had become a troop transfer ship. The engine was in disrepair. He was placed into a compartment on the first deck with four other prisoners. Now, the vessel held five thousand prisoners from concentration camps. The rumors were that when the ship's bow was full with 10,000 prisoners. It would be towed to Sweden—and freedom.

On April 30, 2945, three Swedish ships, *Magdalena*, *Lille*, and *Matthiessen* sailed to Sweden hospitals with 448 French prisoners. On May 2, the British Second Army reached the towns of Lübeck and Wismar. Three days after Hitler's suicide on May 3 and one day before the German surrender, the SS *Cap Arcona*, now full with 10,000 prisoners, was ready to be towed to Sweden.

Kare was awakened in his cabin. An air raid siren wailed on shore. He could hear panic on deck. He rushed to the sound and saw SS guards and *Kriegsmarine* personnel distributing life jackets amongst themselves. They lowered lifeboats and abandoned ship.

Kare could hear anti-aircraft guns on the shore. He looked at the sky. A squadron of RAF planes blasted their guns, diving in the direction of the SS *Thielbek*. Panic erupted on the SS *Cap Arcona* deck. SS guards shot their guns, pushing the prisoners back into the ship's interior. Several prisoners were shot and lay on the deck. Blood spewed. Some yelled in panicked voices, "The guards took all the life jackets! We are doomed!" Prisoners began jumping overboard. SS guards on the boats shot at every prisoner in the water with machine guns. Kare looked in the direction of the SS *Deutschland* and then at the SS *Thielbek*, which was now on fire and sinking. He glanced at the sky again. There were RAF Hawker Typhoon Aircrafts diving, blasting their guns on the SS *Cap Arcona*. The deck was full of panicked prisoners jumping overboard like rats running from fire. The 400 SS guards on boats in the bay were busy shooting at them. It was like a shooting gallery. Exploding rockets hit the SS *Cap Arcona*'s deck. The blast of the rockets shook the ship, igniting the SS *Cap Arcona*. Diesel and oil filled the air.

Kare froze for a moment, and then retreated inside the interior away from the guns. He said to himself, *We are all doomed. Why is the RAF attacking prison transfer ships? Did the British coordinate it with the Swedes*? He became convinced that the Gestapo had orchestrated this show. There were no Swedes or Red Cross; it was a theatrical show to kill them all. Now, the SS *Cap Arcona* was shaking from explosions.

Kare climbed on deck. He needed to get out and jump into the water to survive. If only he had a life jacket. Suddenly, it struck him that, during the time of filming of the *Titanic*, a life jacket had been lying on the deck and interfering with filming the scene. He had removed it and stuffed it behind the nearest metal storage compartment on deck. He wondered if it was possible that the life jacket was still there after three years. Rushing on deck, now full of smoke and dead bodies, Kare lost his bearings. Fires blazed and bullets zigzagged in the air, ricocheting with loud metal clinks. Kare crawled on his hands and knees, trying to find the metal storage box along the ship deck. His hands stretched, feeling for the storage box and found it. He reached his hand behind it, but the space was empty. A rocket exploded nearby, and Kare was almost thrown overboard. He crawled again, this time on his belly toward the next storage box. He used the side walls of the ship deck to feel his way. His clothes were soaked with blood and oil. He reached another storage box. In desperation, with his hands shaking and his mind blank, he pushed his hand behind the box. There it was. Tightly pushed and crumbled behind the metal was the life preserver he had deposited there three years ago. With all of his might, he yanked it out. Lying on the deck next to several dead bodies, he put the life jacket on and tightened it around his body. The smoke on deck was unbearable. His throat was raw, and he was gasping for air. He looked over the railing of the ship. Between the wisps of smoke, he saw that the SS *Thielbek* was no longer there; it had sunk.

Other German ships were on fire. Smoke covered the water surface. The sea was littered with all kinds of debris. Dead bodies floated on the waves. SS guards on boats and on shore continued to shoot all around the bay. A large black oil slick from the sunken ships floated dark on the water. A rocket landed on the SS *Cap Arcona* and exploded on deck. Kare was thrown into the water. He felt sharp pains in his head and hand. In the water, he momentarily sank, but then he floated up. The seven degree Celsius water woke him from the shock. His mind was sharpened now, his thoughts on survival. He looked around and noticed an overturned broken wooden table floating nearby. It was the one the Swedish Red Cross had used on deck when they were processing the prisoners. Now, it was in the water. A bullet-ridden corpse was lying halfway on the table. He got hold of the table, struggled to remove the dead man's shirt, and pushed him into the water. He pulled the corpse's shirt over his lifejacket to conceal himself from the marauding SS guards on shore who were now taking shots at anything floating, swimming, or moving in the water. Holding the edge of the table, keeping a low profile, he pushed himself, floating away from shore, away from the killing zone.

It was low tide in the bay, and the seawater was rushing Kare toward the mouth of the bay to the open sea. Now, as twilight set in, the British aircraft left the scene. In the distance, Kare still heard gunshots from the SS guards. He remembered that there were several small fishing villages downstream where he could find a hiding place. As night set in, Kare climbed onto the table, shivering. He lay on top, paddling with his hand, elated to see distant lights on the dim shore. After an hour of paddling, he was exhausted and wanted to close his eyes, but he knew that sleep meant death. He was bleeding from his head and hand. He fought to stay awake, trying to keep occupied. He reached into his pocket, took out Monika's medallion, and looked at it in the semidarkness. Monika's face leapt from the medallion. He placed it in front of him, looked at it and thought, *Oh, Monika, I lift my aching arms to you. I toss this troubled night for you. Oh, Monika, please guide me through.* Lying on his stomach with his hands outstretched, he told himself, *Keep paddling, keep paddling.* Behind him, he saw a searchlight and heard gunshots. He paddled faster. *I'm paddling toward you, Monika.* He lost all concept of time. Exhausted, he reached the fishing village. All was quiet now; just a half moon was shining on calm water. Kare maneuvered his floating platform to the nearest fishing boat. A dog started to bark on shore. He docked his platform next to the fishing boat. Grabbing the edge and standing, with his last bit of strength, he flipped himself onto the deck of the boat. The dog on shore kept barking. He must have sensed Kare's movements. Kare crawled to the small front cabin and tucked himself in the front corner, shivering but alive. He passed out and dreamed.

He was a young boy in bed. Father was sitting next to him. He felt the warmth of the man's body against his cheek. Father was reading to him the Nordic myths of the sinister Valkyrie spirits of the dark angels of death, who soared over the battlefields like birds of prey and picked the dead heroes, gathered them up, and bore them away to Valhalla.

Kare woke from his dream. A shadow stood in front of him. He was blinded by sun. *Am I dreaming?* he thought to himself. He looked up to see the silhouette of a woman. *Is she the Valkyrie female shielded-maiden? Is she to guide me to the doors of Valhalla?* The pain in his hand and forehead reminded him he wasn't dreaming. *I have been discovered. I am doomed.* The woman reached for him and gently pushed him. He fell on the deck on his back. Exhausted, he had no strength in his hands from paddling all night.

"*Legen Sie sich hin und bleiben Sie ruhig!* (Lie down and stay quiet)," she said in German. Then she left.

Kare thought to himself, *I need to get out now before she brings the SS guards.*

He was on his knees when the woman came back. A bearded man stood behind her. She said, "I told you to lie down."

Kare had no choice; he lay on his back. Looking at her face, he figured she was in her forties. She had a rough face and wore no makeup, giving a masculine appearance. She wore a scarf over her brown hair, which was neatly combed back. There was no life in her eyes. She knelt down and examined his wounds. The touch of her hands was warm and gentle. She said, "I will be back." Then she left. The old man stood looking at Kare in silence. With a pipe in his mouth and a knitted hat on graying hair, he stood, eyeing Kare, not saying anything, puffing smoke.

The woman returned. This time, she had a bucket of warm water, some cloth, and a block of brown laundry soap. She knelt down and began to wash his face, hands, and head wounds. Kare looked into her eyes but saw no reaction. She allowed him a hint of a smile. Kare was covered with diesel oil, his face black as the night. Now, he figured she could see who he was. The old man suddenly took his pipe out of his mouth, pointing toward Kare. He opened his mouth and said, "I know you from somewhere."

Kare looked at him and said, "I don't think I know you."

After a few seconds, the old man replied, "Now, I remember! Three years ago, you hired me with a fishing boat, filming a movie at the bay. What movie was it?"

"*Titanic.*"

"Yes! *Titanic*! What are you doing here?" Looking at his striped uniform, he asked, "Are you from those ships at the bay?"

"Yes."

The woman finished washing him and wound homemade bandages on his forehead and hand. "Poor bastard!" the man said. "Do not worry! We will not turn you in to those killers. You are safe with us." He helped Kare to shore and hid him in his cellar. It was May 4.

The next day, the old man came to the cellar. He said to Kare, "I just heard on the radio that the war is over! Germany surrendered to the Allied forces!"

Tent 120

A long British Light Scout Car arrived in the fishing village. Besides the driver, there was a gunner and a sergeant in charge of patrol. Kare, dressed in civilian clothes, cautiously approached the patrol. Speaking with a British accent, Kare identified himself as an SOE Agent, code name Blue Angel. The sergeant was surprised to find a British agent in a small, remote fishing village. He made a radio call to headquarters, which was now located in the former German barracks in the Port of Lübeck. The field radio cranked and came alive. A voice came out, "Bring the Blue Angel to headquarters."

Kare bid farewell to his German fishermen family who had given him a safe haven for a few days. He wished Magdalena good luck. She was a widow; her husband had died on the Russian front. She deeply distrusted the Nazi regime. She blamed the loss of her husband on unnecessary war with the Soviets. She called the Nazis "butchers" and "swine." Her father, Ludwig, the old fisherman with the pipe, whose ancestors had come from Denmark, was a veteran of World War I and had been a prisoner of the British during that war. He hated all wars and hoped that this would be the last one he saw in his lifetime. He distrusted his fellow neighbors and had hidden Kare in his cellar until this day, May 8, 1945. Kare promised that, given the opportunity, he would be back. He climbed into the Scout Car and drove away.

Kare was back at the same location at the Port of Lübeck. Just a month ago, he had been a prisoner and a slave; his masters had been the SS guards. Now, they were the prisoners and were confined in the navy barracks. The slaves were the masters now. Kare was hoping that they would be tried in a court of justice for war crimes.

He walked, for the last time, to see his tormentors sitting defeated behind barbed wire. He recognized some of the SS guards from the SS *Cap Arcona*. None of them looked into his eyes.

A transmission came from London. It was a message from Major Stanley:

> *9 May 1945*
>
> *Congratulations, my boy, on your successful mission! Glad to hear that you are alive. You are ordered to travel to headquarters in Oldenburg for debriefing as soon as possible. Congratulations! You are now commissioned as first lieutenant in the Intelligence Corps.*

At the British Headquarters in the Bay of Lübeck, Kare asked the British Major General of the 11th Armoured Division a burning question, "Why did the British bombers bomb the transport ships in the bay?"

He was given a written report that accounted the events of May 4, 1945. The report concluded the following:

The pilots of the RAF stated that they were unaware that the ships were laden with prisoners who had survived the camps. Some elements of the British command knew of the occupants but failed to pass on the information. The RAF commanders ordering the strike reportedly thought that the ships carried escaping SS officers, possibly fleeing to German controlled Norway with dilapidated and completely rusted ships.

A RAF pilot of No.193 Squadron reported, "We used our cannons to fire at the chaps in the water … We shot them up with 20-millimeter cannons in the water. Horrible thing, but we were told to do it and we did it. That's war."

Reconnaissance mission over the Bay of Lübeck on the 4th of May, 1945 by F-6 Mustang. The British plan took aerial photos that showed two laid wrecks, SS *Thielbek* and SS *Cap Arcona*, in the Bay of Neustadt. Severely damaged and set on fire, the SS *Cap Arcona* eventually capsized. The capsized hulk of the SS *Cap Arcona* later drifted ashore and the wreck was beached. The death toll was estimated at 5,000 prisoners.

"There were photos of burning ships, listed as SS *Deutschland*, SS *Thielbeck* and SS *Cap Arcona* and of emaciated survivors swimming in the frigid Baltic Sea; other bodies of victims washed ashore."

Kare questioned the report and lack of coordination between the British high command and the RAF squadron commanders ordering the strike. *They should have known better,* he thought. It was just a few days before the Germans surrendered, ending the war.

Kare reflected on the events that had occurred over the past few days. He had survived drowning at sea, had faced death, and now welcomed life. He saw his immersion at sea as a dipping in the "living waters." It had cleansed him from the horrors of the past. It had given him a rebirth and a quest to find his lost love, Monika. But a hard question lingered: Had she had his child? Then he found himself haunted by memories of Gabby. *What shall I tell her? Does she remember me, the one who went far away into the silent land? Now, I am back, telling her that I love someone else.* With a sad heart, he sat to write to Gabby.

10 May 1945

Dear Gabby,

The fog of war has lifted, thank God; we are victorious. Four years have passed since we parted, and from me, there was only silence. Forgive me.

I was sent on a secret mission to Germany, and my survival was in doubt. What can I say, dearest Gabby? Life gives you reason to cry. I have no words to describe my journey.

I survived the concentration camps, I survived drowning, and against all odds, managed to stay alive. I am a different person now; seeing death has made me humble.

Dear Gabby, I remember our last embrace on that gravel road. I said, "I love you," and made a promise to honor that love. Love is most beautiful; it showed me the light and joy. Now, it breaks my heart to ask for your forgiveness. I didn't earn your love. I am in love with someone else; her name is Monika.

Oh, dear Gabby, how can I describe my life's horrors of the past few years? We are like two branches on one stem growing apart. I grieved for my father's death, and my mother was in the concentration camp. Is she dead or alive? I need to find out. My journey now has just begun to find Monika and my child. I have come to realize that the only people I need in my life are the ones who need me in theirs, even when I have nothing else to offer them but myself. Indeed I am free—not perfect, but blessed, to have your parents, who gave me a gift, a treasure, which I will never be able to repay. It made all the difference in my life.

Dear Gabby, accept me as your humble friend. You were my first love and the sweetest, but the first cut is the deepest.

"I awaken at dawn and discover I have gone my way and left you free."

Please answer me. The silence is unbearable.

Your devoted friend,
Kare

Kare was given a British uniform and travel documents, and then was put on a special transport to the British headquarters at Oldenburg. Before leaving for Oldenburg, Kare asked the major of the Special Service Brigade, "Sir, can you make arrangements to deliver food provisions to my German rescuer as thanks for saving my life?"

"I promise to do so on the next patrol in the area."

As he and the Major drove toward Oldenburg, Kare saw the devastation of the war. Citizens and soldiers of Germany had emerged from their cellars, shelters, foxholes, and trenches into peace; however, it still remained a dangerous world. Dead horses and dead people littered the ground. Columns of German prisoners were marching along the roads as US and British tanks and trucks rode by. Destruction was everywhere; streets were reduced to rubble. Vast numbers of refugees and displaced people were on the move. *To where?* Kare asked himself.

The major seated next to him in the jeep said, "In 1936, Hitler asked the German people to give him just ten years and they would not recognize the face of the country. The persistent Allied bombing of German cities pulverized them into ruins and rubble of bricks. It was the only promise that Hitler had delivered to the people of Germany."

Now, the German government had collapsed, and the people had to fend for themselves as best they could. Kare saw crowds of hungry Germans begging for morsels of bread from the passing military trucks. All of the refugees made their way to the British-occupied zone of Germany. They were vengeful toward the Red Army in the east. Kare was not surprised after seeing how the SS had treated the Soviet prisoners of war at the prison camps. The dead Russian souls were crying out, "Revenge!" The drunken, victorious Russians took revenge on ordinary, defenseless German folks.

The major continued talking and quoting statistics to Kare, "More than sixteen million Germans are now refugees. Half a million civilians are dead. Three million dwellings have been destroyed. One and a quarter million dwellings are heavily damaged, and who knows how many millions died in concentration camps." *The Germans will have to answer for it,* Kare said to himself.

In the Oldenburg British headquarters, Kare was debriefed. The intelligence officer wanted information from Kare about everything that he had seen or learned about the production of V-2 missiles.

During Kare's work as editor with the film crew, he had kept important clippings of film that had covered the production and testing of the V-2. He had saved those clippings in a glass jar, which he had buried in the camp just before abandoning the Dora complex. Now, he would have to travel back to the camp to retrieve them.

It was strange for Kare as he walked through Dora as a free man. He stopped in front of tunnel B where the V-2 rockets had been assembled. Looking at the dark entrance, a sober truth sunk in. He was blessed to have survived the brutal camps of Buchenwald and Dora, the Devil's inferno that swallowed thousands in the flames of their crematoriums. He sat on the ground in silence, head bent between his knees, questioning his purpose in life. He had been in Hell and had been challenged by life and death. There, his soul was purified and spiritually transformed to allow him to ascend to *Gan Eden*, earthy paradise. Now, he felt a new surge of energy, a life force, the Philosopher's Stone Elixir of Life. In this changed world, he needed to realize life's new hope and the potential for his rebirth.

The Dora camp was now completely abandoned, except for American soldiers removing and dismantling the rockets and hauling them away. Kare dug out his jar with the important test clippings inside.

Back in the British HQ in Oldenburg, Kare received a message from Major Stanley in London:

25 June 1945

Congratulations! The clippings showing the test of the V-2 rockets are of great importance to us. You have regards from your uncle and auntie, Laura and Gabby.

Kare asked Major Stanley to give him two weeks of personal leave to travel in Germany. He needed to find Monika. Permission was granted. Two days thereafter, Kare received a letter from Gabby:

27 May 1945

Dear Kare,

I am overjoyed to hear that you are alive and well. Your letter touched my soul. I feel your pain, hope, and despair spring up from your pages.

Dear, there is a saying: If you love flowers, don't pick them. Because if you do, they will die. If you love the flower, let it be. Love is not a possession. Love is about appreciation.

Dear, I felt your love that magical evening in the greenhouse. Our hands met, our lips met, our hearts spoke soft and low as lovers. It will always stay with me. Let it be our secret that we'll carry to our graves.

My love, my friend, I am delighted to hear that you found your love, Monika. I pray for you. Go on your journey and find Monika and your child. When you do, they are welcome in my arms.

We can say sorry to each other a million times. The truth is that our journey through life is like a crooked road with many bumps along the way.

Now I must confess to you, I love someone else. Lt. Chatwin and I are engaged to be married soon.

Oh, dear, I can't wait to hug you again, my dear cousin. We are all hoping to see you soon. Laura, father, and mother are sending you their best regards.

I will write you more in a few days. Please write to me.

Your devoted friend,
Gabby

A heavy stone lifted from his chest. After all, Gabby had found her love, and it was not him.

Kare obtained documents authorizing him to travel to Berlin. He did not recognize the city. It was in ruins. Soviet military police women were directing traffic. Berlin was divided into zones: Russian, American, and British. Kare wandered through the streets. The Brandenburg gate was heavily damaged. Next door, the Adalon Hotel had been bombed and destroyed. People were lined up to drink from water trucks. German housewives hunted for anything that would burn. Wood was the only fuel available. Food was in short supply. Here and there, people stripped the carcasses of dead horses lying on the roadside for meager meat. Kare stopped on the sidewalk. In front of him was a civilian with amputated legs. He was selling his personal possessions on the sidewalk. He begged Kare to buy something. Rummaging through a pile of old records, to his astonishment, Kare found an old 78 rpm record. The label read, "Tommy Dorsey Orchestra, 'Getting Sentimental over You.'" It was the music that he had danced to with Monika during the New Year of 1942. It was so long ago. He gave the civilian one US dollar. The man kissed Kare's hand in thanks and urged him to buy more.

Kare needed to get to Potsdam, now occupied by the Red Army. It was a Russian zone. He hitched a ride on a US military transport. Potsdam had been relatively untouched by the war blitz. Except that some military sites had been bombed, the city was just as Kare remembered. He arrived in the evening and got hold of a collapsible military shovel. Immediately, he headed to Sanssouci Park. There was nothing out of place. The Schloss Sanssouci Palace shined brilliant yellow from the dissenting sun to the west. The Chinese tea pavilion, there in the woods, was a jewel untouched, waiting for his visit. Kare's heart beat hard. He wanted to find out if Monika had ever opened his envelope, which he had given to her in 1942. He had told her to take everything from inside the treasure box. It was for her survival during the war. He easily located the spot where he had buried his treasure. Now, night fell in the park; it was all quiet, no visitors on site. It was moonless. He immediately proceeded to dig. The earth was soft and easy to dig into. With a few strokes, he reached the stone that he had placed on top of the box. All looked untouched. His hands began digging fast, his mind thinking only of the treasure. He removed the stone and saw his metal box, seemingly untouched as well. Kare reached toward the metal cover and opened it. It was empty. Kare was relieved. Sweat ran down his forehead. *Monika had been here*, he said to himself. *But, why did she leave the box?* He proceeded to remove the box. He opened it. There was a paper inside. Kare, with his hands trembling, rushed to the nearest streetlight. He carefully unfolded the paper. With anticipation, heart pounding, he read:

14 February 1943

Dear Kare,

I don't know if you will survive to read this letter. I want to tell you how sorry I am for treating you like that with harsh words during our last time together. The words I said, I wish I could take back. But, I realize it cannot be done. I hurt you, and I am sorry. I want you to know that I love you and always have. If you are angry with me, I understand. How foolish was I? I always believed in angels, and I am praying every day for your well-being. If you are not alive to read this letter, I shall meet you in the afterlife. I will tell you that I will always be yours, and we shall walk on clouds hand in hand.

I am leaving my address. You can find me at the village of Grohn near Bremen. There is a village church. It is on the same block as my Uncle Herbert's hardware store. The street is Amound Fahr Strasse. He lives on the second floor. I will be staying with his family for the duration of the war.

Yours,
Loving Monika

Tears streamed down Kare's face. He folded the piece of paper and discarded the treasure box. Then he ambled back to Potsdam. As he walked, deep in thought, he decided to stop where Heidi had lived. *Perhaps she is still there*, he said to himself. He reached the house. The lights were on. He knocked on the door. "Who is there?" a voice came from inside.

Kare recognized it as Heidi's voice. His heart pounded. "It is I, Kare Hoffmann. Open the door."

There was a silence. Then the door opened with such force that it almost ripped from its hinges. In the light was Heidi. Behind her stood her husband, Theodore. They looked as if they had encountered a ghost. Kare removed the military beret. His hair was short, and there was a scar on his forehead. Smiling for a moment, they were frozen in space. Then a cry of happiness came from Heidi. She rushed into his arms, kissing him all over his face. Theodore stepped right behind her, hugging Kare. Then he invited Kare inside. Heidi stood with her hands clasped, crying and looking at him. "I knew you would come back," she said. "I knew you would survive. Sit down and tell us all about yourself."

Kare said, "I will." Sitting at the dining table, he said, "First, I must know where Monika is." He pulled the letter from his pocket, not finishing his words.

Heidi put her hand on Kare's and said, "The last time I heard from Monika was in 1944. Then Bremen was bombed. We have not heard from her since. She has your child, a beautiful girl. Monika named her after me, Heidi, and her middle name is Esther, after your mother. She must be two and half by now." Tears ran down her cheeks. "Kare, she is waiting for you. You must find her. She loves you. She told me, swearing that she would not marry anyone else. You are her first and last love. Please find her."

Then Theodore said, "Kare, I helped Monika dig your treasure. I urged her to put that letter into the box. Monika gave us some gold and reichsmarks. It has made a difference in our lives." He stood up and went to the cabinet, fetching some gold coins. "Kare, this is what is left. It is yours."

Kare pushed the coins away. "No, it is yours. I gave it to Monika, and she gave it to you. I am happy that it made a difference in your lives."

Kare spent a long night telling them the story of his survival. It was the first time in a long time he slept in peace, dreaming of Monika.

Hugging Heidi, saying goodbye, Kare left Potsdam in a hurry the next morning. His quest was to find his love. Hitching a ride on a military transport toward the east, he arrived in Bremen exhausted and unshaven. Over a thousand raids had been mounted against Bremen. The British and Americans had bombed the city heavily; sixty percent of it lay destroyed. Monika's address was not close to the city center or military instillation, but evidence of destruction was everywhere. Monika's address was the village of Grohn. It was a few kilometers from the center of the city of Bremen. Her uncle's hardware store was not too far from the village's only church. Kare stopped at the British Third Infantry headquarters in Bremen and asked for directions to the village of Grohn. The Sergeant in charge unfolded the map of the surrounding villages of Bremen. He pointed to the village. He warned Kare that most of the village had been destroyed during the British offensive. The sergeant offered him a ride to the village.

The sergeant had been right. Except for the church and some surrounding buildings, nothing was standing. It looked deserted. Kare was driven to despair. Grohn was no more. It was rubble under bricks. The only sign of the hardware store was a broken sign in the brick pile. Kare lost all hope. He asked the Sergeant what had happened to the survivors. "They mostly perished after months of bombing," he said. "Those who managed to stay alive left Bremen for Oldenburg, now a large refugee center."

Kare walked toward the still-standing church. There was no door, so he was able to walk right inside. There were holes in the walls; beams of light streamed in and shone on the pews. The church was full of debris, and everything was covered in grey soot. He stood, looking toward the altar, deep in thought. *Where should I continue looking for Monika? I will need the help of the Red Cross.*

A voice came out. "Can I help you?"

Kare turned around. An old man stood behind him. "Oh, I was just looking at the old church," he said.

The old man was unshaven and dressed in a black stained suit. He introduced himself, "Wilhelm. I am the priest in the village. This is my church—or what's left of it." He pointed his hand toward the altar.

"I am looking for Herbert's family. They had a hardware store. Do you know if they survived the bombing?" Kare's heart was now beating fast as he hoped for any news as to the whereabouts of Monika.

The priest answered, "Herbert died in the bombing. I am sorry to tell you the bad news. Are you a relative?"

Kare's heart was unnerved. "No, I am looking for my friend. Her name is Monika."

The priest paused and then said, "A blonde from Berlin with a baby girl? Yes, she was with us in the bomb shelter. She left with a few refugees to Oldenburg … east."

Kare could not believe his luck. Blood rushed through his veins, and suddenly, he felt a strange strength overtaking his body. He hugged the priest, who was taken aback by Kare's sudden move. Kare said, "Thank you!" and ran toward the door.

"Did you find what you were looking for?" the Sergeant asked as he tossed a cigarette butt into the street.

"Yes, bloody good news!" Kare said. "How can I get to Oldenburg?"

"Sir, tomorrow, a transport is heading to the headquarters. You can hitch a ride."

Kare did not sleep that night. At dawn, he was outside the Sergeant's temporary office, which was in a large, half demolished house. A lone British soldier on guard paced, waiting for his relief. Within a few hours, a military supply truck arrived from Oldenburg. By noon, Kare was on the truck headed to the British headquarters. He arrived in Oldenburg by late afternoon. He rushed to the Red Cross headquarters, housed in the city next to the temporary British military government office in the old city hall.

At the front desk, a receptionist told him that the offices were closed for the day. Kare waved her away and asked to see her supervisor. A young woman wearing civilian clothes with a Red Cross band on her arm greeted him. Kare identified himself as a British intelligence officer on official business. He needed to see the list of refugees in the Red Cross camps. No questions were asked, and the supervisor told him, "There are over forty thousand listed on our roster. You are welcome to look at it. What name are you looking for?" she asked.

"I would like the ledgers of letters *D* and *F*," he said.

Four ledgers were brought for his search. Each ledger book contained five thousand names alphabetically. Kare started to search *D*. Monika's family name was Daecher. Running his finger through the names, he found several similar names, but not the right spelling. Monika did not appear on these pages. Disappointed, he searched the letter *F*. He came up with the same results; many women named Monika but none with the family name, Freude Daecher. He wondered if it was possible that she had used his family name, Hoffmann. He asked for the ledgers for the letter *H*. He ran his finger nervously through the names, but there was no Hoffmann to be found. Kare was disappointed and dumbfounded. He decided to repeat the search, this time using a piece of paper as a guide. He searched the list of names but had no luck. He came up empty handed. Tired now, he closed the ledgers, stood up, and was ready to leave. Hope began to fray.

"Did you find what you were looking for?" the supervisor asked. She was ready to close her office door.

"No. I will have to file an official search request through the Red Cross," Kare said.

"You can do it tomorrow morning. We open at eight. We also have a ledger of the Red Cross staff and employees who are living in tents in the camp, working in the field hospital. Would you like to look at it?"

Kare's face lit up. *Of course! Monika is a nurse! Is it possible that she is working in the Red Cross hospital?* His hope sprang back up. He was given one more chance to find her name. It was a short list. He opened the ledger with trembling fingers. He pointed to the letter *D* and carefully moved down the list, reading each name. There it was, staring him in the face: *Monika Freude Daecher.* His fingers froze on the page. He looked again, rubbing his tired eyes. Had he made a mistake? No, it was her name. Her tent number, 120; row, J; and Camp, W, instantly became permanently lodged in his brain. "Eureka!" he shouted out loud. The supervisor came in. "I found what I was looking for," he said, smiling. "Where is tent 120, row J, camp W?"

She invited him to her office. A map hung on her wall. Tent numbers and rows were color coded on the plan. "Here," she said, pointing her finger. "It is not too far from the field hospital."

Kare kissed her on her cheek. She was taken by surprise. "Thank you! You are an angel!" he said as he rushed to the exit door.

Now, a dark night had fallen as Kare arrived at Camp W. There were rows and rows of military tents surrounded by barbed wire. At the makeshift gate was a British guard with a rifle, sitting in a chair. Kare identified himself and was given permission to enter. A wooden sign showed the tent numbers and row numbers. Kare did not pay any attention to the displaced people around the camp. All he wanted was to find Monika. He found tent 120. Frozen, he looked at the tent. A dim light shone through the tent's cracks. Kare, in an excited voice, called, "Fräulein Monika, are you there?" Someone moved in the tent. Kare said again, "Monika, are you there?"

A flap door of the tent opened. A woman holding a little girl came out. Kare looked at her. It was not Monika. She had dark hair and was dressed in an unkempt dress and a light coat. The child rested her head against the woman's shoulder and clutched a baby doll. Kare's heart stopped beating. Cold sweat appeared on his face. He was speechless, staring at the woman. She said, "Who is looking for Monika?"

Kare opened his mouth. "I am Kare Hoffmann. Does Monika live in this tent?"

The woman examined Kare. He was an unshaven, strange man asking for Monika, wearing a British uniform with a backpack slung over his shoulder. Then she said, "What is your name again?"

"Kare Hoffmann."

For a moment, she said nothing. The two stared at each other. Then she said, "Monika is not here now. She is in the field hospital tonight."

An electric shock moved through his body. The thought that he had found her was unbelievable. He wanted to run to the hospital. He swallowed hard and controlled his emotions. Then he said, "Whose child is that?"

"Monika's."

Kare's eyes lit up. *My child,* he thought. He came closer. He said, "Heidi!" to the child. The woman was surprised that Kare knew the girl's name. "Heidi, my darling." Kare touched her. The child pulled closer to the woman.

She asked, "Who are you?" and was slightly frightened.

Kare asked, "Where is the hospital?"

"Just a ten-minute walk," the woman said. "You will find her there." She smiled and pointed her finger in the direction of the hospital. Kare took another look at the little girl. She definitely resembled Monika.

Kare began walking, then running slowly. Then he sprinted quickly between the rows of tents, oblivious to everything around him. Breathless, he reached the field hospital. It was a combination of large tents. At the entrance was a desk. He asked the nurse in charge, "Where can I find Monika Freude Daecher?"

She looked at her sheet and said, "Ward B. That way."

Kare composed himself and walked slowly between two rows of beds. Doctors, nurses, and civilian personnel were milling around the patients' beds. Rows of light bulbs hung in the middle of the tent. The smell of disinfectant and alcohol was in the air. Kare found Ward B and slowly entered it. A nurse wearing a British uniform greeted him. "Can I help you, sir?" she said in English.

Kare replied, "I am looking for Nurse Monika."

"You can find her there," the nurse said, pointing to the back rows of beds. "She is on duty tonight."

"Much obliged," Kare said. He looked at the last row of beds. There she was, with her back to him, her golden hair flowing down her back, a white handkerchief neatly wrapped around her head. She was bandaging the leg of a young man. Kare froze; he felt his heart beating in his throat. He could not believe that he had lived to see this day. Then he decided to retreat slowly back to the front of the ward.

There was a small administrative office, partitioned with dividers. He asked a nurse on duty, "Do you have a record player?"

The nurse answered, "Yes. It is connected to the public address system." She pointed to the record player and the radio on the desk.

Kare asked, "Can you play this record?" He removed his backpack and gave her the 78- rpm record. Within minutes the music of the Tommy Dorsey Orchestra's song, "Getting Sentimental over You" filled the ward. Kare walked toward Monika again. He stood a few feet behind her, looking at her back. The sound of the song made her body freeze. She stood motionless: "*Never thought I'd fall, but now I hear love call. I'm getting sentimental over you. Things you say and do just thrill me through and through. I thought I was happy that I could live without love. Now I must admit, love it is all I'm thinking of.*"

She turned around. Their eyes met, and a stream of tears rolled down her face. Kare felt tears flow down his cheeks. It was a long moment before they rushed into each other's arms, hugging and kissing. Kare felt her warm body against his, their hearts beating together. Looking in his face, she said, "Forgive me, Kare, for my harsh words in the past. My despair enflamed the dark tide of my veins. I misspoke. Every day, I kneeled to God in my suffering and asked for your forgiveness. I was lost. In my heart, I knew that it had not been our last 'adieu.' I knew that you were alive, and now that you have found me, I can live again."

She held his face with her two hands. They hugged and cried on each other's shoulders. Applause erupted in the ward. Now, the patients sitting in their beds smiled and clapped, realizing that two lovers had found each other.

After a long moment, Monika said, "I have a surprise for you." Holding Kare's hand, she led him to another ward. There, she stopped in front of a bed. Kare looked at a white-haired woman, worn to a shadow, then he rushed into his mother's arms, hugging and kissing her. It was a miracle that Lila had survived the concentration camp. She had been liberated by the American Advance Forces.

Kare asked Monika, "How did you find my mother?"

She said, smiling and crying, "When the new patients came into the hospital, I looked at the names. There was an unusual name, Lila Esther Schonkoff. I remembered you mentioning that name. I knew she must be your mother. I asked her if she had a son by the name of Kare Hoffmann. Her eyes lit up. She was dying, but when she heard your name and my story, she wanted to live again."

Two weeks later, in the Red Cross Field Hospital, a wedding ceremony was witnessed by Lila, little Heidi, and the hospital staff. The wedding was officiated by a US Military Hebrew chaplain. Kare and Monika stood facing each other, holding hands, gazing at each other. Tears rolled over Monika's cheeks. A *tallit* (Jewish prayer shawl) was held over Kare's and Monika's heads by four volunteer soldiers. She was given a Hebrew name, Rina (Joy). The betrothal blessing was recited by the chaplain.

Kare held the ring and declared, "Behold, you are betrothed unto me with this ring according to the Law of Moses and Israel." He then placed the ring on Monika's forefinger.

The chaplain announced, "*Mazal tov*! You may kiss the bride."

Six months thereafter, Lila, Kare, Monika, and their daughter, Heidi, traveled to Amsterdam to his Uncle Jacob's home, who escaped the Nazis to Canada. Jacob gifted the house to Kare. There, in a tearful reunion, Kare met his Uncle Andrew and Aunt Sally. Andrew gave Monika a wedding gift—his mother, Miriam's, two silver Shabbat candelabras.

Rio de Janeiro

Six days before Easter, 1950, the Rio Carnival Samba Parade filled the streets of Copacabana. There, in the crowd was a man with a child on his shoulders holding the hand of a woman who was dancing the samba. Kare turned to Monika and said, "I promised you that I would take you to this enchanted place."

"Yes, you have fulfilled my dream."

They danced hand in hand to the sound of Batucada, moving their feet to the sound of the beat. As they danced, Kare noticed the reflection of sunshine glittering off of metal. He looked up and saw the medallion of Madonna and Child hanging from his daughter's neck. With thoughts of all he had been through, pride suddenly blazed inside him. He looked around as if seeing the world for the first time—the blue ocean, the sky, the carnival, now moving and winding like a colorful snake in a mysterious and magical way. In the midst of all this, he looked at Monika and his child. He knew that he was the luckiest man in the world to be dancing here in this sun-graced, resplendent city with those he loved.

Then he will judge disputes between many nations and settle arguments between many people. They will hammer their swords into plow blades and their spears into pruning shears. Nations will never fight against each other, and they will never train for war again.

—Prophet Micah 4:3

Printed in the United States
By Bookmasters